MURDER AT WALDENMERE LAKE

AN IRIS WOODMORE MYSTERY

MICHELLE SALTER

D1312780

B

Boldwood

First published in Great Britain in 2023 by Boldwood Books Ltd.

Cover Design by Lawston Design

Cover Photography: Lawston Design

A CIP catalogue record for this book is available from the British Library.

Paperback ISBN 978-1-83751-048-1

Large Print ISBN 978-1-83751-049-8

Hardback ISBN 978-1-83751-047-4

Ebook ISBN 978-1-83751-050-4

Kindle ISBN 978-1-83751-051-1

Audio CD ISBN 978-1-83751-042-9

MP3 CD ISBN 978-1-83751-043-6

Digital audio download ISBN 978-1-83751-044-3

Boldwood Books Ltd
23 Bowerdean Street
London SW6 3TN
www.boldwoodbooks.com

For Mum & Dad

PROLOGUE
WALDENMERE LAKE

November 1918

Silently, the metal beast began to descend. Water closed over it, ripples subsided and no trace was left – nothing to say it had ever been there. Waldenmere was motionless once more.

The soldiers watched the man scramble to shore. His uniform was caked in mud and he struggled to stay upright in the waist-high water. They heard him swear when his torchlight flickered and died.

After the man had gone, they crept from their hiding place and returned to camp. The soldiers would say nothing of what they had seen. Soon they'd be gone from here, back to their old lives.

War was over. Peace was just beginning.

1

WALDEN, HAMPSHIRE

May 1921

'Waldenmere is not for sale.' General Cheverton burst into the office, waving the latest edition of *The Walden Herald*. He marched past my desk, his silver-topped cane tapping on the wooden floor. 'Good afternoon, Miss Woodmore.'

Elijah, who'd been dozing in his chair, woke with a start. He struggled to his feet as the general slapped the newspaper on his desk. It contained an article suggesting the army was about to sell Waldenmere to the highest bidder.

The Walden Herald's headquarters consisted of two rooms above Laffaye Printworks. Its editor, Elijah Whittle, ran operations from his smoke-filled den, where he could keep an eye on me and anyone entering the main office. I was the only permanent reporter. The rest of the newspaper's staff were housed in the printworks below.

'Waldenmere belongs to the British Army.' General Cheverton lowered his tall frame into a chair.

'It should belong to the people of Walden.' Elijah rummaged through the papers strewn across his desk, searching for his cigarettes.

I stopped typing so I could listen to their conversation.

'I know townsfolk are sentimental about the lake.' The general took out his pipe and Elijah passed him a box of matches. 'But our plans won't cause any disruption. We just want to give our war heroes somewhere peaceful to recuperate.'

'I've heard the army doesn't have the funds for a convalescent home.' Elijah took back the matches and lit a cigarette.

'It's in hand.' A halo of smoke circled General Cheverton's mane of grey hair. 'These things always take time.'

'Why not let the council buy the lake? That way, its future is more secure.' Elijah was fast disappearing behind his own cloud of smog.

'It's not at risk. Townsfolk will always be welcome at Waldenmere.'

'They were forced to keep away during the war.'

I coughed as tobacco fumes wafted across my desk.

'There's a difference between active soldiers and veterans. Now the training camp has gone, local people can enjoy the lake alongside recovering soldiers.'

The general puffed contentedly on his pipe while Elijah took long drags from his cigarette. They appeared to be enjoying their exchange.

With fifty-two acres of open water, Waldenmere was the perfect location for a convalescent home. Before the war, the lake had been used to trial floatplanes and prototype battle tanks had been tested on its marshes. In 1914, a military camp was erected on the lake's shores and remained there for five years.

Locals had been hostile towards the army camp and most were in favour of the council buying Waldenmere. However, General Samuel Cheverton was a popular figure in Walden and many would be swayed by his view.

I was torn between my personal attachment to the lake and a sense of obligation to those men who'd given so much for their country. Deep down, I wanted Waldenmere to go back to the way it had been in my childhood and had misgivings about an institution looming over its shores. The lake was an old friend to me and I didn't want it to change.

Elijah hefted himself out of his chair and fished a whisky bottle and two glasses from the filing cabinet. I started to type. He smiled at my futile attempt to pretend I hadn't been listening and kicked his office door closed.

The only sound was the noise of the printing presses below. I decided to leave them to their whisky and coax any gossip out of Elijah in the morning. It was nearly six and George might be waiting for me downstairs.

I took out my powder compact and checked my face in the tiny mirror. Picking up my jacket and bag, I was about to leave when Elijah reappeared.

'Make sure you're here by nine tomorrow. We have an appointment with Mrs Siddons at the council offices.' He slammed the door shut before I could ask any questions.

I went downstairs and emerged onto Queens Road into a sticky heat. The smell of ink chemicals rose through the grate of the printworks, replacing the clinging odour of tobacco fumes from above.

'At last.' George was standing in the doorway of the printworks, his jacket was slung over his arm and his tie hung loosely around his neck. He tossed his cigarette to the ground and we strolled along the road until we reached the shortcut to the lake. By taking a footpath that ran through the woods and then curved alongside Grebe Stream, we could follow the flow of water until it wound its way into Waldenmere.

'You're late. Don't tell me something newsworthy has happened in Walden?' George worked in the council offices on the high street. When he finished at five-thirty, he'd stroll down to Queens Road to wait for me. He was never in a hurry to catch the train home to Basingstoke. Instead, we strolled by the lake together and at some point, he'd end up at the railway station.

'It's this lake business. General Cheverton paid us a visit to put us right about the army's plans.'

'What did he say?'

'Apparently, Aldershot Military Estates, the army unit that holds the land deeds, has no intention of selling Waldenmere to anyone.'

'I'm not sure that's true.'

'He admitted they don't have the funds to build the convalescent home yet. But he's adamant it will go ahead. I think he just wanted to chew the fat with Elijah. The whisky bottle was out by the time I left. Have you heard anything?'

'Nothing I can tell a reporter,' George teased. 'You should ask your friend, Mrs Siddons.'

'I will. We've got a meeting with her tomorrow at the council offices. Has she taken up residence there?' I could imagine her commandeering an office.

'She has. I'm exhausted.'

I noticed he walked a little stiffly and tried to slow my pace without him noticing. 'I don't imagine Mansbridge is happy about that.'

The previous year, Mrs Siddons had become MP for Aldershot and the third woman to take a seat in the House of Commons. She'd done it by standing as the Liberal candidate in the local by-election and beating the Conservative candidate, Councillor William Mansbridge.

He yawned. 'She's had us digging out old maps and finding out about boundary lines.'

'Does that mean she's the one behind the plan for the council to buy the lake?'

He nodded.

'Excellent. That means it has a chance of happening.'

He didn't seem convinced, but I knew how influential Mrs Siddons could be. Even before she'd entered Parliament, she'd moved in political circles and had the ear of Prime Minister Lloyd George.

'How did you become friends with the famous Mrs Siddons?' he asked.

We left the footpath and pushed our way through the bracken to reach Bog Myrtle Glade and the seclusion of our bench.

'She was kind to me after my mother died.' I didn't want to talk about that. I looked over at the lake. Bathed in sunshine, it was beautiful. The air was still and the only sound came from a warbler singing from the cover of the reedbeds.

'Will Elijah be with you tomorrow?' George stretched out his leg. I suspected he was in pain, but I knew better than to ask.

I nodded.

'Does he know...' He trailed off. I guessed he wasn't sure how to describe our relationship.

'No. No one does.' I felt a little embarrassed. Tomorrow's encounter could be awkward.

'Shall I pretend I don't know you?' His dark eyes crinkled in amusement.

'Of course not. Just don't...' It was my turn to fumble for the right words.

'Don't what?' he whispered into my ear, his nose touching my face.

'Don't let on that we've been spending so much time together.' I kissed him lightly on the nose to temper the meaning behind my words.

'I get the picture.' He moved away from me to the end of the bench. 'I wouldn't want anyone to get the impression we were anything more than casual acquaintances.'

'I'm just worried about your reputation.'

He laughed and slid back to wrap his arms around me. Few people knew our bench existed. It had been there so long the roots of an ancient oak had grown over its iron legs. The canopy of the tree hid us from view – we could glimpse the lake in the distance, but no one could see us.

'Water hides its secrets,' George observed.

'What do you mean?' I touched his cheek, tracing the line of a faint scar that ran along his left temple before disappearing under a mess of dark curls. The same shellfire that had injured his left leg had also grazed the side of his face.

'Look at the land and you'll find tell-tale signs of war, but water swallows everything up. When this place was an army camp, it was all mud and machinery.' George motioned towards the reedbeds. 'You can still see traces of it – bits of metal here and there, old boundary stones. But the lake stays the same. It doesn't reveal anything.'

'When I lived in London, I'd dream about Waldenmere.' I followed his gaze across the water. 'It was comforting. The lake was something constant, unchanging. I found it reassuring when every-thing else was chaos.'

'Is that why you came back?' He took my hand and placed it around his waist. I moved in closer.

'It was my father's idea. He thought we'd be happier here. I wasn't so sure, but I couldn't get a job with any of the London newspapers. Elijah's an old family friend and he offered to take me on at *The Walden Herald*.'

'Don't you miss London?'

I smiled. George couldn't understand why anyone would want to leave the city to settle in a small market town in Hampshire.

'Sometimes,' I admitted. 'But I'm not sorry we came back.'

'Nor am I. Otherwise, we may never have met.' He trailed his finger down my cheek and gently turned my face towards his.

* * *

'What's this meeting about?' I asked Elijah. 'The lake?'

'I'm assuming Mrs Siddons is behind the proposal for the council to buy Waldenmere. No doubt she'll let Mansbridge think it's his idea.'

When I walked with George, I'd learned how to discreetly slow down if I saw signs his leg was aching. With Elijah, I found it more difficult not to stride ahead. Despite our gentle progress, he was still red in the face by the time we arrived at the council offices.

'Here's George Hale,' Elijah panted. 'I'll buy him a pint in the Drunken Duck later and see what he's got to say about all this.'

'Elijah, how are you?' George slapped him on the back.

'Hello, George. You know Iris, don't you?'

George gave a formal nod in my direction and I reciprocated with a polite incline of my head. I could see the laughter in his eyes.

'Mrs Siddons is with Councillor Mansbridge in the meeting room. I'll show you up.'

Elijah leant heavily on the polished oak bannister, breathing hard as he made his way up the curved staircase. George and I followed, exchanging sidelong smiles.

'See you tonight?' he mouthed.

I held up six fingers to indicate the time. He nodded.

Elijah turned at the top of the stairs and noticed the last few seconds of this exchange.

'I'll see if they're ready for you.' George left us to wait in a small antechamber.

'You and George friends, eh?' Elijah raised his eyebrows.

'We've chatted a few times.' I pretended to examine the portrait of a bearded man who looked a bit like King George. The plaque revealed he was Alderman Redvers Tolfree.

'Hmm, well, be careful. He's likeable enough, but I'm not sure your father would approve.'

With my father away on his travels, Elijah had the vague notion he should adopt a sort of parental role. Fortunately, he hadn't got a clue how to go about it.

'Don't worry. I'm not planning on marrying him,' I replied and instantly regretted it. Elijah's eyebrows shot up again.

'What are you planning on doing with him?' His tone was cynical.

'We enjoy each other's company.' I felt my cheeks flush. I didn't plan on marrying anyone, but I relished having a boyfriend – especially a secret one.

'I know you think you should be able to do anything a man can do, but I'm afraid the world doesn't work that way.'

'The world's changing.' I kept my eyes fixed on the portrait of Alderman Tolfree.

'Not that fast, it isn't. Don't risk your reputation on the likes of George Hale. Walden's a small town with wagging tongues.'

It was a relief when George reappeared. He ushered us into an austere meeting room dominated by a huge mahogany table. The walls were clad in dark wood and hung with portraits of former council leaders.

'Please take a seat.' Councillor William Mansbridge stood to greet us. His six-foot frame and black hair and beard made him a distinctive figure in Walden. 'Thank you, George.'

George left the room and Mrs Siddons got straight down to business. She was resplendent in a dark blue satin gown with glistening sapphire earrings and a sapphire ring from her famous jewellery collection. 'I'm sure you're aware of the rumours circulating regarding the future ownership of Waldenmere. We'd like you to inform your readers of the current state of affairs.'

I took out my notebook. I knew from experience Mrs Siddons could impart a lot of information in a short space of time.

'It's true Walden Council has expressed an interest in buying the lake. However, no agreement has been reached with Aldershot Military Estates. The army may wish to retain Waldenmere if they can find the funds to build a convalescent home for war veterans.' She gave a politician's pause. 'This may seem like a noble idea, but it doesn't take into account the impact this type of establishment could have on the town. The council would raise objections to such a development.'

Councillor Mansbridge didn't appear as comfortable as Mrs Siddons about this, but he leant back, allowing her to take the lead.

'General Cheverton believes he can drum up enough investment to enable the convalescent home to go ahead,' Elijah commented.

Mrs Siddons sighed. 'He'd better start tapping his contacts to stump up the cash soon because time's running out. A third party is interested in buying Waldenmere and they have deeper pockets than the council and army put together.'

'Who?' I demanded. Even Elijah looked startled. This hadn't been mentioned before.

'London and South Western Railway. They plan to build a four-storey hotel on the northern side of the lake, next to the station.'

'No,' I gasped.

2

'Take notes, but don't ask any questions. And don't show any hostility to the man. Understood?' Elijah sat in the corner of the carriage, his hat resting on his lap.

To my amazement, he'd managed to secure a meeting at short notice with Sir Henry Ballard of London and South Western Railway. Like many people, I sometimes underestimated my boss. His shambling gait and vague air belied the fact that he was extremely astute, with an extensive network of contacts from all walks of life.

'I'll mention the concerns of the townspeople; he'll expect that. But he needs to know we'll present his side of the story too.' Elijah waved his cigarette at me. 'He'll give us more information that way.'

The London train pulled out of Walden Station and I stared out at the shimmering lake. I couldn't imagine a hotel looming over Waldenmere. The idea was preposterous.

London and South Western Railway's head office was inside Waterloo Station. A secretary escorted us into a drab room with grimy windows that overlooked the platforms. The smell of burnt coal seemed to have permeated the wallpaper. A large map covered one wall, dotted with key railway stations across the south of the country. It showed where railway hotels had already been built and indicated proposed sites for new ones. It already displayed an outline of the Waldenmere Hotel.

Whereas his office was plain and workmanlike, Sir Henry Ballard was flamboyantly dressed in a chequered waistcoat and polka-dot bow tie. He followed my gaze and pointed to the map. 'The latest addition to our chain.'

'If you're successful in buying the lake,' Elijah corrected.

'Of course.' Sir Henry raised his hands in concession. 'We still have matters to settle. But I hope to have a team of men on site before the year's out.'

'You'll appreciate your plan has caused some unease. Locals are worried about the damage that could be done to Waldenmere. And they're concerned about the numbers of visitors a large hotel will bring to the town.' Elijah relayed these facts without emotion. 'Walden is a quiet place.'

And we want it to stay that way, I was tempted to add, but remained silent.

'I understand, Mr Whittle. Change of any sort causes unrest. But once the hotel is up and running, locals will soon adjust to its presence.'

'But most of your hotels have been built in cities or coastal resorts. Walden is a small and relatively new town. We've only had a council for about twenty years,' Elijah commented.

'I know Walden's history and the part the railway played in its creation. Don't forget that.' Sir Henry tucked his thumbs into his waistcoat pockets. 'Waldenmere is a major attraction for visitors. The last thing we want to do is detract from its appeal. But... a few modifications may be necessary.'

'What do you mean, modifications?' I didn't like the sound of this. Elijah coughed in my direction.

'Nothing that need worry you, Miss Woodmore. I know large-scale building works can be frightening when you first witness them.' Sir Henry smiled at me. 'Hasn't that always been the case since the dawn of the railway? Yet, where would we be now if we didn't have trains to take us from one end of the country to the other, eh?'

'I'm just curious to know how you go about modifying a lake.' I forced a smile, irked by his patronising manner.

'An excellent question. Let me enlighten you.' He spread out a map across his desk. It showed Waldenmere with a hotel standing next to the railway station. 'As you can see, the water runs into the lake from Grebe Stream by Heron Bay on the south side. On the north side of the lake, not far from the railway line, there's a weir with a sluice that we can raise to let the water flow into Walden Brook and onto the River Hart. By temporarily draining the lake, we can create a northern bay similar to Heron Bay.'

I was infuriated by his presumption that he could buy Waldenmere and change it to suit his needs.

'Our hotel will be close to the railway station and the new bay will sit in front of it. We can form a shallow bathing area by cutting away the existing reedbeds and shipping in tons of sand. A promenade will run alongside the bay, leading to a boathouse on the north-east corner of the lake to facilitate boating. Once the work is complete, we'll return the water level to normal.'

I struggled to hide my dismay at the thought of my beloved lake being turned into a seaside resort.

'I'm sorry if I'm frightening you with my talk of construction.' He stroked his moustache. 'When the railway first came to Britain, vast swathes of countryside were ravaged, much to the alarm of those living in the vicinity. Once those lines were in place, everything soon returned to normal.'

On his desk was a photograph of a well-dressed woman with two young girls, presumably his wife and children. They were standing on an immaculate lawn in front of a palatial manor house. I wondered how the Ballard family would feel if LSWR decided to route a railway line through their garden.

'Are you suggesting we focus on the benefits the hotel could bring to the town?' Elijah prompted.

Sir Henry beamed at him. 'Precisely, Mr Whittle. Think of the advantages a hotel would offer. It will create new and exciting jobs and local merchants will be delighted by the increase in trade. I'm sure the good people of your town will flock to be seen in the hotel's bar and restaurant.'

I tried unsuccessfully to picture the inhabitants of Walden in suits and evening dresses, sipping cocktails in the lounge of the Waldenmere Hotel.

'For a fee, day visitors will be allowed to join our paying guests in the swimming pool or bathe in the lake during the summer months.'

'Locals bathe in the lake for free all year round,' I couldn't resist commenting.

'But at the hotel, they'll be able to recline on sun loungers, order drinks from the bar and bask in the beauty of the lake in luxurious surroundings.'

'You seem confident Aldershot Military Estates will agree to sell.' Elijah's fingers twitched and I could tell he was longing for a cigarette.

'I've spoken to my fellow board members here at LSWR. They fully back the scheme. I'm confident we'll be able to make Aldershot an offer it can't refuse.'

'What about Mill Ponds?' I scrutinised the map. 'Isn't that where you want to build your promenade?'

'The old house that was a training academy? I'm sure we can get the army to throw it in as part of the deal.'

'The army doesn't own Mill Ponds.' I was jubilant at having

found a flaw in his plan.

Sir Henry seemed taken aback. 'Are you sure? It was used to train officers during the war, wasn't it?'

'That's right,' Elijah said. 'General Cheverton gave it over to the war effort. An Officer Cadet Battalion was there from 1916 till 1918. But the general never moved out and still lives at Mill Ponds.'

That wiped the smile from Sir Henry's face. 'It's something I'll need to investigate.'

'Do you have a drawing of what the hotel might look like?' Elijah asked.

Sir Henry took down a photograph that had been pinned to the wall. 'This is the South Eastern Hotel in Deal in Kent. It has eighty bedrooms, lifts to the upper floors and electric lighting throughout. It sits right on the seafront with its own promenade. Beautiful, isn't it? Can you picture it on the shores of Waldenmere?'

I couldn't hide my horror at the thought of such a vast building towering over the lake. It was monstrous.

Even Elijah, who'd remained impassive throughout, looked shocked by the size of it. We thanked Sir Henry for his time and left him poring over the map, frowning over the problem of Mill Ponds.

* * *

'How can this be allowed to happen?' I exploded. Elijah beckoned me to keep my voice down. We'd walked over Waterloo Bridge and found a table at the Lyons Corner House on the Strand.

He picked up the coffee pot and filled our cups. 'I'm flabbergasted LSWR considers Waldenmere a suitable location for a railway hotel. They usually prefer big cities or seaside towns.'

I chewed on my fish paste sandwich, shaking my head in disbelief. 'Can't the council do something?'

'Mrs Siddons may have her connections, but the railway

companies are too powerful. I'm not sure she'll have enough influence to stop this.'

'And LSWR is likely to be the highest bidder, isn't it?'

'Probably.' He drained his coffee and refilled his cup. 'Even with Horace's help, the council is unlikely to be able to match the financial clout of the railway.'

'Mr Laffaye? How's he involved?' Horace Laffaye was the owner of *The Walden Herald* and Laffaye Printworks.

I moved the plate of sandwiches towards Elijah. He'd survive on coffee and cigarettes unless prompted. He ate a ham sandwich without enthusiasm.

'He's been meeting with the council to try to help them broker a deal with Aldershot Military Estates.'

'How?' I tucked into a slice of fruit cake. I was starving, even if Elijah wasn't.

'He's using his military connections to put pressure on Aldershot to sell to the council.'

He and Horace had much in common. Both had contacts in high places, though Elijah also had some rather shady connections in distinctly low places.

'Mr Laffaye won't appreciate tourists on his doorstep,' I commented. 'Or a hotel ruining his view.'

Horace Laffaye's house overlooked Heron Bay. He was already opposed to the plans for a neighbouring convalescent home. A hotel across the lake would be even less welcome. Horace wanted Walden and Waldenmere, to stay just the way they were.

'He'll loathe it. He doesn't like disruption. He had enough of that during the war with the army camp.' Elijah scowled into his coffee cup. A cloud of gloom seemed to have descended on him.

I could guess why. Horace wasn't just his boss. The two shared a close personal relationship. I'd come to realise they were partners in life as well as business, not that it could ever be publicly known.

If Horace decided to move away, Elijah would be heartbroken. And if *The Walden Herald* folded, he'd also be out of a job. I thought it unlikely that Horace would part with Elijah. He'd want him to come too. And where would that leave me?

We lapsed into silence while I finished the rest of the food and he drained the coffee pot.

After lunch, Elijah went to meet with an old colleague for a drink and I took the opportunity to go to Dolly Dawes Hair Salon. My short bob was considered too modern for provincial Walden and I couldn't find a local hairdresser who'd attempt it.

I met Elijah back at Waterloo at four o'clock.

He eyed my hair suspiciously. 'Planning on seeing George later?'

'No.'

'What happened to young Baverstock?' He climbed into an empty carriage and sank into a seat by the window.

'Nothing's happened to him,' I said in exasperation. 'He was just a friend.' I had been keen on Percy Baverstock, however he'd proved to be unpredictable with his affections.

'So George is more than a friend?' Elijah smirked.

'I didn't mean that.'

To my relief, he grunted, drew his hat over his eyes and was snoring within minutes.

I woke him up as we pulled into Walden Station. Stepping down from the train onto the platform felt like entering a gentler, more tranquil world after the bustle of London. We strolled out to the station concourse and at the same time, both stopped.

In unison, we turned to look towards Mill Ponds.

'Do you think the general will sell?' I asked.

Only four houses were situated around the lake. On the south side was Heron Bay Lodge, home of Horace Laffaye. His neighbour was Mrs Siddons in Grebe House. To the east was Sand Hills Hall, belonging to Colonel Thackeray. And on the north-east corner stood Mill Ponds.

'I can't see it. Rumour has it Colonel Thackeray's been trying to persuade the old boy to move out and let them convert Mill Ponds into a convalescent home rather than building on Heron Bay. But the general's determined to stay put.'

'He's not likely to be persuaded by the railway company then.' I felt more optimistic.

'Let's ask him.' With an abrupt change of direction, Elijah turned away from the road into town and took the lake path to Mill Ponds.

Five minutes later, we were strolling up the long driveway towards the red brick house. It was an impressive building, though it had seen better days. The roof and chimneys were in need of repair, but there was still a grandeur about the place. If these walls could talk, they'd tell tales of wartime plots and official secrets.

Elijah rapped on the oak front door. All was quiet, so we went around to the side of the house, where the French doors to the general's study were open.

'General Cheverton,' Elijah called, peering into the room.

I turned to look towards Waldenmere. Heavily scented pink and lilac rose bushes provided bursts of colour against the silver backdrop of the lake. With a view like that, I didn't blame General Cheverton for not wanting to leave his home.

Hearing a strange gasp, I spun around.

'Stay here.' Elijah held up his hand to stop me.

I hung back, but curiosity got the better of me. I followed him into the room, my eyes drawn to a vivid splash of red.

The general's body lay at an awkward angle on the floor, blocking the doorway into the study from the house. His mouth was open and his white shirt was stained with blood. A shotgun lay on the rug beside him.

3

_____

I clamped my hand over my mouth. Elijah walked over to the body and raised a lifeless wrist. Blood seeped from General Cheverton's chest.

'He's dead.' He went to the telephone, dialled the operator and asked to be put through to the station house.

I inspected the room. Papers were scattered across the desk and a drawer of one of the cabinets was open. It gave the impression the general had been searching for something. Or someone had.

Elijah put down the receiver and shooed me back into the garden. 'Ben Gilbert's coming over.'

'So much blood.' I exhaled, realising I'd been holding my breath.

'God knows what he was doing with that shotgun.'

We walked back towards the driveway. 'It happened not long ago, by the look of it.'

He glanced at me in surprise. 'You've seen dead bodies before?'

'Many. I was a volunteer at Lewisham Military Hospital towards the end of the war. And I saw my mother's body,' I added, then wished I hadn't as the image of her came back to me.

He reached into his pocket for his cigarettes. With shaking hands, he lit one and inhaled greedily. He offered me the packet, but I shook my head.

'Do you think he shot himself?' My eyes were drawn back to the house.

'More likely an accident. He wasn't as sharp as he used to be. Or maybe there was something wrong with the gun. It looked old.' He drew deeply on his cigarette.

I tried to block out the scene in the study and turned to the lake. A pair of swans glided through the water, watched by a crow perched on the branch of a willow. The view was ludicrously peaceful compared to the violence we'd just witnessed.

A scream jolted me back to the present and we ran to the house. Betty Akers, General Cheverton's housekeeper, was standing by the study door, staring in horror at his body.

Elijah stepped across the room, took her hand and guided her into the garden. I couldn't help peeking again at the dishevelled corpse before I followed them.

'The general,' Betty muttered.

I took her hand from Elijah's. 'We're waiting for the police to arrive. We thought the house was empty.'

'I've only just got back. I went straight to the kitchen.' Betty began to gabble. 'I've been into town to fetch something nice for his supper. I'm a bit late as I was chatting with your Lizzy. I unpacked the shopping and went to see if he'd like a cup of tea and...'

A bicycle swung into the driveway and PC Ben Gilbert dismounted. 'The doctor's on his way. Superintendent Cobbe is coming over from Aldershot. Elijah, will you show me the body? Iris, could you take Mrs Akers to the kitchen?'

Given the rarity of any serious crime in Walden, I was impressed by how assured Ben was. The town didn't have a police station, just the station house Ben shared with PC Sid King.

I took Betty by the elbow and steered her towards the door of the scullery. In the familiar surroundings of her kitchen, she seemed to revive.

'Sit down, Miss Iris. I'll make tea.' She busied herself by the stove, heating a kettle of water.

The kitchen was cavernous, with a series of smaller spaces leading from it, including the scullery, larder and laundry room. All manner of pots and pans filled the shelves, but most looked as though they hadn't been touched in a while. However, judging by the smell of fruitcake, the baking tins were still in regular use.

'Why don't I do that?' Despite its size, I could see which items in the kitchen Betty favoured. On the lowest shelf of the sideboard was a row of faded rose-patterned plates and matching cups and saucers.

Betty hesitated, then sank into a heavily cushioned chair and wept. I pottered by the stove to give her time and privacy to cry.

'He was definitely dead, wasn't he?' She sniffed into her handkerchief.

'I'm afraid so.' I poured boiling water into a tarnished silver teapot and took cups and saucers from the sideboard, examining a row of recipe books on the shelf. I wondered how often Betty got to prepare exotic dishes nowadays.

'It was that horrible old shotgun of his. He should've got rid of it years ago. It must have gone off by accident.'

'It looks like it was a gunshot wound. The doctor will examine him.' I thought of the way the papers on his desk were scattered about, but that could have been due to a breeze through the open doors. 'Was he working in his study today?'

'He doesn't do much in there apart from writing the odd letter. Most of those cabinets haven't been opened since the war.'

'A drawer of one was pulled out. Perhaps the general was searching for something?' I placed a cup of tea by her side.

'He was an orderly man as a rule, though he'd make a mess when he couldn't find something. He tended to forget where he put things. Usually, it was his spectacles or his pipe. Then he'd turn everything out to try to find them.'

'What's in those filing cabinets?'

'War records. For the soldiers that were here. They should go over to Aldershot, but no one's ever come to take them away. I think the army thought they'd get this place and the general would move somewhere smaller, but he was having none of it.' She raised the teacup to her lips, but tears began to spill down her pink cheeks and she put it back in its saucer.

'Is it just you and the general living here?'

She nodded. 'All the trainee officers left at the end of the war. We had a house full of them at one time. And makeshift dormitories in the grounds.'

I imagined the kitchen bustling with staff, with dozens of soldiers to feed.

'A girl comes in of a morning to help me with the cleaning...' She suddenly looked bewildered. 'What am I going to do? What will happen to Mill Ponds?'

'Don't worry about that now. When the police have finished here, you're coming home with me.'

Betty dissolved into tears.

Ben Gilbert poked his head around the door. 'Is she up to answering some questions?' he whispered.

I went over to him. 'She's becoming more distressed. I want to take her home to Lizzy.' Our housekeeper, Mrs Elizabeth Heathcote, had been friends with Betty since they were girls.

He nodded and disappeared. A few minutes later, he returned to say he'd arranged for us to be driven home in Superintendent Cobbe's car.

Betty and I sat in the back while Elijah got in the front. The

car pulled away and I looked back at the tall figure of the superintendent standing outside the open doors of the study. I shuddered at the thought of the general's body lying beyond him on
the rug.

We made the short journey to 9 Chestnut Avenue in silence,
apart from the sound of Betty's sobs.

'Come upstairs with me,' Lizzy instructed. 'You're going to lie
down on my bed while I make up the spare room.'

Elijah slumped into one of the high-backed leather armchairs
in the drawing room. I went to Father's drinks cabinet and poured
us each a brandy before sinking into the chair opposite him. I shivered. It was too warm to light the fire, but I felt chilled.

'I'm sorry you had to see that.' Elijah rubbed his eyes. 'It's not
something a woman of your age should have to witness.'

I shrugged. 'I saw worse at the military hospital. I was with a
Voluntary Aid Detachment when you and Father were in France.'

'It must have been a harrowing experience.'

'It was unbearable at times but then so was sitting at home
doing nothing. I joined in 1916 and started looking after refugees at
the Park Fever Hospital in Hither Green. Then I was moved to
Lewisham Military Hospital. That came as a shock.' I forced a
laugh.

'I can imagine.' He ran nicotine-stained fingers through his
thinning grey hair.

Tending to the refugees had been hard but rewarding work. It
hadn't prepared me for the horrors of a military hospital. I shuddered as I recalled my time on the wards. Some days had seemed
like a blood-soaked nightmare, an unrelenting parade of torn limbs
on stretchers.

'I thought my role would be to talk to the men and write letters
for them, that sort of thing, but they had me carrying slop buckets
and swabbing wounds. I felt sick most of the time. I realised I'd

make a terrible nurse.' The brandy burned my throat although the sensation wasn't unpleasant.

He gave a weak smile. 'I wasn't exactly cut out to be a soldier. Unfit and over fifty when I joined your father in the Intelligence Corps. I had no idea what I was letting myself in for. Officers like Colonel Thackeray weren't keen on us non-military types, but General Cheverton was always kind. I'll miss the old boy.' His voice was gruff. 'I'm not sure I'd have survived the war without him and your father.'

'Father didn't tell me until after the war that he'd spent time at Mill Ponds. It was what made him decide we should come back to Walden.' I took another sip of brandy, its warmth starting to thaw the chill.

'We weren't there for long. The place was bursting at the seams. They'd billeted commissioned officers in the house while lower orders were camped out in tents in the grounds.'

'It was kind of the general to give up his home like that.'

'The old boy loved having the place overrun with soldiers. Every day was an adventure for him back then. Never seen him so alive. And he looked after his men. Not like Thackeray. But Thackeray was the one running the training courses for the battalion.'

'I've heard my father say he could be rather harsh at times?' I posed the question carefully. In fact, my father had said little about his wartime experiences but I'd always sensed an underlying hostility between him and Colonel Thackeray whenever they met. I could tell by the stiffness in Father's manner that he disliked the colonel, although they were always scrupulously polite to one another. I was close friends with the colonel's daughter, Alice Thackeray, and I knew Father was fond of her too.

Elijah grunted. 'Thackeray's a snob. Not just a common or garden snob. It runs deep with him.'

'What do you mean?'

'At the start of the war, to get a commission, you had to have come from a University Officer Cadet training unit or at least a public school one. But by 1916, they were in desperate need of officers, so they set up the Officer Cadet Battalion. If you had a bit more intelligence than your fellow soldiers, you were in with a chance of getting into the battalion, much to Thackeray's chagrin.' He drained his glass. 'When it came to training cadets, he didn't judge men on their abilities, but their social background. If you were working class, you were straight off to France to be cannon fodder.'

I closed my eyes, remembering my father's letters. Certain things he'd written at that time started to make sense. Or rather, things that he'd alluded to but not been able to say. 'Father wanted to write about it, didn't he?'

My father and Elijah had been journalists for *The Daily Telegraph* for many years. During the war, Father had become frustrated with the propaganda circulated by the government and military – and especially newspaper proprietors. He'd left the paper to become a freelance writer, working for various news syndicates.

'We both did. But we were suffering heavy losses and badly needed officers. Thackeray knew how to train them. It would have been considered treason to write anything against the war effort.' He sighed. 'No one would have published it, anyway.'

'Is that when you decided to leave *The Telegraph*?'

'I knew your father would go freelance once the war was over. I'd planned to retire. Take up gardening or something.' He smiled. 'Horace already had the printworks and thought a local paper would be a profitable business venture. He decided to launch *The Walden Herald* and asked if I'd run it.'

Like General Cheverton, Elijah was not a man suited to retirement. He was happiest when he was working and I'd long suspected Horace had created *The Walden Herald* out of love.

I got up and refilled our glasses. It had been a long day. Was it only this morning we'd sat in Sir Henry's office when he showed us his plans for the hotel?

'What do you think will happen to Mill Ponds now? I can't bear the thought of it falling into Sir Henry's hands.'

Elijah's face crumpled. 'The timing couldn't be worse.'

'If LSWR buys Mill Ponds, they could go ahead and build a hotel, even if they don't manage to get Waldenmere, couldn't they?'

'It's possible. It would put a stop to Sir Henry's plans for promenades and boathouses if he can't get the lake. But yes, the hotel could still go ahead.'

'The general's death is highly convenient for Sir Henry, then?'

'When he hears about this, he'll do everything he can to get Mill Ponds and Waldenmere.' Elijah stared morosely into his glass.

I thought of General Cheverton's bloodstained body lying on the rug. 'What went on when I was in the kitchen with Betty? Did the doctor come?'

He nodded. 'I stayed in the garden most of the time. The doctor and Superintendent Cobbe were inside for a while. When they came out, the superintendent asked what we'd touched when we were in the study. He wanted to know if we'd handled the body or the gun or moved any of the general's papers.'

'Why would he think we'd touch anything?'

'Because someone had. A drawer of one of the cabinets was open. He thinks someone was looking for something.' He placed his glass on the table and lit a cigarette.

'Probably the general himself. Betty said he was always losing his pipe or spectacles. He could have been searching for a letter or something and pulled open the drawer to find it. Then picked up the shotgun and it accidentally went off?' Even to my ears, this sounded an unlikely scenario.

Elijah leant forward and lowered his voice. 'Cobbe said the shotgun didn't kill him.'

I gaped at him. 'It must have done. Even I could tell it was a bullet wound. Why doesn't he think it was the shotgun?'

'Because it hadn't been fired.'

4

'I heard what happened. I wanted to see if Betty needed anything.'

The following morning, I came down to breakfast to find my friend, Alice Thackeray, seated at the kitchen table.

'I've persuaded her to stay in bed a while longer.' Lizzy was at the stove filling our old brown teapot with boiling water. 'She's done in.'

When my father was away, I usually ate my meals in the kitchen with Lizzy. Had I known we were going to have Alice and Betty to breakfast, I might have suggested we use the dining room. But Alice seemed happy where she was.

'You look dreadful, love,' Lizzy said. 'Why don't you go back to bed?'

I rubbed my eyes, trying to wake up. I'd spent a restless night dreaming of General Cheverton, alive and laughing, only to turn into a grey corpse. I was aware my face was pale and blotchy and my hair was sticking out in odd directions.

'Ben Gilbert's coming over. Betty was too upset to answer questions yesterday but Superintendent Cobbe wants him to take a statement from her. And me.' I glanced at my watch. He'd be arriving soon.

'I still can't believe it.' Alice poured me a cup of tea. 'Poor Uncle Samuel.'

He'd been more like a grandfather than an uncle to Alice but the childhood title had stuck.

'Does he, I mean, *did he* have any family?' I wanted to know who would inherit Mill Ponds.

'No children of his own,' Alice replied. 'Just Nathan, his nephew.'

'The general's wife died in 1911. Betty nursed her through her last year.' Lizzy joined us at the table. 'She adored her mistress.'

'Betty and the general loved it when the house was full of people. She cooked and cleaned for all the soldiers stationed at Mill Ponds.' Alice became tearful. 'What's she going to do now? Betty likes looking after people.'

Lizzy nodded. 'She was a great comfort when I lost my Albert. I don't know what I'd have done without her.'

Lizzy's husband had died in 1912. We'd moved to London the year after his death and she'd chosen to come with us. But she'd never taken to life in the city and had been delighted by our return to Walden.

'I wonder what will happen to Mill Ponds?' I hoped it would stay in General Cheverton's family, safely out of Sir Henry's reach.

'I think it will go to Nathan,' Alice said. 'Father suggested converting it into a convalescent home, but Uncle Samuel wasn't keen.'

The doorbell rang and Lizzy pushed back her chair. 'Iris, take Ben into the drawing room. I'll go upstairs and see how Betty is.'

'Tell her I'll call again later.' Alice followed me out into the hallway.

I let Ben in and pretended not to notice the whispered

exchange and brief touch of hands as he and Alice crossed on the doorstep.

Ben sat in the leather armchair and took out his notebook. 'Tell me what happened yesterday afternoon when you and Elijah arrived at Mill Ponds. What time was that?'

I recounted the previous day's events, explaining about our meeting with Sir Henry Ballard and our sudden decision to call on General Cheverton. 'The train got in at a quarter past five. We walked to Mill Ponds from the station. I suppose it was about twenty past five when we knocked on the door.'

'Did you see anyone on your way over there?'

'A few people got off the train. As far as I can remember, they all walked towards the town. We were the only ones to cut across the concourse and take the lake path.'

'You didn't see anyone by the lake or near the house?'

I shook my head. 'It was quiet. Betty said she went out at around three-thirty when the general went upstairs for a nap.'

He frowned in thought, tapping his pen on his notepad.

'Do you think it was a burglar?' I asked. 'They might have seen Betty leave, noticed the French doors were open and took a chance?'

'That's what it looks like. The general was shot as he stepped into the room.' He seemed unsure.

'Why the doubt?'

'Because there was money in the general's desk and some valuable items in the study. But nothing was taken as far as we can tell.'

'Nothing at all?'

'We can't be sure. We need Mrs Akers to take a look around. A few papers had fallen to the floor. The drawer of a cabinet was pulled out. We think someone was looking for something and the general disturbed them.'

My mind went back to Sir Henry's talk of promenades and

boathouses. 'Do you think this could be connected to the sale of the lake? Maybe someone trying to get their hands on Mill Ponds?'

'Superintendent Cobbe thinks it's more likely someone was snooping around to see what they might find and panicked when the general appeared with his shotgun.' Ben's tone hardened. 'But they must have been carrying a gun.'

'Did you go to Mill Ponds when it was an officer training academy?'

'Briefly. A lot of men from around here passed through its doors at one time or another.'

'You must have got to know General Cheverton.' I was beginning to realise how different Walden would have been at that time, overrun with soldiers from Waldenmere Camp and Mill Ponds.

Ben nodded. 'He was a kind man. Told me I was captain material. He pushed for me to become an officer.'

'What happened?' I suspected Colonel Thackeray was what happened.

He shrugged. 'I was shunted around for a time. Then the general pointed me in the direction of the military police. I wasn't sure at first, but in the end, it made me realise what I wanted to do with my life.'

On my return to Walden, I'd been shocked to find the serious-faced little boy I'd played with as a child had transformed into a burly young policeman. I could understand why Alice had fallen for him. He was honest and dependable and she'd had enough volatility in her life. But I was afraid there were too many insurmountable obstacles to them being together.

'I'm going to find out who did this.' Ben's usually warm brown eyes were cold with anger. 'I owe it to him.'

* * *

I dumped my bag on my chair and went through to Elijah's den. His ashtray was overflowing and there were three empty coffee cups on his desk. He added another sheet of paper to the growing pile of notes in front of him.

'Are you writing about the general's murder? Possibly a burglary that went wrong, according to Ben.'

'I'm writing General Cheverton's obituary.'

'Oh, of course. Can I help?' I'd forgotten we'd have to publish an obituary. 'Do you know much about him?'

'A fair amount. He was a career soldier, been in the army all his life. Rose up through the ranks and was awarded medals for bravery. He'd been married for nearly forty years when his wife died. The general's been on his own since then.'

'What do you think will happen to Mill Ponds?'

'It's likely his nephew will inherit. I know Nathan Cheverton. We spent some time together in France.'

'What's he like?' I sat down uninvited.

He sighed, resigning himself to the interruption. 'He was in a bad way then and his war didn't get any better. He wasn't like his uncle. He should never have been made a captain. Military life didn't suit him.'

I knew better than to ask how bad it got. Most men I knew, including my father, didn't talk about their wartime experiences. 'But he became an officer while more capable men like Ben Gilbert got passed over?'

Elijah smiled. 'You remind me of your father sometimes. Yes, that about sums it up. It wasn't Nathan's fault. He didn't want to be an officer, but as the nephew of a general, he didn't have much choice. He hated having to send men into battle. It still haunts him now.'

'Does he ever come to Walden? I can't recall ever seeing him with the general.'

'Nathan hasn't been here since the war. He never wants to set foot in Mill Ponds again. Not that he blames his uncle, but he hated his time there and what he was forced to do.'

'Why wasn't Ben Gilbert made a captain?' I suspected I knew the answer.

'Rumour has it, Thackeray opposed it. He reasoned you couldn't have the son of a blacksmith giving orders to men who were socially his superior.' He lit a cigarette. 'Not the "done thing", according to him.'

'Did General Cheverton agree?'

'He gave Thackeray free rein when it came to training the men. In some cases, the general would intervene, mainly using his contacts or influence to help soldiers out. I believe he arranged for young Gilbert's transfer to the Royal Military Police. The general had a nose for sniffing out where a person's talent lay, nudging them in that direction.' He gave a wheezing cough. 'Unfortunately, he was blind where Nathan was concerned.'

'Where's Nathan Cheverton now?'

'He lives in London. Last I heard, he was trying to sell his paintings to earn a living.'

'He's an artist?' I'd imagined him working in a bank or something.

'A good one. But his paintings aren't the sort people want to hang on their walls.'

'Why? What are they of?'

'War. Exploding shells, barbed wire and fallen men.'

I was quiet for a moment. Every day, I was thankful my father had come home to me in one piece. 'Can I help you with the obituary?'

'I'd like you to check a few facts for me.' He stubbed out his cigarette. 'You've spoken to Ben Gilbert today?'

'He's not convinced it was a burglary. He said money was left in the desk drawer and there were valuable items in the study that could have been easily pocketed. Perhaps a soldier held a grudge against the general? Some bitterness over the way they were treated?'

'I can't see it. He was well-liked. Thackeray was another matter, but the general looked after his men. And they respected him for it.'

I hesitated. 'You don't think this has anything to do with the sale of Waldenmere?'

He stroked his chin. 'I don't see how. You saw Sir Henry's surprise when we mentioned Mill Ponds. He didn't know it belonged to the general.' He paused to light another cigarette. 'As ruthless as LSWR can be, I can't see them suddenly dispatching someone to Walden to carry out a teatime assassination, can you?'

I'd thought about this. 'We left Sir Henry at eleven-thirty that morning. The general was killed between Betty leaving at three-thirty and us arriving at five-twenty that afternoon. He could have arranged something in that time.'

He snorted. 'Don't let your imagination run away with you. It's a coincidence.'

I wasn't so sure. 'Ben needs Betty to go back to Mill Ponds to see if anything's missing. I think I should go with her.'

'So you can have a nose around the general's study?' He waved his cigarette at me with a smile.

'To support Betty. But I wouldn't mind taking another peek while I'm there,' I admitted.

* * *

Ben Gilbert was waiting for us in the study. The room smelt of the spicy tobacco General Cheverton had smoked. The sight of his pipe lying on the mantelpiece made Betty cry.

All eyes were inevitably drawn to the bloodstained rug near the door.

'Does anyone else come in here apart from you and the general?' Ben asked.

Betty shook her head. 'The girl who helps me clean the house isn't allowed in here.'

'Why don't you start by the door and work your way around the room,' Ben suggested. 'Tell me if anything is missing or in the wrong place.'

Betty ran her hand over a globe that stood in the corner of the study. Then she moved over to the mantelpiece. 'That's the general's snuff box. Real silver. It would fetch a bit. And that dagger is from India. Those are real rubies on the handle.' She touched all the ornaments in the room, telling a tale about each.

She stopped when she reached the filing cabinets and pointed to the key in the lock of one. 'This shouldn't be unlocked. It contains the records of the officers that were here during the war. They should all have gone over to Aldershot by now, but no one's ever collected them.'

Ben examined the cabinet. 'Can you tell if any papers are missing?'

'I wouldn't know what was supposed to be there.'

She went over to the desk and picked up a photograph of Lady Cheverton. 'Beautiful lady in her day. The general always kept her picture in front of him when he worked. The frame's ivory; it's quite valuable.' She peered into the open desk drawer. 'The keys to the filing cabinets are kept in here.'

'How many keys are there?'

'Four. Three are still here. And that's the fourth.' Betty pointed to the unlocked cabinet.

I examined the labels on the front of the drawers of the four filing cabinets. The records were kept in alphabetical order. The open cabinet drawer was labelled A to E.

Betty was rummaging through the top drawer of the desk. 'His gun isn't here.'

'What gun?' Ben was by her side in an instant.

'He kept his old service revolver in here. He'd take it out and clean it sometimes.'

Ben asked Betty to step aside and made a thorough search of the desk. 'It's gone.'

'Do you think it's what was used?' I asked.

Betty stifled a sob. 'I'm going into the garden.' She buried her face in her handkerchief.

'What do you think?' I said to Ben when she was out of earshot.

He walked over to the door. 'The general was upstairs and heard someone down here. He fetched his shotgun...'

'And confronted the person?' I continued.

'They panicked and picked up the gun they'd found while they were searching his desk...' Ben pointed his fingers.

'And shot the general with his own revolver?' I finished.

5

I walked briskly up the slope to Sand Hills Hall, then realised Elijah was some way behind me.

Colonel Thackeray's father had bought the hall in 1854 when the army first settled in Aldershot. It was similar to Mill Ponds in structure but had the advantage of overlooking the lake from the top of a sandy hill that backed on to dense woodland.

I stopped to wait for Elijah by the remains of a wooden track which had once been used to launch floatplanes. The track had run from the top of the hill down on to a jetty and out into the water. All that was left of the top half were a few wooden posts, but the lower section still held together, jutting into the water like an abandoned pier.

Holly, the Thackerays' maid, answered the door and Colonel Charles Thackeray came out to greet us. I'd been a frequent visitor to the hall over the years after becoming friends with Alice at the age of eleven.

'Mr Whittle, do go through to my study. Iris, Alice is in the drawing room with her mother if you'd like to join them.' He looked askance at the trousers I was wearing.

'Iris is here to assist me and take notes. I hope that's acceptable to you?' Elijah's politeness didn't hide the fact that my inclusion was not negotiable. He'd arranged the meeting to discuss the army's position on Waldenmere in light of the general's death.

'Oh, yes. Of course. Working girl and all that.' He gestured for us to follow him into his study. The colonel walked cautiously. Inner ear damage from a grenade attack had left him with a sense of imbalance. He refused to use a stick, so Elijah and I shuffled awkwardly behind him.

I couldn't remember ever having been inside the study before. The door was always closed when I called to see Alice. It was an austere room, with framed maps hung on dark green papered walls. Rows of books on military history lined the shelves of a heavy mahogany bookcase. French doors led into the garden in an arrangement similar to General Cheverton's study.

'How is your father, Iris?' Colonel Thackeray gestured to a pair of leather-covered chairs before sitting behind his vast desk. 'Well, I hope?'

'I believe so. He was in Germany last time I heard from him. The country has suffered greatly since the end of the war.'

He stiffened. I sensed his disgust and wasn't surprised when Elijah took over the conversation.

'Thank you for agreeing to see us, Colonel Thackeray. The general's death must have come as a dreadful shock to you and your family.'

'We were all terribly fond of Samuel. It's sickening he should have been killed in such a way. You found his body, according to young Gilbert. Have you any idea what occurred?'

'The assumption is the general disturbed an intruder and they fired in panic. It didn't look like a professional job.' Elijah rubbed his chin. 'In my limited experience of these matters, I'd say the shot was fired haphazardly but unfortunately still managed to hit its target. It was a tragic end to such a distinguished life.'

'Shot by a coward and thief.' Colonel Thackeray thumped the desk with his fist. 'With his own revolver, too.'

'Do you know what sort it was?' Elijah asked.

'A Webley Mark IV. His old service revolver. He'd had it since the Boer War. I'm trying to get Army Intelligence involved. That superintendent from Aldershot seems competent enough, but young Gilbert hasn't the experience. We need someone with more intelligence to get to the bottom of this.'

I wondered if he made this type of comment in front of Alice. If he did, she would have to endure it in silence.

Nodding diplomatically, Elijah continued. 'Let's move away from this sad subject to the matter of the lake. Recently, I attended a meeting with Sir Henry Ballard regarding London and South Western Railway's interest in buying Waldenmere.'

'Damned man.'

For once, I agreed with the colonel.

'Are you aware of Aldershot Military Estates' current plans?'

'I'll be frank with you, Mr Whittle. Having spoken to some of my colleagues, we're in somewhat of a quandary.' He tapped his cigarette case on the table. Then, seeming to remember what it was for, he held it out to Elijah.

'Does that mean you may be about to sell?' Elijah gratefully took a cigarette, having politely refrained from lighting his own.

'I'm loath to admit it, but it's a possibility.' The colonel's hand shook as he struck a match.

'You're abandoning plans for a convalescent home?' Elijah sounded hopeful.

Colonel Thackeray brought a cigarette slowly to his lips. It was balanced precariously between unsteady fingers. 'It means we wouldn't be able to build on Heron Bay as planned. But we may be able to find suitable premises.'

I suspected he was thinking of Mill Ponds.

'Are you aware of the proposal to build a hotel near the railway station?' Elijah asked.

'I think you're probably better informed there than I am, Mr Whittle.' The colonel gave a deep sigh. 'I won't deny Sir Henry Ballard has approached us regarding the land. We had a heated discussion on the matter. I wanted to send the odious man away with a flea in his ear, but some of my colleagues felt differently.'

'Sir Henry plans to build a four-storey, eighty-bedroom hotel on the northern side of the lake, adjacent to the railway station.' Elijah clearly wanted to emphasise the extent of the building work planned.

The colonel dropped his cigarette. 'I hadn't expected anything of that size.'

'He showed us a picture of what he proposes.'

'On the northern side, you say?' Colonel Thackeray swept the smouldering cigarette into an ashtray. 'Perhaps we could still build on the southern side. Did he mention any plans for Heron Bay?'

Horace Laffaye would love that, I thought. A hotel on one side and a convalescent home on the other.

'No, he didn't. He spoke of temporarily draining Waldenmere to build a bay on the northern side with a promenade, bathing site and boathouse. And a raised swimming pool overlooking the lake,' Elijah threw in for good measure.

'Good God.' The colonel appeared suitably horrified. 'Drain the lake? Why on earth would he do such a thing?'

'It would only be a temporary measure to facilitate the construction of the new bay. He intends to demolish the reedbeds and bring in tonnes of sand to create something similar to Heron Bay.'

'Preposterous, completely preposterous.' The colonel sank back in his chair.

I silently agreed with this sentiment.

He seemed to consider the matter for a few moments, then suddenly leapt up. Startled, I jerked back in my chair.

'This must be stopped. A four-storey hotel? It would destroy Waldenmere and be the ruin of Walden.' Colonel Thackeray took a map from the shelf and spread it over his desk.

I tried not to stare at the wounds to his hand as he pointed at the map. The same grenade attack that had caused his inner ear imbalance had resulted in the loss of the ring and little finger of his right hand.

'What about Mill Ponds? Surely it would be in the way of this idiotic promenade and boathouse?'

'Sir Henry was under the impression Mill Ponds belonged to the army and would form part of the deal. It was the reason I decided to call on General Cheverton that afternoon. To tell him about LSWR's plans,' Elijah explained.

'You don't think Ballard could be involved?' The colonel stared out of the French doors towards the lake.

'Not unless he knew the contents of the general's will,' Elijah replied. 'Do you know who will inherit?'

Colonel Thackeray shook his head. 'I'd hoped we could persuade him to bequest Mill Ponds to the army for use as a convalescent home. That way, the chaps in Military Estates would have more incentive to retain ownership of Waldenmere. But the general was always rather cagey on the subject. I suspect he's left it to Nathan.' His expression showed what he thought of Nathan Cheverton. He slumped back into his chair. 'I don't think there's any more I can tell you.'

The sudden energy the colonel had displayed only moments before vanished as fast as it had materialised. I'd been aware of his volatile nature but it was the first time I'd seen for myself how quickly his mood could change. Living with Colonel Thackeray couldn't be easy.

Elijah nodded and we stood to leave. It was clear there was nothing more to be gained from the meeting.

6

Alice appeared in the hallway and I guessed she'd been waiting for us to emerge from her father's study.

'Thank you for writing such a lovely tribute to General Cheverton, Mr Whittle. It was touching to read how he influenced so many lives, especially those young men under his command.'

'I wrote what I knew of the general.' Elijah appeared bashful, much to my amusement. 'He'll be greatly missed.'

Alice nodded gravely. 'I wonder, is Iris still working, or could I possibly steal her away for the rest of the afternoon?'

'I think we've finished for one day.' He smiled at Alice but barked at me. 'You can make up the time tomorrow.'

I grinned as Holly shut the door behind him. 'Alice Thackeray, you can wrap the most cantankerous of men around your little finger.'

I followed her into the drawing room, where Florence Thackeray was seated by the window. Alice's spaniel, Bear, lay beside her.

'Iris. How's life at *The Walden Herald*?'

'It's become quite lively recently.'

I'd been awestruck the first time I'd met Florence. She'd turned heads with her flaming red hair and startling green eyes. As a plain child, Alice had confided she felt invisible when standing next to her glamorous mother. But the years had passed and Alice has become a beautiful young woman while the light had gone from her mother's intense emerald eyes and flecks of grey dulled her once vivid hair.

'Is Mr Whittle behaving himself? No secret drinking in the office?'

'Mother,' Alice remonstrated.

'Everyone knows Elijah Whittle likes a drink.' Florence waved a slender hand in the air. 'It's common knowledge. Ask anyone in Walden.'

'Elijah's always professional.' I was irritated by the truth of her words. 'He's an experienced journalist and I'm learning a lot from him.'

'Oh, ignore me. Who can blame him?' Florence rose from the window seat. Her movements were slow and laboured and she had a desolate look on her face.

'Are you feeling unwell again, Mother?' Alice reached down to pick up Bear.

'I'm fine, darling.' She kissed the top of Alice's head. 'Just a little tired. It's the shock of Samuel's death. I'll leave you and Iris to chat. I need to speak to Cook about the funeral arrangements. We're going to hold a reception here afterwards.' She left the room, leaving behind the lingering scent of her floral perfume.

'How has she been?' I asked. One of the things that had drawn Alice and me together at school was that our mothers weren't the same as everyone else's. Back then, Florence was always socialising or going away somewhere. Alice had sometimes feared her mother wouldn't come back. But over the years, Florence had lost her vitality and seemed to radiate an almost tragic air.

'She hasn't been the same since the war. It was difficult for her.

She couldn't entertain the way she had before. And we lost most of our maids to the war effort. Mother and I had to muck in with the cooking and housework. You can imagine how she hated that.' Alice played with Bear's ears and he gazed adoringly at her. 'We're lucky to have found Holly. It's so difficult to keep maids nowadays.'

Compared to the suffering other families had endured, it was difficult to feel too much sympathy for Florence. However, having just experienced Colonel Thackeray's strange mood swings, I suspected that keeping maids was the least of her problems.

'And food was scarce. She never really understood how rationing worked,' Alice continued. 'Uncle Samuel and Nathan helped out when they could, bringing us chocolates and other treats.'

'Do you know Nathan Cheverton well?' I asked.

She blushed. 'Sort of. When he was here, we'd paint together. He's very good. He'd teach me different techniques. I miss that.'

'Was he close to the general?'

'They were fond of each other. But Nathan didn't fit in with the battalion. With the other officers, I mean. He was always a bit bewildered.' She laughed. 'He never seemed to know what he was supposed to be doing.'

'How did your father feel about him?' I couldn't imagine Nathan meeting the colonel's exacting standards.

She gave a faint smile. 'Disappointed. I think that's how Father felt about him. He'd like me to marry someone with military connections and saw Nathan as a possible candidate. Fortunately for me, he soon went off that idea.'

'Good grief.' I was glad my father was too absorbed in his work ever to contemplate looking for a husband for me. 'Surely Nathan would be too old?'

'Nearly twenty years older than me.' She shuddered.

'Did he like you? In that way, I mean.'

'I'm not sure.' She blushed again. 'We got on well together when we painted. Before he left, I had an unpleasant encounter with him.'

'Did he try it on with you?' I immediately felt protective towards her.

'Not exactly. It was here, in the drawing room. Father was away and I've no idea where Mother was. Nathan was upset because he was about to go over to France.'

'What did he do?' I was intrigued.

'He wrapped his arms around me and held me tightly. He said he needed to hug someone and that he missed his mother.'

I resisted the urge to laugh. 'What did you do?'

'There wasn't much I could do. My arms were pinned by my side and I couldn't move. It was suffocating. Then he kissed the side of my head.'

'How horrible for you.'

'He wasn't aggressive, more agitated. It probably only lasted a moment or two, but it felt like an eternity. I was so relieved when he let go of me.'

'I can imagine. Did you say anything to him?'

'I think I said, "I hope you keep safe". He thanked me and left.'

'How polite.' I smiled. 'You handled the situation perfectly. The poor man was obviously traumatised. It happened to me a few times at the hospital but there were always doctors and nurses around to help. Being grabbed in your own drawing room must have been frightening.'

'Not the sort of social situation one's accustomed to dealing with.'

We laughed.

'I felt rather embarrassed. I decided not to tell anyone, for Nathan's sake. Father would have overreacted and I didn't want to cause any bad feelings between him and Uncle Samuel.'

'Didn't you tell your mother?'

'She kept disappearing.' Alice gave a rueful smile. 'I thought at one stage she might leave for good. You know what she was like when we were at school.'

I nodded. I'd hated the way Florence had neglected Alice. 'I'm sorry I wasn't here. It must have been lonely.'

'It wasn't much fun,' she admitted. 'I had no one I could talk to.'

We jumped at the sound of a door slamming. Bear let out a frightened yelp.

'Florence!' Colonel Thackeray bellowed.

Alice closed her eyes at the noise of something smashing. It sounded like a vase hitting the tiled floor of the hallway.

'Bloody railway companies,' the colonel shouted. 'Greedy bastards, the lot of them.'

'Sorry.' Alice stroked Bear's head. 'Father hasn't been himself since Uncle Samuel's death.'

'Our interview may have upset him. Perhaps we should go for a walk until he calms down?' I hoped the colonel wasn't about to thunder into the room. I wouldn't relish being on the receiving end of his temper.

'I need to see to him.' She put Bear down on the carpet and stood up. 'You'd better go.'

'Are you sure you'll be all right?'

'It's just Father in one of his moods.' She gave a hollow laugh. 'This way.' She directed me out through the French doors.

I could still hear Colonel Thackeray bellowing as I walked across the lawn. My instinct was to go back to Alice – the fear in her eyes had shocked me – but I had to respect her wish for me to leave.

7

It was market day and the high street was packed. Elijah would mutter curses under his breath whenever anyone dared to get in his way. His former gloom had returned and I guessed he was fretting over the prospect of Horace moving away and the newspaper closing.

The market was held in the square outside the council offices but as usual it had spilt over onto the high street. Townspeople were used to taking their carts around the side roads when food stalls blocked their way but it was unlikely visitors unfamiliar with local roads would be so tolerant of this weekly diversion.

I sidestepped out of the path of a market trader carrying a basket of fish on his head. I didn't want to turn up at the council offices smelling of haddock. Once again, we'd been summoned by Mrs Siddons. This time, to discuss a public meeting regarding the sale of Waldenmere.

At the council offices, George and I greeted each other with self-conscious mumbles and avoided eye contact as we made our way up the curved staircase. Elijah smirked in amusement. It was the most cheerful I'd seen him all morning.

As soon as we were seated, Councillor Mansbridge started to speak, presumably to pre-empt Mrs Siddons. 'In the interests of fairness, we intend to hold a public meeting in the town hall to give each party interested in buying Waldenmere a platform to present their case to the townspeople. Aldershot Military Estates has informed us that they haven't yet reached a decision on whether to sell. Certain high-ranking officers have been trying to raise funds for the convalescent home.'

'You mean General Cheverton and Colonel Thackeray?' Elijah said.

William Mansbridge inclined his head. 'I believe so. I think the general's death has brought matters to a head. Unofficially, I've been told if the money isn't found soon, the army will sell to the highest bidder—'

Mrs Siddons interrupted. 'This would leave the council and LSWR in direct competition. By opening up the issue to public debate, we'll give the good citizens of Walden the opportunity to have their say. And maybe nudge the army into making a decision in our favour.'

Councillor Mansbridge frowned.

'A tourist hotel would have a significant impact on the quality of life we enjoy here.' Mrs Siddons' emerald drop earrings swayed as she spoke. 'An increase in train services and a surge of visitors would disrupt the familiar routine of our town. I'd like *The Walden Herald* to focus on that when you publish details of the meeting.'

'Isn't this about fairness?' William Mansbridge complained. 'Surely the paper should be impartial and give an equal voice to each party?'

Mrs Siddons ignored him. 'This is about what's best for Walden and its growing population. The lake is what first attracted people to this area and it's why the town was formed. It needs to be preserved the way it is.'

I nodded in agreement.

'But does the council have sufficient funds to compete with LSWR?' Elijah asked.

Mrs Siddons gave a politician's answer. 'That remains to be seen. We want the town to flourish, but it has to grow in the right way, not become a tourist destination. We'd rather see new homes, a bigger school and other amenities for families, not large hotels that would destroy the character of the town. I'm sure the majority of your readers will agree with this sentiment.'

'That still leaves the question of where the council would find funding for these amenities and the purchase of the lake.' Elijah wasn't to be fobbed off.

'The government wants to try to ease overcrowding in the city by encouraging people to move to more rural locations. They're keen to help towns like ours grow if there's sustainable employment in the area. We're fortunate we have many thriving industries in this corner of north-east Hampshire. The government is aware Walden could provide decent homes for many families.'

I guessed she'd already been pulling strings in Parliament to try to raise the cash. And from my experience of campaigning with her the previous year, if anyone knew the right people to tap, it was Mrs Siddons.

'If the council is successful in obtaining the land, would it build houses around Waldenmere?' Elijah asked. Horace Laffaye liked his privacy and wouldn't welcome the arrival of new neighbours.

'No. The development of the housing estate at Crookham is already going ahead, so we meet the criteria for providing new homes.' Mrs Siddons had made good her election pledge of the previous year. 'But I've made it clear to central government that the appeal of the new estate is its rural location and proximity to the canal and Waldenmere. If the lake were privately owned, the area would be a less enticing proposition to families wishing to relocate.'

Elijah nodded in approval. William Mansbridge sighed. It was clear *The Walden Herald* would not be impartial.

* * *

I strolled to the town hall the following week, enjoying the warm evening sunshine. Lizzy and Betty had decided to accompany me purely so they could see Mrs Siddons. To my and Alice's amusement, they seemed to have formed a Mrs Siddons admiration society and liked to discuss every detail of her dresses and jewellery.

It was hot for June and I'd swapped my usual working trousers for a light green summer dress. I told myself it was because I was representing *The Walden Herald* at a public meeting and not because I planned to sneak off with George afterwards.

Lizzy and Betty went to find a couple of seats at the back while I waited outside, watching the great and good of Walden slowly trickle into the hall.

When the article on the proposed sale of Waldenmere had first appeared in *The Walden Herald,* talk in the town had been of little else. But that was before the murder of General Cheverton. Townsfolk had started to feel decidedly unsettled and I was curious to see how tonight's events would play out.

Mrs Siddons was expected to take the stand for Walden Council, while Colonel Thackeray would speak on behalf of the army. Sir Henry Ballard was also rumoured to be making an appearance.

Ben Gilbert appeared relaxed as he watched for any signs of a disturbance. The meeting was due to begin at seven – too early for any rowdiness from the regulars of the Drunken Duck.

'Working tonight?' he asked.

I nodded. 'I'm waiting for Elijah.'

'He's not happy about all this, is he?'

'Why do you say that?' I was alarmed. I knew the reason for Elijah's concern but it would be dangerous for anyone else to suspect the true nature of his relationship with Horace. Especially a policeman.

'It's caused some heated debates in the Duck.'

'Nothing serious, I hope?' My concern grew. Elijah could become argumentative after a few drinks.

'Just a few minor altercations. Everyone's got an opinion about this hotel business. And the general's murder has prompted whispers about a conspiracy involving LSWR.'

I was more than willing to add fuel to this fire. 'General Cheverton was an obstacle in their way. I think people are right to be suspicious.'

'If it was a hitman, it wasn't the most professional shot I've ever seen.' Ben evidently didn't believe this theory.

'If they had to find someone to do the job quickly any petty villain would have done. The general was an old man. They probably thought he was an easy target.'

'But we're pretty certain the gun used was the general's service revolver. I suppose it's possible they'd planned to bludgeon him to death, then came across the gun.' He shrugged.

'Hey, Ben.' George strolled towards us, his jacket hooked over his shoulder and his dark curls swept back. 'You should see the car that's coming around the corner.'

'I see you two know each other.' This made me slightly uneasy. Ben was one of my oldest friends. And although he had a close relationship with Alice, it was unlikely it was as close as the one I was enjoying with George. For some reason, I didn't want Ben to disapprove of me.

'Councillor Mansbridge regularly summons PC Gilbert to the

council offices to remind him that he's personally responsible for upholding the moral values of the town.' George did a convincing imitation of William Mansbridge's deep, pompous voice.

Ben laughed, then gave a low whistle as a gleaming black Daimler pulled up. The chauffeur opened the rear door and Sir Henry Ballard bounced out. I watched the pair go over to take a closer look, irritated by their enthusiasm. George looked more rakish than usual next to smartly uniformed Ben.

'You look jolly pretty,' said a familiar voice in my ear. I swung around.

Percy Baverstock was smartly dressed in a grey flannel suit, his floppy hair falling over his forehead as usual.

'What are you doing here?' My breath quickened.

'I'm here to save Waldenmere, of course.'

'Of course.' I tried to regain my composure. 'How do you intend to do that?'

'Walk with me to the railway station afterwards and I'll tell you all about it.'

'I can't.' He was standing close to me and I could see that George's attention was no longer on the car.

'You didn't reply to my last letter,' he whispered. Then he took a step back. 'Here comes the boss.'

Elijah was ambling towards us, panting. He ignored the crowd around the Daimler and came over to slap Percy on the back. 'Young Baverstock. What brings you here?'

'Important business, sir.' Percy gave a mock bow. 'I'll reveal all to your star reporter after the meeting.'

'Will you, indeed?' Elijah glanced over at George and smiled. 'I hope my star reporter gives you her full attention.'

Inside the hall, most people had veered towards the back or middle. Elijah headed straight for the front.

'Oh, Mr Whittle.' Horace Laffaye was sitting at the centre of the front row, immaculately dressed in a blue suit with a pale pink rosebud in his buttonhole. A Panama hat rested on his knee. It was hard to imagine this softly spoken man trading on Wall Street. He indicated to the seat beside him.

I sat on the other side of Elijah while Percy, who seemed determined to stay glued to my side, took the chair next to me. I glanced around to see if I could spot George, only to find he'd placed himself directly behind us. I could feel his eyes boring into my back as Percy leant over to whisper in my ear. I noticed Elijah and Horace looking on in amusement.

I gritted my teeth and turned to face the front. This was going to be a long meeting.

8

The hall filled up in the few minutes before the clock chimed seven. I turned to inspect the audience, ignoring George's stare. Lizzy and Betty were seated in the back row and there were a few other women dotted around, including Miss Millicent Nightingale, a teacher at Walden Elementary School. But the majority of the crowd were male, most of them local business owners.

Just after seven, the large frame of Councillor William Mansbridge filled the small stage. Rows of faces looked up at him expectantly.

'Good evening. It's gratifying to see so many of you here tonight. I want to begin by expressing my own sadness at the death of General Cheverton. I know the whole town is still in shock at this tragic event. Not only was the general a distinguished officer and gallant soldier, he was also a popular and highly respected citizen of Walden. He will be greatly missed.' He bowed his head for a brief moment before continuing. 'Now, to the matter at hand. I'm not surprised by this large turnout. In recent weeks, I've talked with many of you as I've walked around the town and been asked numerous questions regarding the future of Waldenmere. Tonight's meeting is to give you the opportunity to hear from each of the parties interested in buying the lake and question them yourselves. As Waldenmere is currently owned by the army, it seems only fair to let the present incumbent speak first. Therefore, I'd like to invite Colonel Thackeray to take to the stage.'

The colonel climbed the few steps up to the platform to a smattering of polite applause. At one point, he stumbled. Florence watched from her seat with her lips pursed. She made no move to assist her husband.

The colonel steadied himself and then turned to face the audience. 'General Cheverton cared about his men and he cared about Walden. I know I would have his full support in what I'm about to say.' His hand shook as he referred to the notes he held. 'The town of Walden has a proud history of serving the military. The British Army first acquired Waldenmere as part of a land deal that dates back to 1854. Since then, the military has been present on the lake in one form or another, trialling floatplanes and testing prototype tanks. As you know, we occupied its shores for the duration of the war.' His voice became grave. 'We lost many men during that long conflict. Many more are still suffering. I'd like to use Waldenmere to give something back. The tranquillity it offers makes it the ideal location for a convalescent home for our war heroes.'

Murmurs of agreement came from the audience.

'I want to reassure you that the home will in no way stop local people from enjoying the lake as they always have. We just want to allow our veterans to share in its beauty and provide them with the peace they need to recuperate.'

More murmurs of support came from the crowd but others seemed reticent. I didn't doubt the colonel's sincerity and it might have melted some of my hostility towards him if I hadn't witnessed his recent outburst and the fear it had brought to Alice's eyes. When I'd returned to Walden after a five-year absence, I'd been shocked to see how the war had aged the colonel. His once dark hair had become grey and his tall frame stooped. He'd always been a formidable-looking man and that hadn't changed, but his former vigour seemed to have been replaced by rage and bitterness.

'Does the army have the funds to build suitable premises?' Elijah asked.

'Here's the situation as it stands,' Colonel Thackeray barked as though he were addressing an officer of a lower rank. 'Aldershot Military Estates has evaluated the situation and will require some financial help if it's to retain the lake and fund the construction of a building large enough for our needs.'

'How many veterans would the home accommodate?' Elijah didn't flinch at the colonel's glare.

'Up to fifty, if we can get it kitted out properly. To help raise funds, my wife and I will be hosting a garden party at Sand Hills Hall.' He glanced at Florence, who returned a forced smile. 'I hope you'll all come along and spend what you can to help our war heroes. Let's show our wounded men how grateful we are to them for all they've sacrificed for our country. I believe building a convalescent home is the right thing to do and I know many of you feel the same.'

The colonel cautiously made his way down the steps to polite applause. The reception wasn't unanimous but there was certainly support for the plan.

Councillor Mansbridge took to the stage once more. 'I'd like to introduce you to someone you won't be familiar with. Sir Henry Ballard is a director of London and South Western Railway. As I'm sure you'll appreciate, he's a busy man. He's taken the time to come to Walden to speak to us this evening about the plans his company has for redeveloping part of the lake and building a hotel. Sir Henry, could I ask you to make the next address, please?'

Smiling at everyone he passed, Sir Henry made his way down

the central aisle of the hall. Surprisingly, given his somewhat corpulent frame, he skipped up the steps in a few graceful bounds.

'Good evening, everyone. I'm delighted to be here in Walden. You must all be very proud to live in such a beautiful town.' He beamed down at the crowd, unfazed by the hostile eyes that stared back at him. 'I know our plan to buy Waldenmere has come as a shock to you but I don't want you to be alarmed. Our intention is not to spoil a much-loved lake. If anything, we want to make it better. The railway has already brought much prosperity to Walden. We want to add to that by giving the town its first hotel.'

If Sir Henry hoped his enthusiasm would be infectious, he was soon dissuaded of that view. The more he bounded around the stage, describing the Waldenmere Hotel with its swimming pool, cocktail bar and promenade, telling the audience how it would brighten their lives, the louder the chorus of disapproval grew. In the end, Councillor Mansbridge had to intervene. He motioned for quiet and asked if there were any questions.

Elijah was the first to speak. 'When we last met, you mentioned you wished to acquire Mill Ponds. Is that still your intention?'

'That matter is on hold, given the tragic circumstances. I'm sorry I never got to meet General Cheverton; I understand he was a remarkable man. His death is clearly a great loss to the town and you have my condolences.' His solemn manner gave the impression he was as shocked as everyone else by the general's death. Nevertheless, he was still the one who potentially had the most to gain from it.

Ted Cox, publican of the Drunken Duck, got to his feet. 'We don't want a hotel. Or a swimming pool. Or a promenade, for that matter. It's not the bloody seaside. Walden's not a holiday resort. It's a quiet town. We don't want tourists here with cars and the like.'

Shouts of 'hear, hear' came from the crowd.

'That's not exactly a question, Mr Cox.' Councillor Mansbridge motioned for quiet. 'But I take your point. Does anyone else have anything to add?'

Jim Fellowes, owner of the Walden Emporium, stood. 'Why would you need to drain the lake? It's fine the way it is.'

If Sir Henry had anticipated local tradespeople would welcome the idea of a hotel, he was wrong. Ted Cox and Jim Fellowes were the spokesmen for the Walden business community. Other trades-folk would follow their lead.

Sir Henry beamed down at the unreceptive crowd. 'As I explained, the partial drainage of the lake would only be temporary while we construct the foundation for the promenade. For a short time, the weir will allow levels to fall while the work is in progress. Once the base of the promenade is in place, the water will be returned to its normal level.'

'You'll find all sorts of things down there.' Ted Cox sniggered. 'Those soldiers chucked in everything but the kitchen sink before they left. Maybe some dynamite too.'

This provoked laughter from the audience. Sir Henry seemed perplexed. Colonel Thackeray started to get to his feet to respond, then appeared to change his mind and sat down again.

'Is that true?' I whispered to Elijah. 'Did the army dump stuff in the lake?'

'I was still in France then though I've heard the rumours. Eyewitnesses saw all sorts of things being thrown in.'

Councillor Mansbridge seemed momentarily uncertain as to what to do next. He decided to keep things moving rather than be diverted by this revelation and gestured to Mrs Siddons. Resplendent in a plum-coloured silk gown that would have Lizzy and Betty swooning, she swept him aside before he could introduce her.

'Take the weight off those sizeable feet of yours, William. I'm the last act of the night so you can stand down.'

This caused more laughter from the crowd.

'I think everyone here knows me. My name is Sybil Siddons and I'm proud to be your Member of Parliament. I'm not an elected representative of Walden Council. So, what am I doing here tonight, you might ask?' No one did dare ask. She smiled down at her audience. 'I've been involved in politics for many years and I've made many useful contacts during that time.'

I knew this was true from a trip I'd made with her to the Houses of Parliament the previous year.

'Central government is keen to help towns like ours grow. But we must grow in the right way. We need a bigger schoolhouse, a local hospital and homes with amenities for families.' She paused and shook her head. 'Not a huge hotel to cater to the privileged few.'

Unlike Colonel Thackeray, she held no prompt cards. Instead, she looked directly at the people in the hall and gestured towards them.

'Waldenmere must be part of that growth. It's our local beauty spot, the jewel in our crown. It should belong to us. I believe I can secure the necessary funding for Waldenmere to become a public amenity. Just as it should be.'

I scanned the hall. The crowd was looking on with approval.

'The ownership of Waldenmere shouldn't be about who has the deepest pockets. It's not a bag of flour that can be bought by the pound from Mr Fellowes' excellent Emporium.' She smiled at Jim Fellowes, who shrank back in embarrassment. 'This should be about what's best for Walden. For its current citizens. And its future citizens, our children. For them, we must take control of the destiny of our town and our lake.'

Cheers echoed around the hall.

'I'm here tonight because I care about the people of Walden. You're my neighbours, my friends. I want us all to continue living in this wonderful town and enjoying our peaceful life here together, which is why I propose that Walden Council buys Waldenmere.' She stretched out her hands to the audience. 'And keep it just the way it is. Do I have your agreement?'

The hall was on its feet, applauding loudly.

'Unanimously agreed.' With that, she swept from the stage as though this was a *fait accompli*, not waiting for any questions.

I watched in awe as she made her way down the central aisle, vigorously shaking hands with her friends and neighbours. Percy went over to speak to her and I took the opportunity to give him the slip by discreetly following Elijah and Horace out of the hall. Lizzy and Betty were in the crowd around Mrs Siddons.

Outside, Sir Henry's Daimler had gone but Horace's had taken its place.

'Would you care to join me for a nightcap, Mr Whittle?' Horace was saying. The chauffeur opened the rear door and Elijah climbed in.

George was waiting by the side of the steps, chatting with Ben. I turned in their direction, but not fast enough. Percy appeared by my side.

'I look forward to hearing what you have to reveal to my star reporter,' Elijah called out of the car window before it moved off.

Ben strolled over. 'Hello, Percy. What brings you back to our neck of the woods?'

'This delightful creature.' Percy put his arm around my shoulder. 'I was sorry to hear you have a murder on your hands, PC Gilbert. No time for dominoes in the pub now.'

This was a reference to a comment he'd once made about the town being so quiet the local bobby did nothing but sit in the pub and play dominoes all day. Until the death of General Cheverton, this hadn't been far off the mark.

Ben smiled. 'I still have time for the odd pint. I'm knocking off for the night now if you'd like to join me.'

'Sadly, I must get back. I'm going to walk Iris home, then head to the station.' Percy gripped my arm.

'George, you coming?' Ben asked.

'Why not?' he said through gritted teeth. He cast me a meaningful glare before walking away.

'Alone at last.' Percy had a wicked grin on his face.

'What is it you want?' I gave up on trying to salvage the evening and set off down the high street.

'Do you know that chap?' Percy sped after me.

'Ben? Yes, of course I know him.'

'No. The other one. George?'

'He's a friend of mine.'

'He didn't seem terribly keen on me walking you home. I can tell these things, you know.'

'Very astute of you.'

'You didn't reply to my last letter.' He quickened his pace to keep up with me.

'I've been busy. Besides, I had nothing interesting to write.'

'It didn't work out with Constance, you know.'

'You told me in your letter.'

'I thought perhaps you and I could go to the pictures again like we used to.' He paused. 'I realise I may have been a bit insensitive that night you met me at the Foxtrot Club.'

'I didn't notice.' This wasn't true. I'd gone dancing, thinking we were about to embark on a romance. The evening hadn't turned out as I'd expected.

'I'm sorry if I was. I'd like us to be friends again like we were before.'

'We are friends.'

'So you'll come out with me sometime?'

'I'm too busy.' I wasn't going to let him off that easily. 'Anyway, tell me how you plan to save Waldenmere.'

'Do you remember the day we first met, when you came to one of the society's talks?' Percy was a member of the Society for the Promotion of Nature Reserves.

'At the Natural History Museum?'

'Yes, the speaker was Mrs Juliet Rendall.'

'I remember. She was very good.'

'She lives near here. In Odiham. Waldenmere's special to her. When I mentioned I'd met Mrs Siddons, she told me to get down here and offer our support.'

'How?' I slowed, suddenly interested.

'The idea is to lobby Parliament to give Waldenmere legal protection as a nature reserve. Mrs Siddons thinks it might have legs. I've arranged for Juliet to meet her. Do you think you can get Elijah to run a campaign in the paper?'

I smiled. 'I think I could arrange that.'

9

Elijah was pulling at his tie. I resisted the urge to adjust it for him. His dark tweed suit was too heavy for the warm June day and he was red in the face.

My black woollen dress was little better but it was the only one I had that was suitable for the occasion.

I'd written to tell my father of General Cheverton's death and he'd replied, asking me to represent him at the funeral. Although the service was held in the familiar surroundings of our local church, St Martha's, the general had been laid to rest with full military honours. Soldiers in dress uniform rubbed shoulders with locals in their Sunday best.

In the churchyard, Ben Gilbert came over to join us.

'Any news?' I fanned myself with the order of service.

Ben shook his head. 'Nothing so far. We've searched the grounds of Mill Ponds and the nearest section of the lake but there's no sign of the gun that killed the general. We don't have much else to go on.'

'Have you interviewed Sir Henry Ballard?' I wanted to see him rattled by being implicated. It might put him off buying Waldenmere.

'No. We have no reason to.'

I was disappointed. 'I know it's difficult to prove, but he could have arranged for someone to kill the general.'

'Just because you want him to be guilty doesn't mean he is.' Elijah examined the congregation, scribbling down a list of all the noteworthy attendees.

'But apart from him, who else would benefit from the general's death?' I wasn't willing to let Sir Henry off the hook just yet.

'Only one person,' Ben replied. 'And he doesn't have an alibi for the time of the murder.'

Elijah looked up sharply. 'Nathan Cheverton?'

Ben nodded. 'He could do with the money.'

'I can't see him doing something like that.' Elijah returned his notepad to his breast pocket. 'He was probably in London at the time. Doesn't he have someone who can vouch for him?'

'He wasn't in London. He was at Wildmay Manor.'

Elijah sighed. 'Poor Nathan.'

'Does he suffer from shell shock?' Wildmay Manor was the country residence of a wealthy banker. It was set in acres of privately owned countryside. During the war, it had been converted into a hospital for soldiers suffering from mental ailments.

Ben nodded.

'Then the staff will be able to vouch for him.' Elijah searched his pockets for his cigarette case. It had been a long service and we still had refreshments at Sand Hills Hall to come.

'He wasn't around that afternoon. He's a voluntary patient. He can come and go as he pleases,' Ben said. 'He was out painting, according to one of the nurses. No one saw him after lunch until about seven o'clock that evening.'

'Where does he say he was?' I asked. Wildmay Manor was only six miles from Walden.

'Painting by the lake,' Ben replied.

'Waldenmere?'

'He's not sure. The manor has its own lake.'

'He doesn't know which lake he was painting?' I said incredulously.

'He gets confused.' Elijah sprang to Nathan's defence. 'He's been through a lot.'

'Is he here?' I was curious to see this man.

'Over there, talking to Mrs Akers.' Elijah pointed his cigarette in Betty's direction.

Nathan stood at the entrance to the church, talking to Betty and Reverend Childs. He was a tall man with a shock of greying brown hair and a slightly bewildered expression. I could discern a slight resemblance to his uncle, more in his stature than his features.

'How's he coping?' I asked.

Elijah frowned. 'It's difficult to tell. He wasn't in the best shape before his uncle's murder. He was fond of old Cheverton, even though they were cut from different cloth.'

Colonel Thackeray approached Nathan with Florence and Alice trailing behind. Nathan seemed pleased to see Alice and she smiled sweetly at him. At the same time, she glanced over at me and gave a slight flicker of her eyebrows. I winked back at her.

'Is that Finlay with Superintendent Cobbe and Horace?' Elijah pointed towards a corner of the churchyard where the three men seemed to be having an intense discussion.

Ben nodded. 'Captain Finlay Fortesque.'

I looked over to where a tall, thin man in uniform with a small, neat moustache was talking to the superintendent. I'd seen him once before with Elijah and Horace.

'Military intelligence?' I remembered. He was one of Horace's contacts.

'They're looking into the assassination angle. A German spy still operating in this country,' Ben explained. 'The superintendent thinks it unlikely, but it keeps Colonel Thackeray off our backs. He's been complaining that us provincial officers aren't up to the job.'

'I wouldn't mind having a word with Finlay.' Elijah dropped his cigarette and headed over with Ben in tow.

The congregation seemed no nearer to making a move, so I wandered further into the churchyard. Earlier, I'd noticed some fresh flowers on my mother's headstone. Her grave was tucked away in a quiet corner close to an ancient yew tree. Propped up against the headstone was a sprig of purple lilacs tied with green and white ribbon – the colours of the suffragettes. I picked them up and sniffed the pungent scent.

At regular intervals, these flowers would appear, always purple with green. My mother's old comrades honouring her. At first, I'd resented them, but I'd come to accept she would always be remembered for the part she played in their fight.

'Iris,' Elijah said gently, 'it's time to go to Sand Hills Hall.'

I put the flowers back against the headstone and we left the churchyard together.

* * *

'Woodmore? Oh yes, I know your father, Thomas.' Nathan jerked his hand towards me and splashed whisky onto the Thackerays' woven rug. 'Fine man. What's he up to these days?'

I explained that my father was travelling in Germany, writing about the situation in the Rhineland for a news agency.

'I have friends in Cologne. They're practically starving. Scarcely any meat or butter to be had. Dreadful, just dreadful.' Nathan spoke loudly, causing heads to turn. In a room filled with military men, this remark earned him a few disapproving tuts. I was used to this when I mentioned the situation in Germany. Nathan's sympathy surprised me.

Under the circumstances, I decided to change the subject, in case he became too vocal on the issue. 'Are you staying at Mill Ponds?'

'No, haven't been near the place. Suppose I'll have to at some point.' He shuddered with what seemed like genuine horror.

I wondered what made him so afraid of going to the house.

'Think I'll head back to London tonight.' Nathan slopped more of his drink onto the rug. 'Why don't you come with me, Elijah? We can go to a club. Have some drinks, play some cards.'

Since arriving at Sand Hills Hall, Nathan had latched on to Elijah and seemed to look to him for guidance.

'Not tonight. Another time.'

'I'll miss the old boy, you know. Don't want to be here, though. Not keen on this place.' It wasn't clear if he was referring to Sand Hills Hall or Walden. His speech was starting to become erratic and difficult to follow. 'Won't come back again. Can I go now, d'ya think? No, must see Florence and dear Alice first.'

'I think they're in the garden.' Elijah guided him through the French doors. It seemed sensible to encourage him to leave. He was becoming increasingly incoherent.

'Attractive woman, Florence.' Nathan staggered slightly and Elijah took his arm. 'Shame what happened...' The sentence petered out and Nathan looked guilty. 'Shush, mustn't say any more.' He put his finger to his lips.

This aroused my curiosity, but it wasn't the time to ask what he meant.

Nathan suddenly spotted Alice and grabbed her hand. 'Beautiful girl,' he said to her. She took a step back in alarm. 'Want to paint your portrait. Haven't done many but going to try. In oils.'

'How interesting.' Alice moved closer to her mother.

'We were just leaving.' Elijah tried to prise Nathan away. 'Thank you for your hospitality, Mrs Thackeray.'

'So kind of you to come, Mr Whittle.' Florence followed Elijah's lead, helping to guide Nathan away from Alice and towards the driveway. 'It's good to see you again, Nathan. You must take more care of yourself.' It was said with a mix of affection and sadness.

'In white. Don't like black.' Nathan was pointing to Alice's dress. 'With your hair loose.' Several heads turned to stare at him.

'Perhaps you've time for a quick drink at the Duck before you catch your train?' Elijah tugged at his arm.

'Good idea. Fine fellow.' Nathan slapped him on the back.

Florence appeared relieved this distraction had worked and nodded her thanks to Elijah.

'Let's hide like we used to.' I took Alice's hand and we headed to a bench in the kitchen garden that was out of sight and sound of the house, stopping to pick a handful of strawberries on the way.

'Poor Nathan,' she said.

'He's in a sorry state, isn't he? Are you all right?'

'I'm glad you and Mother were there. It was kind of Mr Whittle to take him away.'

'Elijah will look after him.' Or, more likely, get drunk with him. 'How have things been with your father?'

'He's much calmer. I think arranging the funeral helped.'

'You're always welcome to come and stay if you'd like to get away for a while.' I was careful not to say too much. 'Though you'd have to share with me now that Betty's in the guest room.'

'Thanks. But everything's fine. Father's temper is usually short-lived. He went through a lot during the war, you know.'

I noticed her defensiveness and tried to reassure her. 'I'm sure he did. And the general's death must have been upsetting for him.'

'Father used to spend a lot of time at Mill Ponds. I think it was a refuge for him when he wanted to get away from Mother. For Uncle Samuel to die there in such a horrible way. It must have been dreadful for you to have found him like that.'

'Today brought it all back to me,' I confessed. 'I suppose I saw worse sights at the hospital, though it's different when it's someone you know in their own home.'

'I wish I could have volunteered in a hospital.'

'You did valuable work here.' I was glad she hadn't seen the horror of the wards. I knew her well enough to realise being so close to the pain and suffering of others would have scarred her too deeply.

'The Walden Women's Group occasionally tended to wounded soldiers, but mainly we helped families struggling financially with their menfolk away.'

'How did you become involved with the group?'

'Mrs Gilbert put up a poster outside the town hall. She organised a collection of food and clothes to distribute to needy families. I asked if I could help. Mother wasn't keen, but she didn't stop me. We thought we'd disband after the war, but we've kept going. Now we help soldiers with disabilities. We've been able to find jobs for some, though others can't work and we try to give financial support to their families. Mrs Gilbert is an absolute miracle worker when it comes to getting donations. The group would never have got off the ground without her.' Alice took a strawberry from the pile in her lap and bit into it.

'Is that how you and Ben became close?'

She blushed.

'Or do you just happen to find yourselves by Waldenmere at the same place at the same time?' I teased.

'Who was that man I saw you with by the lake the other day?'

I wasn't used to having the tables turned on me by Alice. 'When was that?'

'On Tuesday evening. You were walking close together and laughing. He had dark, wavy hair. You know who I mean.'

'Oh, that would have been George.'

'What does he do?'

'He works at the council offices as a clerk for William Mansbridge.'

'What's his background?'

I smiled at the question. 'He grew up in Basingstoke. When he was at school, he was awarded a scholarship to Winchester College. He enlisted in 1916 and was sent to France. He was injured a year later but stayed in the army, working in the office of General Bartlett.'

'How was he injured?'

'Caught in machine-gun and shellfire, carrying wounded men back to the trenches. He was awarded a Military Medal. He doesn't talk about it. I looked up his citation. It said, "He continued to search for injured men throughout the night and managed to evacuate many wounded soldiers from the front line at great personal risk".'

'Gosh.' She glanced at me from under her lashes and said with an innocence that didn't fool me, 'You went out of your way to look up his citation?'

I grinned. 'I'll admit it, I like him. But it's not serious. I don't think he'll stay around here for long.' I tried to sound as if I didn't care. 'He's working for the council so he can save up enough money to travel.'

She hesitated, then said, 'I like Ben. A lot.'

'He's a vast improvement on Nathan.' I shuddered at the

thought of Alice saddled with poor Nathan Cheverton. 'Your mother must have realised he was unsuitable?'

'She never took it seriously. She knew what Nathan was like. Not that he was that bad in those days. He and Mother were very fond of each other. I suppose they're of a similar age. He was someone she could confide in when Father was away.'

Nathan and Florence? I wondered what Nathan had been about to say when he'd stopped himself. Could he and Florence have had an affair in the colonel's absence? If General Cheverton had found out, it would have caused a scene. Although, I had to admit, it was unlikely Nathan would have waited all this time to retaliate. But secrets did have a way of coming out later.

10

Percy had sunk into the depths of one of Mrs Siddons' plush red velvet sofas. His long legs jutted out, nudging an occasional table that was perilously close to toppling.

Elijah and I had received an invitation from Mrs Siddons to call on her at Grebe House, her elaborately decorated home. With an ivy-covered gabled roof and rows of pretty arched windows, Grebe House was in the enviable position of overlooking Grebe Stream as it flowed into Heron Bay.

'I'd like you to meet Mrs Juliet Rendall, a founder of the Society for the Promotion of Nature Reserves. And you know Percy.' Mrs Siddons was wearing an amethyst silk gown with matching marcasite and amethyst necklace. I stored up the details to share with Lizzy and Betty later.

'I'm pleased to meet you, Mrs Rendall.' Elijah nodded politely. 'Perhaps you could tell me why the society formed? And when?'

Juliet Rendall was a striking woman of about thirty. Her blue eyes were quite dazzling, set against pale skin and luxuriant dark hair. Despite her height, she managed to assume a more upright position on the sofa than Percy.

'We started in 1912. Our intention was to secure legal protection for sites across the country considered worthy of preservation due to their importance to nature.'

I'd heard her give a talk at the Natural History Museum the year before and remembered how compelling she'd been as a speaker. I'd gone along to investigate another matter but her knowledge and commitment to her cause had captured my interest.

'As you'll have guessed, Waldenmere is one of the sites the society believes is of national importance,' Mrs Siddons said. 'And Mrs Rendall is an expert on its wildlife.'

'I've been studying Waldenmere for years and many of its habitats have been lost because of army occupation. The marshland surrounding the lake forms one of its most interesting environments.'

'I hope you don't mind me asking, Mrs Rendall, but if the army's occupation has already destroyed many habitats, how worthy is it of preservation?' Elijah gingerly shifted his weight, aware he was dangerously close to joining Percy in the depths of the sofa.

'Please, call me Juliet.' She smiled at the question. 'It's a good point. But nature has a way of adapting. Since the army left, an extraordinary number of species have re-established themselves.'

'Look at all the herons that have returned to nest at Heron Bay.' Percy struggled to sit up. 'And some wonderful aquatic plants are reappearing in Willow Marsh.'

'Has the society been successful in obtaining government protection for any other sites?' Elijah asked.

'Not as yet,' Juliet admitted.

'But we will,' Percy said with conviction. 'Give us time.'

'It's another string to our bow.' Mrs Siddons waved a finger at Elijah. 'We need all the ammunition we can muster to persuade the government to fund the purchase of Waldenmere.'

'You feel the society could add some weight?' Elijah seemed doubtful.

'Don't be cynical, Mr Whittle. When we hold a second public meeting, Juliet is going to talk about the history of Waldenmere and what we could potentially lose if developers are allowed to destroy valuable natural habitats.'

I was sure Mrs Siddons hadn't a clue what those natural habitats were but a little thing like that wouldn't stop her from persuading people they needed to be saved.

'Not many people know Walden was originally home to two lakes.' Juliet swept her long dark hair back from her face.

'Really?' This had Elijah's attention. 'I've lived in Walden for years and never heard of a second lake.'

'It was believed to have been destroyed in 1567.'

'Really, 1567. How interesting.' His tone indicated it was anything but.

'The lake has a fascinating history.' Juliet was undeterred. 'It's manmade, hence the weir that will enable Sir Henry to lower the water level. It's likely a natural watercourse was dammed to create two lakes. Fish and waterfowl would have provided a vital source of food for the local population.'

'Juliet probably knows more about Waldenmere than anyone,' Percy said with some pride.

'What happened to the second lake and where was it?' I was interested, even if Elijah wasn't.

'Maps show it was north of the current lake, on the other side of where the railway line is now. It's thought that in a heavy storm in 1567, a great flood washed away the head of the second lake,' she explained.

'Don't you think your readers will be intrigued to learn about the history of Waldenmere and how it's become an important place for wildlife?' Mrs Siddons prompted Elijah.

He seemed to struggle to find a response to this.

'We truly want to help. Of all the sites I've visited, Waldenmere is the most special to me. I'd hate to see it destroyed by developers. If the lake is turned into a holiday destination and overrun with tourists, at least I'll have recorded what was there for posterity, along with my predecessors.' Juliet's tone was measured and thoughtful. She was more understated than Mrs Siddons but I thought the two of them would make a formidable team.

'What do you mean, your predecessors?' I asked.

'The naturalists who came to Waldenmere in the last century and recorded their findings. That's how we know which species have already been lost. Some journals are in the Natural History Museum. Others are closer to home in the herbarium at University College, Reading. Perhaps you'd like a trip to the museum? I can show you records from over fifty years ago.'

I nodded. 'I'd like to write an article on the history of Waldenmere and the second lake.' I ignored Elijah's withering glance. 'I think our readers would be interested to know how it's weathered the activities of its previous owners. I could list all the species that have already been destroyed to highlight why it needs protection.'

'Excellent.' Mrs Siddons nodded. 'Juliet and Percy will be able to supply you with all the information you need.'

'We'd be delighted.' Percy beamed at me.

Mrs Siddons' butler, Mr Grosvenor, opened the door for a maid, who came in bearing a tray of tea and scones.

'You'll have to make do, I'm afraid. There has been some conflict in the kitchen and I am currently without a cook,' Mrs Siddons said dryly. Mr Grosvenor sniffed and left the room without comment.

Elijah chewed morosely on a solid scone. While Mrs Siddons enthused at the prospect of Waldenmere becoming a nature reserve, he clearly didn't think this was about to cause Sir Henry any headaches.

* * *

'Oh, Mr Whittle.'

Elijah and I were returning to the office when Horace Laffaye appeared, dressed in a pale grey suit, a Panama hat covering his closely cropped white-grey hair.

He was standing by the gate of his house on Heron Bay, arguably the prettiest aspect of the lake. A natural curve of sand surrounded by trees formed a picturesque bay, offering a panoramic view of the water. Behind it, tucked away in a copse of trees, stood Heron Bay Lodge, a stylish wooden-clad house with a high veranda that overlooked Waldenmere.

'Oh, Mr Whittle. Could I have a word? It would save me a trip into town. Perhaps a small nip of brandy could persuade you? Or is it too early?'

No doubt Horace knew of Mrs Siddons' invitation and wanted to hear all about our meeting.

'How can I refuse?' Elijah turned to me. 'I'll see you back at the office.'

I waved at Horace and continued along the footpath until I was out of sight of the house. Then I found a patch of grass in a clearing and sat down to study the lake.

Bright yellow marsh marigolds decorated the shoreline. Partially hidden by reeds, a grey heron stood motionless, scrutinising the water. Near my feet, a pair of mallard ducks waddled out of the lake, eight feathery little ducklings stumbling after them.

I needed to learn more about the habitats that Sir Henry's hotel would destroy so I could write an article that would shock people into understanding what they were about to lose.

'What are you doing down there?'

I looked up to find Percy watching me. 'Appreciating the nature of Waldenmere.'

'Where's Elijah?'

'Gone for a drink with Mr Laffaye. He lives over there.' I pointed to Heron Bay Lodge.

'He'll be a while then.' He flopped down and lay back on the grass.

'Maybe, but I still need to get back to the office.' I noticed how tanned his skin was. He looked as if he spent more time outdoors than in the museum.

'No, you don't. You need to work on your article with me.'

'With Juliet. Tell me about her?'

'She's extremely knowledgeable. Her father was a professor of botany at the university in Reading and helped form the herbarium there in 1900. Juliet and her brother, Robert, followed in his footsteps.'

'Is her husband involved too?'

'He was. She lost her husband and brother in the war.'

'God, how awful.' I couldn't imagine being a widow at such a young age.

'She saw action herself. She was a mechanic and an ambulance driver in the Women's Army Auxiliary Corps. Then she trained as a nurse. She's incredible.' His tone was reverential.

'You sound like you're in love with her.' I knew from personal experience how easily Percy could lose his heart.

'More in awe.' He pushed his hair out of his eyes, looking self-conscious. 'I've never met anyone like her.'

'Why don't you ask her out dancing?' I'd never known Percy not to invite a good-looking woman to go to his favourite club in Soho.

'She's over thirty. And a widow.'

I snorted. 'You're twenty-six. Thirty isn't old.'

'No, I suppose it isn't.' He didn't seem to have considered this. 'It just sounds old.'

'For a woman?' I'd seen the way he looked at her. I suspected that if she gave him any encouragement, he wouldn't hesitate, despite her thirty years of age.

'When you put it like that, perhaps I have been dismissive of the older woman. I shall give it some thought. Opens up whole new possibilities.'

'As if there aren't enough possibilities already.'

He laughed. 'I know you think I'm fickle. Perhaps you're right. But I do care for Juliet. She's been through such a lot but still manages to keep her convictions. I admire that about her.'

'She seems very committed.'

'She adored her father and brother and wants to continue their work. Waldenmere is particularly close to her heart. I'm going to do everything I can to help her with this.'

'Me too.' I nodded.

He reached out to take my hand. 'What about you? Have you been out dancing with anyone else?'

'No.' I pulled my hand away.

'What about that fellow the other night? The one who looked like he wanted to throttle me?'

'Lots of people want to throttle you.'

'George, that was his name,' he said, as if just recalling it. 'Are you seeing him?'

'We're friends.'

'That means you're seeing him. Is it serious?'

'He's fun. I like his company, that's all.'

'You used to like my company,' he complained.

'I need to get back to work.' I stood up.

He jumped up, flicking his floppy hair from his face. 'Let me show you something before you go. It's a flower I haven't seen here for years, so I was thrilled when I spotted it again.'

I couldn't resist following him. We left the footpath and pushed our way through the bracken until we were in a damp, grassy glade.

He knelt to point out a tiny flower with delicate pink petals surrounding a brown and yellow centre lip. 'The Bee Orchid. So called because the flower resembles the bee it's trying to entice into pollination. Before the war, there were more but the army trampled the ground and compacted the soil. They'll return in time if we can create the right conditions again.'

While his long, angular body had seemed awkward in the confines of Mrs Siddons' decorative drawing room, he was at home in this outdoor setting. I had to admit, I still found him attractive, if annoying.

I crouched down to examine the flower. 'It's beautiful.' It was incredible in its design – a perfect imitation of a bee.

He was pleased by my reaction. 'I thought you'd like it.'

'I don't think I've ever seen one before. I used to come here with my mother to collect wildflowers.'

When I thought of my mother, it was in two separate periods. The time we'd spent in Walden when I was young, collecting wild-flowers and paddling in the lake. One summer, we'd picked a single bloom of every flower we could find. Mother, a city girl, had delighted in discovering the names of each. Then came our time in London when she was a suffragette. I preferred to remember those earlier years, but I'd long since forgotten the names of all those flowers. It was time to rediscover them.

'Come to the museum. I'll show you some of the paintings we have of Waldenmere and its wildlife.'

'I'd like that.'

'And I'll take you to the pictures afterwards.' With that, he kissed my cheek and bounded off before I could reply.

* * *

Elijah returned to the office smelling of brandy and cigars. He headed into his den, his face a picture of gloom.

'Did Mr Laffaye have anything interesting to say?' I hovered by his door.

'He wants me to go to London to talk to Nathan Cheverton.'

'About Mill Ponds?'

He nodded.

'Why is Nathan so scared of going there? To Mill Ponds, I mean?'

'Brings back memories of the war.'

Or memories of his uncle's dead body? 'Why does Mr Laffaye want you to go and see him?'

'To try to persuade him not to sell Mill Ponds to London and South Western Railway.'

'Has Nathan definitely inherited it, then? Surely it can't happen that quickly?'

'He's heard on the grapevine that, subject to probate, a deal's already been done.' He looked deflated.

'That can't be true.'

'I'm afraid Horace's informants are nearly always correct.'

11

'Here comes Boadicea.' Alice laughed as Mrs Siddons made her way across the Thackerays' lawn. 'Who drew that wicked cartoon?'

'I don't know. Elijah won't tell me,' I replied. 'But I'm determined to find out.'

An anonymous cartoon had appeared in *The Walden Herald* depicting a helmet-clad Mrs Siddons, leading 'her people' of Walden to victory.

'Keep that damned woman away from me,' Colonel Thackeray growled. 'Too damn full of herself for my liking.'

'Who's that with her?' Florence Thackeray asked.

'Mrs Juliet Rendall and Mr Percy Baverstock, from the Society for the Promotion of Nature Reserves,' I replied.

'Good grief, I've heard everything now.' The colonel shook his head.

'What are they doing in Walden?' Florence ignored her husband.

'Mrs Siddons plans to petition the government to make Waldenmere a nature reserve.'

'I don't want to talk to them. Deal with it, Florence.' The colonel limped away. Alice shot me an apologetic look and trailed after him. She was acting as host at the garden party alongside her father, while Florence had commandeered me as her right-hand woman to ensure everyone behaved themselves.

Florence appeared momentarily flustered but recovered and smiled graciously at the new arrivals. 'So kind of you to come.'

'We must support our veterans.' Mrs Siddons wore a wide-brimmed lilac hat and carried a lilac parasol. 'Your garden is glorious, Mrs Thackeray. What beautiful sweet peas. They smell divine.'

'Thank you. They're Alice's favourite flower. Mrs Rendall, Mr Baverstock, Iris has been telling me about your society. I believe you'd like to see the lake become a nature reserve?'

'We think it should be given legal protection. When we set up the society, Waldenmere was one of the first sites we put forward for consideration.' Juliet wore a simple blue linen dress that suited her angular figure. 'With Mrs Siddons' support, we're planning to lobby the government.'

'You're familiar with the lake? What made the society think it needed protection?' Florence asked.

'I live in Odiham. My father used to bring my brother and me over to Waldenmere when we were children to study wildlife,' Juliet explained. 'He knew the lake's proximity to the town and railway put it at risk. Once a town starts expanding, there's no saying where it will stop. Nothing can stand in its way, not even a lake. We expected the army would sell Waldenmere at some stage. The war only delayed the inevitable.'

'I wish you every success, Mrs Rendall. I, too, would like to see Waldenmere preserved. I can see the detrimental impact it would have on our town if too much development is allowed.'

'And I support your efforts to fund a convalescent home,' Juliet replied. 'I believe the two could work in harmony if we manage the lake as a nature reserve. Nature is so important to healing. When I

was at Wildmay Manor, I saw how beneficial it was to the men.
Percy told me what your husband said at the public meeting. I was
hoping I might be able to speak with him on the matter.' Juliet
scanned the lawn, but Colonel Thackeray was nowhere to be seen.
Alice was standing on her own, greeting guests.

'I'm not sure where Charles has disappeared to. Perhaps he's in
the tea tent.' Florence gestured in that direction. 'I'm sure he'd be
fascinated to hear what you have to say.'

We'd seen the colonel shut himself in his study and I think we
both suspected he would stay there for the rest of the afternoon.

'Tea, what an excellent idea. I'm parched. I do hope the party is
a great success.' Mrs Siddons led Juliet and Percy away.

Florence's eyes followed them as they walked over to where
Holly was serving tea and cakes. I waited for her to turn her attention back to me but she stood silently, staring at them, a blank
expression on her face.

'Are you admiring Mrs Rendall's dress or Mrs Siddons' parasol?'
I joked in an attempt to bring her out of her reverie. We were
supposed to be checking the beer tent had enough glasses and that
the games weren't becoming too unruly.

She came back to life and gave me a knowing smile. 'I was
admiring Mr Baverstock. Alice has mentioned him. Is he still sweet
on you?'

I squirmed. 'We're just friends. He and Mrs Rendall are helping
me put together an article on why Waldenmere should become a
nature reserve.'

'I wish them every success. I truly want the lake to stay the way
it is.' She noticed my enquiring look. 'Don't get me wrong. I agree
with my husband; our war veterans must be cared for. I'm more
than happy to raise funds for a convalescent home but I don't think
it should be here. We did enough during the war. The town toler-
ated the camp and Samuel even gave up his house. It's time for

Walden to move on. A convalescent home would be a constant reminder.'

'Yes, I suppose it would.'

'You weren't here. You don't know how much we all gave.' Florence sounded almost accusing. 'I don't think Walden is the right place or has the necessary facilities for that type of establishment. It would be better suited to a larger town. Of course, I keep these views from my husband.'

I wondered if these were the only things Florence kept from her husband. 'If you discussed it with him, don't you think the colonel would see your point of view?'

She laughed. 'I'm not encouraged to express an opinion in my own home.' She added in a gentler tone, 'I hope things will be different for you and Alice.'

'It depends on who we marry, I suppose. Or if we marry.' I wondered if I dared broach the subject of Ben.

'You don't sound too keen on the idea?' She gave me an amused glance.

'I'd rather do other things with my life.'

'Good for you. I hope you get to do those things. So, if not Mr Baverstock, what about the dark-haired young man who's been smiling at you from afar this afternoon? What's his name?'

I'd spotted George but hadn't had the opportunity to speak to him. 'George Hale. He works at the council offices. I met him when Elijah and I went to interview the councillors.' This wasn't strictly true but it sounded more respectable than saying George had a habit of hanging around for me after work.

'He's a handsome young man.' Florence's eyes twinkled and for a moment I saw a glimpse of the woman I'd known as a child. 'Is he fun?'

'He makes me laugh.' I couldn't help but smile back at her. 'He doesn't take things too seriously.'

'And you're not planning on taking him home to meet your father?' She said this in a conspiratorial whisper.

I shook my head, unsettled by the question.

'Don't worry. I'm not going to say anything. Why shouldn't you have some excitement? George looks like he'd be good company. Unlike Ben Gilbert. I know Alice has taken a shine to him but he's a little too earnest for my taste.'

So, Florence knew about Ben. 'If Alice wanted to see him, would you object?'

'Not if I thought he could make her happy but I'm afraid he can't.'

'Why not?'

'Because he's the son of a blacksmith.'

'And that matters to you?' I let my annoyance at her attitude show. 'Despite the fact that he's trustworthy, hardworking and respected in the town.'

'Oh, don't be so hot-headed. No, his background doesn't matter to me.' Her sad smile returned. 'But it matters to my husband. He'd never permit Alice to see someone of that class. And Alice loves her father too much to disobey him. Or if she did, she'd feel miserable and disloyal. So, you see, Ben can't possibly make Alice happy.'

I struggled to find an argument with this and hated to admit the truth of what she'd said. 'What if Alice doesn't like any of the men Colonel Thackeray approves of?'

'I pray that some day some young man will come along who fits the bill.'

We both knew this was unlikely.

'I don't think I'll ever get married.'

'I don't blame you. It's not much fun. I was twenty-one when I married. Alice was born the same year. Charles was away fighting in the Boer War, picking up medals for bravery and I was at home minding the baby and wondering where my life had gone.'

How many other women later regretted their marriage choices? Was this why Florence had changed from the beautiful, vivacious woman she'd once been into this world-weary soul?

'Come on.' She took my arm. 'Let's do the rounds and make sure everyone's behaving themselves.'

I was glad the conversation was over. Since my return to Walden, I'd noticed that Florence talked to me like a grown-up, yet she still treated Alice like a child.

The afternoon dragged on and even when it was clear the party was over, people were reluctant to leave. Townsfolk were still in shock over the general's murder and small groups lingered to gossip. I breathed a sigh of relief when the final guests drifted away and the clearing up could begin.

Alice helped Holly ferry all the crockery back to the kitchen while I took down the bunting. Once I'd wound it all into neat bundles, I went in search of the box it was stored in. I wandered towards the hall but stopped when I heard raised voices coming from the open doors of the colonel's study.

'People were wondering where you were, Charles. You arranged the damn party. The least you could have done was to be there to greet your guests.' Florence's voice was high and shrill.

'You managed perfectly well without me. In fact, I'm sure you preferred me out of the way. I saw you simpering over that foppish young chap from the nature society.'

'Don't be ridiculous. I was being polite. Why do you always think the worst?'

'I wish I'd got rid of you when I had the chance.' Colonel Thackeray's voice was low and vicious. 'Alice and I would be happier without you.'

12

It was nearly eight o'clock before I left Sand Hills Hall and walked down the slope towards the lake.

George appeared from under the old jetty. 'I thought it would be safer to wait for you down here. Colonel Thackeray still puts the fear of God into me.'

'What's in the bag?' I asked.

'Beer. Do you want one?'

'I most certainly do.' The quiet stillness of Waldenmere and the cool evening air were bliss after the heat and tension of the afternoon.

'Who was that posh twit who insisted on walking you home the other night?' He took my hand and we began to stroll towards our bench.

'Percy Baverstock. He's a friend.'

'What was he doing with Mrs Siddons today? And who was that with him?' His manner was casual but I could tell he was put out.

'Percy and Mrs Juliet Rendall are members of the Society for the Promotion of Nature Reserves.'

He pulled a face. 'The society for what?'

'They lobby the government to try to introduce legal protection for places they think are important to nature.' I flopped down onto the bench and stretched out my legs.

'What are they doing here?' He opened the bottles and handed one to me.

'Helping Mrs Siddons with a bill she wants to propose to make Waldenmere a legally protected site, a nature reserve.' I took a swig of beer. It was warm but delicious.

'She's kept that quiet from Mansbridge.'

'Has she?' I knew there was friction between them but I thought they were working together on this. 'Doesn't she trust him?'

'I think it's one-upmanship. Mansbridge makes it clear he doesn't like being told what to do by a woman.'

This didn't surprise me. 'She's got more experience in politics than he has.'

'And he knows it. Probably why he's intimidated by her.'

I smiled. 'It sounds like you admire Mrs Siddons?'

'I do. And I enjoy seeing old Mansbridge getting hot under the collar. But I'm employed by the council and he's my boss. He expects me to tell him what's going on.'

'You can tell him about the society. It's common knowledge now.'

'Why's this Percy hanging around you?'

'He and Juliet are helping me with research on an article I'm writing about Waldenmere.' I put the bottle on the bench and gave him a shove. 'At least Percy has an excuse to be seen with me. Mrs Thackeray spotted you looking in my direction today.'

'She's not planning on telling your dad about me, is she?' He dangled the bottle between his fingers.

'No.' I leant into his shoulder. 'She thought you were handsome.'

He laughed. 'I'm flattered, but scared. I wouldn't want to get on the wrong side of Thackeray. Everyone was terrified to go near the untouchable Alice.'

I pulled back. 'Why do you call her that?'

'It's what the lads in my unit used to call her. Your life wouldn't be worth living if you went anywhere near the colonel's daughter. Rumour was that Thackeray kept a tight rein on her in case she inherited some of her mother's tendencies.'

'That's so unfair. Alice is nothing like her mother.' In my haste to defend Alice, I unwittingly revealed more about Florence than I'd intended.

'So you know what I'm talking about?' he said with a grin.

I didn't reply immediately. Then I asked, 'Has there been gossip in the town?'

'Not recently. But there was a rumour Mrs Thackeray was seeing someone while the old man was away during the war and she planned to run off with him.'

'Florence would never leave Alice.' Then I thought of the argument I'd overheard and remembered Alice's fears at school that one day she might come home to find her mother gone. Could Florence and Nathan Cheverton have planned to run away together? Nathan might have lost the charm he'd once had – and as a penniless artist, he wouldn't be able to support Florence in the style she was accustomed to – but he might be more appealing if he inherited Mill Ponds and sold it.

'Did you ever get posted to Mill Ponds?' I asked.

'Briefly, in 1917. I was sent there for training.'

'Did you have much to do with General Cheverton or Colonel Thackeray?'

'The general liked to come and have a drink with us, but Thackeray kept his distance. I was only there for a week. Not officer material.'

'Why not?'

'I'm a working-class boy. Educated enough to be a clerk in the back room but not fit for command.'

'Did you want to become an officer? When you joined up?'

'I didn't have a clue what I wanted. Me and my cousin, Reg, went to the recruiting office together in June '16, soon as we turned eighteen. We couldn't wait to go to war and see a bit of the world.' He gave a bitter laugh. 'All we saw was hell.'

'What happened after you left Mill Ponds?' I wanted to hear everything, but knew he'd tell me nothing.

'I was shipped over to France.' He tapped his leg. 'I got injured.'

'You got a medal.'

'So bloody what?' He gulped his beer.

'Did you ever go back to the front line?'

He shook his head. 'They needed someone to work for General Bartlett. I was lucky, I suppose. My scholarship saved my life. I had enough schooling to do office work.'

'What about Reg?'

'Not so lucky. Killed in Italy. Battle of Piave. Just one week before Armistice.'

'God.' I took his hand. 'I'm sorry.'

He gripped my hand and pulled me towards him, burying his face in my hair. I held him tightly and breathed in the scent of his warm skin.

'Ready to immerse yourself in the world of nature?' Percy was leading me down one long corridor after another. It crossed my mind that we might end up in an illicit underground dancing club.

I felt as if we'd done at least two circuits of the Natural History Museum before he came to an abrupt stop. He swung open the door to a narrow room lined on both sides with shelves crammed full of boxes. Juliet was standing by a long table.

'I've pulled out all the journals relating to Waldenmere. These are just a few of the species that have gone: *Hottonia palustris, ranunculus flammula, ranunculus lingua, potamogeton natans, potamogeton pusillus, elodea canadensis, zannichellia palustris.*' She turned the pages of a volume dated 1870.

'Water violet, lesser spearwort, greater spearwort, broad-leaved pondweed, small pondweed, Canadian pondweed and horned pondweed are some of the plants that have disappeared from the lake since the army took over,' Percy explained. 'Though I think I've seen some water violet blooms in Willow Marsh, near to that old jetty.'

'Really?' Juliet seemed ecstatic. 'That's marvellous. You must show me.'

An animated conversation followed, which made me realise that no matter how interested I became in nature, I was never likely to get that excited over a water violet.

'What caused these species to disappear?' I asked when they'd calmed down a little.

'In recent years, battle tanks.' Juliet peered over the spectacles that were perched on her nose. 'The army tested them at Waldenmere, which caused soil erosion and large quantities of silt ended up in the water, destroying aquatic vegetation. In turn, this reduced the number of other species able to survive in the lake.'

A daunting quantity of records had been filed over the years and we spent the following two hours trawling through them. Juliet and Percy were in their element, delving into every journal with delight. I took copious notes but was overwhelmed by the Latin names and had no idea what I would do with the information. When Juliet decided it was time to call it a day, I gladly tucked my notebook into my satchel.

'Do you have to rush back to Walden?' Percy helped me with my jacket. 'There's a new Douglas Fairbanks film showing. Why don't we all go?'

'Lizzy will expect me back for supper.'

'I'll walk with you to Waterloo Station, then.'

'I can drive you to Walden. I need to get home.' Juliet clipped together the notes she'd made and tucked them into a battered leather case. 'My car's outside.'

Juliet had parked her black Ford Model T on Cromwell Road. A disappointed Percy opened the car door for me and waved us off.

Juliet waved back. 'Percy's a lovely man. He's been my rock, especially when I was in a bad way after the war. Keeping the society going can be a lonely business. I'm so pleased you're keen to help us.'

'I confess, I feel like a hypocrite. Waldenmere is special to me because of my mother. I don't want it to change for personal reasons. But I've never given any thought to its conservation before now.' I sat back in the leather seat, enjoying the ride. I loved travelling in motorcars, except when it was Mrs Siddons driving – that was too hair-raising.

Juliet smiled. 'It usually takes something personal to ignite people's emotions and make them think about the bigger issues. Waldenmere's special to me because of my family.'

'It must have been hard.' I struggled to find appropriate words. 'Losing your husband.'

She nodded. 'And my brother. You lost your mother at a young age, I believe?'

'I was fourteen.' I wondered how much she knew about my mother's death.

'Percy told me she was a suffragette. I was part of a suffragist group, but not a militant one. I mailed out newsletters and handed out leaflets. I didn't take part in any protests.' She glanced over at me. 'I guess campaigning against injustice runs in your blood?'

'I suppose it does.' I thought about Mother. What would she have done to fight Sir Henry? I remembered when she chained herself to the railings outside the home of a well-known politician. 'Perhaps I should organise a protest.'

Juliet smiled. 'As long as no one gets hurt. That goes against my principles. Even when you're up against thugs from the railway companies.'

'Thugs?' I turned to her with interest. At last, someone was thinking along the same lines as me.

'Don't let Sir Henry's grinning face fool you. Those men are ruthless. Not just LSWR. All the big railway companies have been known to use violence to get what they want.'

'What do you mean?'

'Nasty accidents tend to happen to people who stand in their way. I've heard plenty of rumours. I've seen protesters getting roughed up myself. We were trying to save an ancient woodland in Kent from being demolished when men turned up with coshes.' She glanced at me again. 'I'm serious. I don't want anyone to get hurt.'

Someone had already got hurt. General Cheverton. But could it be proved? 'And the railway companies get away with it?'

'Usually. They pay other people to do the dirty work, so it can't be traced back to them.'

'You know about General Cheverton's murder?' We'd left the noise of London traffic behind us and were on the quieter Hampshire roads.

She nodded. 'Are they any closer to finding out what happened?'

'No. According to Ben Gilbert, our local policeman, there's not much to go on.'

'That's what I was afraid of.' Juliet frowned. 'It seems too much of a coincidence that his death gives LSWR exactly what they want.'

'Elijah and I went to see Sir Henry on the day of the general's murder. He acted as though he already owned Waldenmere. But he thought Mill Ponds belonged to the army and he'd get it as part of the deal. General Cheverton was dead by the time we got back to Walden. Could Sir Henry have acted that quickly?'

'It's feasible. He has men on his payroll all over the south. The problem is, it's virtually impossible to prove.'

13

———

'Good grief.' Propped up against my desk was a large oil painting.

'Nathan Cheverton gave it to me. It represents the time we spent together in France.' Elijah was leaning against the door of his den, cigarette in hand.

'Gosh. It's...' I hesitated. 'Very brutal.'

'That about sums it up.'

'He's talented.' I couldn't take my eyes off the painting. It was frantic and messy. A dramatic fusion of mud, blood, barbed wire and guns. Nothing was explicitly depicted, but it didn't have to be. The overall impression was of horror and chaos.

'You should see some of his other pictures. They're captivating, but not in a pleasant way.'

'It's stunning. Vivid but disturbing.' I hoped Elijah would move it into his own office. 'What did he say he was going to do with Mill Ponds?'

'Sell it. He drinks and gambles. The man has debts.' He yawned and rubbed his eyes. I guessed he'd had a heavy night with Nathan.

'To London and South Western Railway?'

'There wasn't much I could do to change his mind. If he could afford to let the army use it as a convalescent home, he would, but he needs cash urgently. He owes money all over the place and his paintings don't raise much.'

'But surely he can't sell Mill Ponds yet?' It was all moving too fast for my liking.

'It will take a while to sort out probate. But he's agreed with Sir Henry in principle that LSWR can buy it for a hefty sum once all the legalities are sorted out. I suspect he's been given some cash upfront on the quiet.' Elijah sounded defeated.

'Upfront? How about before his uncle was murdered?' I stared at the horror of the painting. 'Presumably, Nathan received firearms training when he was an officer? And isn't it likely he'd know where his uncle kept his service revolver?'

Elijah shook his head. 'I can't see Nathan doing anything like that.'

'What about Sir Henry? He could easily have found out Nathan needed money and would sell Mill Ponds if he inherited it. All he needed to do was get rid of General Cheverton.'

'Or it could just be a burglary that went wrong.' Elijah picked up the painting and took it into his den.

I plucked the article I'd been working on from my satchel and followed him. 'Can't the council buy Mill Ponds?' This had to be stopped somehow.

'And do what with it? Their funding will just about cover Waldenmere. They don't need a large house as well.'

'I'm going to talk to Mrs Siddons about it at tonight's meeting. Juliet Rendall is giving a speech.' I put the article on his desk. 'I've written about the damage the army's done to the lake and how much more a hotel would cause.'

'I don't think losing a few flowers is going to hold much sway. I'll look at it later. I've got work to do.' He shooed me out of his office and closed the door.

I knew there was no point in arguing when he was in one of his morose moods. Despite his lack of interest, he'd already found room in the paper for my article on Waldenmere's history.

Before I left, I poked my head around the door. He was staring at Nathan's painting, a tumbler of whisky in his hand.

'I'll see you tonight at the meeting?'

He nodded vacantly.

I left the office and found George in his usual spot in the doorway of Laffaye Printworks. We fell into step as we walked to the lake.

'You look serious.' He waited until we'd reached the secluded footpath before taking my hand.

'It seems Nathan Cheverton has agreed to sell Mill Ponds to LSWR. It could sway the army to do the same with Waldenmere.'

'I think you'll have to prepare yourself for the worst.'

'What have you heard?' I pulled my hand away. 'Has Mrs Siddons got the money from the government to buy the lake?'

He shrugged. 'I'm not sure. Mansbridge seems a bit twitchy. He thinks she's not going to get it.'

'You don't sound too upset.' I knew I shouldn't take my anger out on him but I was frustrated by his acceptance of the situation.

'The lake's beautiful. It will be a shame if it's spoilt. But I don't plan to stay here forever. I admit it doesn't mean as much to me as it does to you.'

'You think Sir Henry's going to win, don't you?' I hated the way everything was working in his favour. It couldn't be a coincidence.

'Like you said, if LSWR buys Mill Ponds, then the hotel can go ahead anyway. The army may as well sell them the lake, too. The railway companies are loaded. I'm not sure the council stands a chance.'

We reached Waldenmere and I felt an ache of loss as I gazed at the water.

'Life's too short to be worrying about hotels.' He put his hand on my shoulder. 'Change is inevitable. You've just got to take things as they come and make the best of it.'

I didn't want to make the best of it. I wanted Waldenmere to stay the way it was. All I could hear was birdsong and all I could see was water and reeds. I didn't want this to be destroyed.

'Come away with me.' George's fingers touched mine. 'I'm going to Italy to find Reg's grave. I promised my aunt I would. A chap from his regiment told me he thinks Reg was buried in a village churchyard on a hill not far from Tezze. After that, we can go anywhere you want. Lie on beaches in the south of France and walk along the boulevards of Nice.'

I shook my head. I'd tried to keep our relationship light-hearted, a flirtatious friendship, but it was becoming more than that and I was feeling vulnerable.

'Are you going to the meeting tonight?' I wanted to get back on safer ground.

He nodded, loosening his tie. 'Mansbridge wants me to be there. I'm going to get a drink and something to eat at the Duck first. Do you want to meet up afterwards? It won't be dark till nearly ten. I can catch the late train home.'

'I can't. Lizzy will wonder where I am.' In fact, I'd already told Lizzy I might be late, but I was questioning whether I'd let things move too fast with George.

'Are you going off me?' He stared at the ground. 'Is it that Percy bloke?'

'Don't be silly. You know I want to see you. But I can't stay out too late. Lizzy will get suspicious.'

We walked to Chestnut Avenue in silence, our fingers lightly touching. George gave me a rueful smile and then turned back towards the town, his hands jammed in his pockets, his head bent low. For a while, I watched his retreating figure. If I didn't have my meetings with George to look forward to, Walden would become very dull. And if the hotel went ahead, I wasn't sure I could stick around to watch my beloved Waldenmere being destroyed.

* * *

That evening, I waited once again outside the town hall to watch the great and good of Walden gather. This time, there was more tension in the air.

Miss Millicent Nightingale made a beeline towards me. 'Miss Woodmore, I just wanted to say how much I enjoyed your article on the history of Waldenmere. I read it out in class.'

'Did you?' I flushed with pleasure. 'I'm glad someone appreciated it. Perhaps if you see Mr Whittle, you could mention it to him?'

I wished there'd been an elementary school in Walden when I was growing up. Alice and I had been tutored in social etiquette at Miss Cotton's Academy for Girls. And, frankly, that had been wasted on me. Miss Nightingale clearly taught her pupils proper subjects like natural history. I was about to say as much when Elijah arrived with George. I felt a twinge of embarrassment. I guessed they'd come straight from the Drunken Duck and prayed I hadn't formed any part of their conversation.

George gave me a polite smile before disappearing into the hall. Elijah, Millicent and I followed, leaving behind fresh air to be immersed in the pungent atmosphere of a room crammed full of people on a hot July evening.

'Oh, Mr Whittle,' a familiar voice called as we made our way down the central aisle. Immaculately dressed, as usual, in a navy linen suit, Horace was motioning for Elijah to join him in the front row.

Not known for his sartorial elegance, Elijah was even more

ramshackle than usual that evening. I felt he was giving up on his relationship with Horace too soon. I sat down beside him and, to my surprise, George reappeared and took the seat on the other side of me. I turned and realised why. Percy was frowning as he searched for the nearest vacant chair.

Councillor Mansbridge took to the stage once more, seeming more anxious and less confident than he had at the previous meeting.

'Good evening, ladies and gentlemen. Tonight, we're going to hear from two more speakers, both representing the interests of Walden Council. First, I'd like to welcome someone who's been visiting Waldenmere for the past twenty years and is an authority on its wildlife. Mrs Juliet Rendall is here to represent an organisation called the Society for the Promotion of Nature Reserves. I think it best to let Mrs Rendall explain what the society stands for and what they hope to achieve here in Walden.'

Councillor Mansbridge left the stage and Juliet took his place, pulling a single card of notes from her pocket.

'Good evening, ladies and gentlemen. I know most of you won't have heard of our organisation, so I'll briefly explain the history of the society. We were founded in 1912 by a group of conservationists concerned about the damage being done to wildlife across the country. Industrial and commercial developments have been responsible for destroying many unique natural environments. Our aim is to secure government protection for sites we believe should be safeguarded due to their importance to nature.'

I scanned the crowd. Some looked sceptical, but she'd caught their attention.

'I've been visiting Waldenmere since I was a child. As you'll probably know, it's the largest freshwater lake in Hampshire and due to its size and surrounding environment, it provides crucial wildlife habitats. It deserves the legal protection that the status of nature reserve could offer.'

Juliet talked for a while about the variety of birds and rare plants found in the marshlands surrounding the lake. She wisely avoided any Latin terms and brought her speech to a close before she lost the audience's attention.

'Are there any other nature reserves?' Miss Nightingale asked.

'Not as yet. We've received a sympathetic response from many MPs, but we've yet to achieve the legal protection we're looking for.'

'MPs are all in the pockets of the railway companies,' Jim Fellowes barked. 'You don't stand a chance against 'em.'

Mutters of agreement came from around the hall. Mrs Siddons took it upon herself to rally the troops and marched onto the stage.

'You're quite right, Mr Fellowes. The railway companies are powerful. But I'm acquainted with many MPs who take the preservation of our rural landscape seriously. We need every weapon at our disposal to secure Waldenmere and I'm fully behind Mrs Rendall's attempt to lobby the government to introduce new laws to protect it. I believe Waldenmere should be a nature reserve.'

'It can't hurt, can it?' Ted Cox's wife, Annie, said. Murmurs of support were heard.

'In the meantime, I'm delighted to announce that the government has agreed to provide the funding we need to put in an offer for Waldenmere.'

This produced loud cheers from around the hall.

'We're not there yet, but it's a major step forward.' Mrs Siddons paused for effect. 'If it's what you want, I'm going to push our case forcefully to Aldershot Military Estates. I want to make it clear to them that it's only right the council has first refusal. Can I see a show of hands from all those in agreement with this course of action?'

There was more cheering and a sea of hands across the hall.

'Carried by all those present.' Mrs Siddons beamed down at her audience.

She was interrupted by the creak of the town hall doors opening. Colonel Thackeray walked unsteadily down the aisle and turned to face the crowd.

'You're too late, I'm afraid.' His face was pale and there was sweat on his brow. 'I've just spoken to my colleagues in Aldershot. The deal's been done. Waldenmere has been sold to London and South Western Railway.'

14

'I'm planning to invite Mrs Siddons to dinner here one night,' I announced.

Lizzy stopped laying the breakfast table. 'What's brought this on?'

'Two reasons. I want to find out if there's anything we can do to stop the hotel.'

Sir Henry had wasted no time. Within weeks of striking a deal with Aldershot Military Estates, a team of workers from LSWR had set up camp on the northern side of the lake. It seemed that despite the distress of the people of Walden, nothing could be done to stop the development going ahead. My article on the destruction of the lake's wildlife habitats hadn't sparked much interest. While national newspapers had reported on the acquisition of Waldenmere, mentioning local opposition to the railway company's plans, it hadn't generated the outcry I felt it deserved.

'I think the battle's lost, but I don't blame you for trying.' Lizzy finished setting out the knives and forks and went to help Betty at the stove. 'We're not going to be able to walk down the high street for fear of being knocked down by a tourist in a motor car.'

I didn't argue, but in my view, the battle was far from over. I intended to do anything I could to frustrate Sir Henry's progress. If I could slow things down, it would at least give the police more time to investigate General Cheverton's murder. And if they found that Sir Henry or someone associated with LSWR was involved, it could trigger the collapse of the whole project.

'What's the second reason for inviting Mrs Siddons to dine here?' Betty placed a dish of crispy bacon and poached eggs on the table. Meals had improved vastly since her arrival but I knew she couldn't stay with us forever.

'I want her to taste your cooking.'

* * *

Mrs Siddons accepted my invitation and the dining room, rarely used in Father's absence, was given a spring clean. Silverware was polished and cut flowers arranged for the table.

It was the first time I'd played host at 9 Chestnut Avenue and I was a little nervous. I filled our wine glasses. 'Why did the army sell to LSWR? You sounded so confident. I thought the council was going to win.'

Mrs Siddons sighed, letting her frustration show for once. 'It was always going to be difficult to compete against LSWR, but I'd hoped with careful negotiation we could have struck a deal with Aldershot Military Estates.'

'Did you have the money?' Rumours had been circulating that despite what she'd said at the public meeting, the government hadn't agreed to fund the purchase of Waldenmere.

'Ministers had signed it off. It would only have been a matter of weeks before it came through.'

'What went wrong?'

'The army acted too quickly. I was nearly there but needed

more time. The railway companies have money at their fingertips. With central government, these things move more slowly. Before I could push it through, the deed was done.' She frowned. 'Nathan Cheverton selling Mill Ponds to LSWR didn't help.'

'But how can the army do this to Walden? After everything the town did for them during the war.' I shared local anger at the callous way the army had behaved.

'The war was expensive. They need money. Evidently, they felt the council wouldn't be able to stump up the cash.'

'Is there nothing we can do?' I didn't like the tone of resignation I was hearing.

'I've made my case to Aldershot and asked them to rethink their decision. I told them they accepted Sir Henry's offer without considering the harmful impact his plans will have on the town.' She took a sip of wine. 'But I fear it would be too costly for them to renege on their agreement with LSWR now.'

'What else can we do?'

'Carry on talking to Juliet Rendall. Your article on the detriment to wildlife made the case well. You may think the nature angle's not a strong one, but it's all we have at present.'

'What about General Cheverton's murder? I still think there must be a connection.' Having seen how fast Sir Henry could make things move, the more certain of this I became. And while Elijah was reluctant to consider Nathan a suspect in his uncle's death, I hadn't ruled him out. He had no alibi for the time of the shooting. He knew how to fire a gun and he was set to make a substantial amount of money from the sale of Mill Ponds.

On top of this, I hadn't forgotten Nathan's strange reluctance to go back to the house. At the general's funeral, he'd said he never wanted to set foot in Mill Ponds again. Elijah put it down to his war trauma, but what if it was guilt?

Mrs Siddons raised a warning finger. 'Don't attempt to write anything that could be construed as libel. Sir Henry and LSWR can afford expensive lawyers. They would destroy you. I know it doesn't feel like much and you'd rather do something more radical, but Waldenmere should have legal protection as a nature reserve. It's the only way forward. Juliet's been working towards this for years, though she's realistic about the prospects.'

I'd hoped for more but knew she was right. 'Juliet told me about other areas of natural beauty that railway companies have destroyed. I can make a direct comparison with Waldenmere without saying anything libellous.'

She nodded. 'We need the article to be picked up by some of the national papers. Will Mr Whittle help?'

'I'll talk to him.' I didn't mention that Elijah had become increasingly morose of late.

'Let's forget about Sir Henry and his damned hotel for one evening.' She touched the corners of her mouth with her napkin. 'This lamb is delicious and so was the soup. Mrs Heathcote is an excellent cook.'

I topped up her wine glass. Time for the next item on my agenda. 'Mrs Heathcote didn't cook this evening. Her food is nowhere near as good as Mrs Akers'. But don't tell her I said that.'

'Mrs Akers?'

'Betty Akers, General Cheverton's housekeeper. She's been staying with us since it happened. The general's death, I mean. She can't go back to Mill Ponds.'

'No, of course not. It must have been dreadful for her to have found him like that. And for you, too.'

'It was terribly upsetting for Mrs Akers. I'm not sure what she's going to do now. When the general and his wife used to entertain, she cooked for all sorts of famous people, even royalty.'

'Does she want to stay in service?'

'Mrs Heathcote tried to persuade her to retire but Mrs Akers is determined to find a new position.'

'I'll see her before I leave. It would be a shame to let her skills go to waste. I'm sure I can find room for her at Grebe House.'

I smiled. 'That would be wonderful.'

She laughed. 'And I thought you asked me here for the pleasure of my company.'

'I did.' I tried to look innocent. 'And to enjoy Mrs Akers' cooking.'

'I'm pleased you invited me.' Her expression became serious. 'I want you to know that you can always talk to me about anything.'

'Thank you.' I wasn't sure what else to say.

'I assume your father's away at present due to work commitments?'

'He's in Germany, reporting on the situation over there for a news syndicate.'

'Do you have any other relatives apart from your aunt and grandmother in Hither Green?'

'My grandparents on my father's side live in Exeter, in Devon.'

'You have a great deal of independence for a woman of your age,' she observed.

The conversation seemed to have taken an unexpected turn. 'I suppose so, though Mrs Heathcote and Elijah keep an eye on me.'

'What I'm trying to say is – this is still a man's world and you need to be careful. When mistakes are made, the consequences are usually more damaging to a woman than they are to a man.'

'That's not fair.' I wondered if she'd spotted me with George. Or did she think I was still keen on Percy?

'It may not be fair, but it's true. If ever you need advice, you will come to me, won't you?'

'Of course,' I replied, although I wasn't sure I would.

It appeared as though she was about to say more, but to my relief, she changed the subject.

When dinner was over, she insisted on Lizzy and Betty joining us, much to their delight. She congratulated them on the food while they soaked up every detail of her ruched scarlet dress, ruby pendant and matching earrings.

* * *

'Did you get what you wanted from your dinner with Mrs Siddons?' Alice asked.

'Not enough to put a stop to that.' I'd been staring across the lake to where Sir Henry's men were at work. 'But at least Betty has a new position.'

'Stop fretting and walk with me.' She crooked her elbow and we linked arms. 'How does Betty feel about cooking for the famous Mrs Siddons?'

I smiled. 'Over the moon.'

'I'm so pleased for her. She's such a dear. Grebe House will be more comfortable than Mill Ponds. It was hard on Betty having to look after Uncle Samuel in that big house on her own.'

'She still misses him. I'm hoping this will help her recover. She's been digging out old recipe books and planning exotic menus.'

'What else did you and Mrs Siddons talk about?'

'How much independence I have for a woman of my age. And how it's still a man's world.' I tried to recall her exact words. 'She seems to feel protective towards me.'

'How funny. She doesn't strike me as the motherly type.'

'Not exactly motherly. More shrewd. She's got some idea that—'

'Is that your friend George?' Alice interrupted, failing to keep the excitement from her voice.

'Hmm.' It was too late to try to avoid him.

'Good evening, ladies.' For once, he looked respectable, with a straight tie and neatly pressed shirt.

'Hello. Aren't you late for your train?' I said in a futile attempt to get rid of him.

'I missed the six o'clock. I thought I'd take a stroll. Aren't you going to introduce me?' His smile said he intended to stand his ground.

'Miss Alice Thackeray, please meet Mr George Hale.' I waved my arm theatrically while giving him a warning glance.

'May I join you on your walk?' He actually made a slight bow towards Alice.

I raised my eyebrows at him.

'Of course,' Alice said before I could reply. 'You work for Walden Council, don't you? It must be fascinating to be involved in local government.'

This was all the prompting George needed. He was soon regaling her with tales from the council offices, followed by his impression of Councillor Mansbridge. Ahead of us on the footpath, Ben turned sharply at the sound of Alice's laughter. He stopped and waited for us to catch up with him.

'Any news on the general's murder?' I asked.

He shook his head. 'Nothing to report, I'm afraid.'

I wanted to know if he'd found out any more about Nathan Cheverton's whereabouts at the time of the shooting, but I didn't want to raise these suspicions in front of Alice.

'I hope you catch the...' George faltered, 'person.'

I guessed his newfound manners were for Alice's benefit rather than mine.

'We will.' Ben glanced from him to Alice, as if measuring up the situation. 'I'll admit, it's taking longer than we'd like. Did you know the general?'

'I met him when I was at Mill Ponds in June '17. Grand old fella.'

George grinned. 'Used to sneak whisky and ciggies into the billets for us.'

'I'd forgotten that.' Ben seemed to relax. 'I was there the year before.'

Alice and I listened to their conversation as we strolled towards the railway station. I was curious to hear their wartime anecdotes.

'You're all so much more worldly than I am,' Alice whispered.

'That's not necessarily a good thing. Mrs Siddons doesn't seem to think so,' I joked.

'You've lived in London and seen so much more than I have. Ben must think I'm rather provincial.'

'He likes you just the way you are and so do I.' I pulled her closer to me. I was glad she hadn't experienced the things I had, but it sometimes created a barrier between us. She was cautious by nature, while I'd become more impulsive. I knew how quickly things could be lost and it made me want to live at a faster pace.

'I wish I could get my hair cut like yours.'

'That's not a good idea.' I could imagine Colonel Thackeray's fury if Alice came home with her beautiful long red hair cut into a short bob.

'And you all have jobs,' she continued. 'Father would never allow me to work. If I'm honest, I'm not sure there's anything I'm good at.'

'I'm not sure Elijah considers me to be good at anything.'

We'd reached the footpath that ran parallel to the railway line where Sir Henry planned to build his promenade and I realised we were gravitating with unspoken accord towards the workmen's camp on the eastern corner of the lake.

'Look what they've done to Uncle Samuel's garden,' Alice cried.

Ben instinctively reached out to put his arm around her shoulder, then withdrew it. A few of the workers glanced over in her direction and one of them gave a low whistle.

Rubbish dredged from the lake was scattered across the gravel driveway of Mill Ponds and the lawn had been trampled by heavy boots. Discarded between battered rose bushes were empty fuel cans, wooden crates and what looked like cooking utensils, even a frying pan with a hole in it.

'Bloody hell.'

At this expletive, I turned sharply to George, surprised he was upset by the mess. But he wasn't looking at the garden. He was pointing at the lake. 'The water's going down.'

It hadn't been noticeable while we were walking, but standing by the shore, it was clear the water level was slowly but perceptibly dropping. A smell of rotting eggs rose from the muddy water.

I stared in dismay. 'Waldenmere's disappearing.'

15

'Sir Henry might not be so keen on our lake if he was to come across an unexploded bomb.' Ted Cox smirked.

Jim Fellowes' eyes widened. 'I won't do anything daft that might harm folk.'

'Nor would I. But it wouldn't hurt to start a rumour that soldiers dumped a few explosives in the water now, would it?'

Jim grinned. 'I get it. When those railway workers come into the Duck, they might happen to overhear us talking about missing bombs?'

'It'd wipe the smile off Sir Henry's face if his men stopped digging.'

I listened to the two men chatting outside the Emporium. News that the lake was already being partially drained had caused outrage in Walden. Most of it directed at Sir Henry. He'd lost none of his enthusiasm for the project, despite being on the receiving end of rude gestures and his Daimler being pelted with rotten eggs as it drove through the town.

Another anonymous cartoon had appeared in *The Walden*

Herald, rather bizarrely depicting Sir Henry dressed as Marie Antoinette handing out cake to the people of Walden.

When I got to the office, I repeated the conversation I'd overheard to Elijah. He seemed to be in a better mood. For once, he'd brewed the coffee himself rather than waiting for me to make it for him.

He laughed. 'People feel powerless. They want to do something.'

'Maybe we should print a rogue story in the paper?' I suggested. 'A few leftover bombs would certainly hinder LSWR's efforts to promote Walden as a tourist destination.'

'I wish we could.' Tempted as he might be, I knew the threat of a lawsuit would deter him.

'Do you think Sir Henry could have hired someone to kill General Cheverton?' I still wasn't prepared to let this go. 'Juliet Rendall says the railway companies can be ruthless. With the general out of the way, Sir Henry got what he wanted.'

He exhaled smoke slowly, considering the matter. 'I've heard stories of the railway companies hiring thugs to carry out beatings. Usually, when protesters get in their way. But arranging the murder of a general? I think that's a step too far.'

'Both Sir Henry and Nathan do well out of this. Perhaps Sir Henry already knew about Mill Ponds when we interviewed him and he pretended he didn't to give himself an alibi? He could even have arranged for Nathan to carry out the shooting.' I wedged open the window a fraction as Elijah blew more fumes across the office.

'Nathan Cheverton would hardly make the most reliable assassin.'

'But you said yourself, it didn't look like a professional job.'

* * *

'This time next year, we could be sitting on the veranda of the Waldenmere Hotel, sipping cocktails by the side of a swimming pool.' George sauntered along the lake path.

I shot him a look of disgust.

'That sounds like fun.' Alice pulled her straw hat low to protect her face from the sun.

'You traitor.' I gave her a shove.

'I'm not sure a policeman's wage would stretch to cocktails at a posh hotel.' Ben took out a handkerchief and wiped the sweat from his brow. 'Mind you, I could do with a dip in a swimming pool right now.'

George's tie was in the pocket of his jacket which rested over his arm. Ben's only concession to the evening's heat was to undo the top button of his tunic.

It was becoming a regular occurrence for the four of us to meet after work and stroll around to the railway station to see what was happening at the hotel site.

'We'd be paying to look at a view that we've always been able to see for free.' I retorted. 'Surrounded by noisy tourists.'

'It will be strange to have rich people visiting Walden.' Alice appeared thoughtful. 'Especially when so many families live in poverty on the outskirts of town.'

'I admit defeat.' George held up his hands in mock surrender. 'I'm a man of simple tastes. Who needs cocktails and a swimming pool when you can enjoy a pint of watery ale in the Duck?'

We weren't the only ones curious to know what was going on at the building site. Other locals had gathered to see what was happening. More rubbish had been uncovered as the water level continued to drop and the piles of debris strewn over the grounds of Mill Ponds were growing at an alarming rate.

Alice inspected the scene with disgust. 'Uncle Samuel would be horrified. How can Nathan let them do this? I never thought him capable of such a thing.'

'I doubt he knows what's going on. He said he didn't want to set foot in Mill Ponds ever again.' I thought of the shambling figure of Nathan Cheverton and wondered whether he'd managed to pay off his debts. I doubted it. Whatever money Sir Henry had given him, I couldn't imagine Nathan spending wisely.

We turned at the sound of a commotion coming from where Sir Henry planned to build his boathouse. Workmen were exclaiming at a huge metal object that appeared to be rising out of the lake. It was firmly submerged in the mud but the water level going down gave the impression it was moving upwards. A sulphuric odour filled the air.

'Good grief.' Ben moved closer to the shoreline. 'Is that a battle tank?'

'Blimey.' George shielded his eyes with his hands, squinting at the machine. 'I remember testing that bloody beast. It was like being shut inside a coffin. The damned thing never moved in the direction it was supposed to.'

'I remember seeing it rolling over the mudbanks. Such a sinister machine,' Alice murmured.

The railway workers were enthralled by their find. One of them took off his boots and socks and rolled up his trousers. He waded into the water and, with some difficulty, managed to climb on top of the tank. We moved closer and watched in fascination as he tried to prise open the hatch.

'You wouldn't get me back inside one of those things again.' George shuddered. 'Not for a million pounds.'

'They caused more damage to our lot than they ever did to the enemy.' Ben frowned. 'It must have been driven into the lake at the end of the war.'

George began to laugh. 'I can imagine the cheering as it went into the water.'

The workman on top of the tank was struggling with the metal hatch. 'Lofty, find me a crowbar,' he called to a tall man standing at the water's edge.

A crowbar was found and Lofty took off his boots and socks, rolled up his trousers and went into the water.

The crowbar did the trick and the hatch lifted. The man peered inside, then jolted backwards. He raised his hand to his mouth, then more cautiously leant forward to take another look. He withdrew again just as quickly, this time falling heavily down into the water. The metal hatch clanged shut. We watched as he waded to shore and fell to the ground, his face ashen.

Ben strode towards him and we followed.

'What's the matter, Jacob?' Lofty bent over his workmate, who was staring in disbelief at the tank.

'There's a body in there.'

16

_____

Ben ordered the workmen to move back. He carefully removed his boots and socks, rolled up his trousers and waded into the water. More nimbly than Jacob, he managed to climb up onto the tank. We watched in anticipation as he lifted the heavy metal lid and peered inside. He quickly withdrew.

'Who's the foreman here?' He scrambled down and strode back to shore.

The men pointed to Jacob, who was still slumped on the ground. Ben turned to the man called Lofty and sent him to the railway station to telephone Aldershot police station for assistance. One of the men handed Ben a cloth and he dried his feet before replacing his socks and boots.

'Is there really someone in there?' I was horrified and enthralled at the same time.

Ben ushered us back to the footpath. 'It's a man's body. George, would you walk Alice and Iris home now, please.'

'Of course,' George replied. 'Come on. Let's get out of Ben's way.'

'Could I take a look?' I ignored the sound of revulsion that came from Alice. 'Just a quick peek?'

'Absolutely not. I need to clear the area before Superintendent Cobbe gets here.' Ben dashed back to the tank to shoo away some locals trying to get a closer look.

'Iris, for goodness sake.' George grabbed my arm. 'Leave Ben to his work.'

'Won't you miss your train?' I was reluctant to leave.

'I'll catch a later one.' He began to walk away, dragging me with him. 'I'm taking you and Alice home first.'

'But who could it be? And how long have they been down there?'

George grimaced. 'The tank must have gone in the lake when the army camp disbanded. That would have been well over two years ago. I pity the poor bloke, whoever he is. It's horrible inside one of those things.'

'It's ghastly.' Alice looked like she was about to be sick.

'But how could it happen? Didn't they notice he was missing?' I couldn't believe no one had known the man was in there.

Alice glanced back towards the tank. 'Things got boisterous in camp after the war ended. Father wouldn't even let me leave the house on one occasion. Some of the men became angry at how long it was taking to get demobbed. Things got a bit heated. Especially as the soldiers from the Officer Cadet Battalion were sent home almost immediately.'

'The officers could leave Mill Ponds, but the soldiers in Waldenmere Camp had to stay where they were?' I asked.

'There was so much paperwork involved. It took time to sort out.' Her tone became defensive. 'The War Office worked as hard as it could.'

'It must have got pretty bad for someone to end up in a tank.' George lit a cigarette. 'I'd heard there'd been mutinies but I thought they were mostly in training camps in France, places like Étaples.'

When we reached the old jetty, I could tell Alice was reluctant to leave, but she started towards the slope. 'I must go. I'll have to tell Father what's happened.'

I glimpsed the dread in her eyes and called after her. 'You can always come and stay with me if you need to.'

She gave a slight nod, then carried on climbing up the slope.

George shot me an enquiring look. 'What was that about?'

I hesitated. 'Her father has a temper at the best of times. This is going to upset him.'

'He wouldn't hurt Alice, though?' I could see concern in his eyes.

'I don't think so.' But I wasn't certain. 'He can be frightening to be around sometimes.'

He threw his cigarette to the ground. 'I wonder what he'll make of this. It's not going to look good for Aldershot, having one of their precious tanks found in the lake, let alone with a body in it.'

'What happened in Étaples?' I asked. 'You mentioned a mutiny?'

'I wasn't there myself but I heard rumours. It was a smelly old training camp in the north of France. Conditions were supposed to be horrendous, verging on torture. Men preferred going back to the front line than staying there.'

'Is that what triggered the mutiny?' The sun was beginning to set though it was still light and I wasn't ready to go home yet.

'A bunch of New Zealanders arrived. Trouble broke out. I've heard all sorts of stories about mutineers fighting with military police. Some of it's probably exaggerated, but there were plenty of arrests.'

'Why wasn't it on the newsreels?'

He shrugged. 'It's not the sort of thing the country wanted to hear, I suppose.'

'What happened to the men that were arrested?'

'Most went to military prison. I think one bloke was executed.' His fingers entwined with mine as we cut away from the footpath and headed to our bench. 'Why do you want to know this stuff?'

'Because people should know the truth. Not what the government or army chooses to tell us. Newspapers should report these things.'

'The war's over. I think most people want to forget about it now.' George pushed a tendril of sweet-scented honeysuckle out of my way. The path had become more overgrown since we'd last visited the bench. 'War is brutal in ways most people don't want to know about.'

'I want to know.' But did I? Perhaps George was right. Perhaps we should put it behind us and concentrate on caring for the wounded survivors.

'You're a strange woman. Forget about mutinies. I don't want to talk about the war.' We sat down and he wrapped his arms around me. 'It's been ages since I've had you all to myself.'

'Why am I strange?' I nestled into him.

'I don't know. You look at things differently.'

'Do I?' I wondered if he thought this was a good or bad thing.

'Why are you here with me now?' he challenged. 'You're not planning to take me home to meet your father, are you?'

'That's not what I want. It's not what you want either,' I retaliated.

'True. I don't think I could handle your father and Elijah.'

I rolled my eyes. 'Elijah?'

'He gave me what he called a polite warning when we were in the Duck. Told me not to get too friendly with you.'

I cringed, imagining the scene. 'I'm sorry if he embarrassed you. I hope you told him it was none of his business.'

He sighed. 'He cares about you. So do I. I told him I was planning to go abroad soon and that you knew I'd be leaving.'

'Did that satisfy him? Or did he just grunt at you?'

He laughed. 'You know him well. Yes, I received the non-committal grunt.'

'The problem is, he knows me too well.' I nuzzled his neck and breathed in the fragrance of his sandalwood cologne. 'I want to make the most of you before you go.'

* * *

I drifted off to sleep that night dreaming of George – the feel of his skin and the heat of his kisses – but I woke the following morning from a nightmare about mutinies, tanks and dead bodies.

When I went down to breakfast, I wasn't surprised to find Alice in the kitchen with Lizzy. Her enthusiasm for my modest home made me smile when I thought of the grandeur of Sand Hills Hall. But having witnessed Colonel Thackeray's erratic moods, I could understand why she preferred the safety of our kitchen.

'How did your father take the news?'

She pulled a face. 'He's furious. He was on the telephone to Aldershot for hours last night.'

I hated the thought of what the colonel could do in a fit of temper.

'I suppose Elijah will put this on the front page?' Her hand trembled as she lifted a cup to her lips and I noticed she wasn't eating anything.

'This is going to make more than just the front page of *The Walden Herald*.' I gulped my tea. 'I have to get to the office.'

I hoped she'd stay behind with Lizzy, but she got up to follow me. 'I'll walk into town with you.'

We took the lake path and I tried to steer the conversation away from the tank although Alice was too agitated to let it go.

'I'm worried people will blame Father.'

'I'm sure they won't.' In fact, it was likely they would, but I could see how anxious she was.

'He's had so much to deal with recently, what with Uncle Samuel's death.' She looked across the lake to Mill Ponds. 'People support the army when we're at war but they're quick to forget. No one wants to know about the atrocities men like my father endured to bring about peace.'

While I acknowledged the truth of her words, she needed to be prepared for the criticism likely to be directed towards the officers in charge of Waldenmere Camp and the Officer Cadet Battalion. Something terrible had to have happened for this man to have ended up dead inside a tank.

'*The Walden Herald* won't be throwing around accusations although we have to cover the story. And I hate to say it, but it may well boost our circulation.'

'Is that important?'

'We're a new publication. We need to broaden our readership to keep going. Mr Laffaye wants to start increasing the print run soon.'

'And if you can't?'

'The paper will fold and I'll be out of a job.'

'If that happens, will you go back to London?'

The sorrow in her voice made me feel guilty. In truth, I would consider returning to London if I didn't have my job. 'If I do, I'll take you with me. We'll share a flat.'

Her eyes lit up. 'Wouldn't that be wonderful? We could go shopping and to the theatre and art galleries. And I'd have my hair cut.'

We continued this conversation all the way into town, both knowing it was an impossible dream.

* * *

A few days later, Ben turned up at the office as we were packing up for the day. I poured him the dregs of the lukewarm coffee.

Elijah ambled out of his den into the main office. 'Do you know who he is yet?'

'No. We need the paper's help with that.' Ben took the coffee and perched on the edge of my desk. 'Superintendent Cobbe has told me I can share some information with you, but you *must* keep it to yourselves until we say otherwise.'

Elijah nodded. 'Do you know how he died?'

'Someone shot him in the back.'

17

'Someone shot him in the back and put him in the tank?' Elijah's tone was a mixture of disgust and incredulity. He motioned for us to follow him into his den. Once we were seated, he closed the door.

Ben took out his pocket book. 'It looks that way. Sir Bernard Forbes, the Home Office pathologist, came down from London. He's been examining him. We'd like you to publish a description of the man. Sir Bernard says he was five foot ten inches tall with sandy hair. He thinks he was between twenty and forty years old.'

I scribbled down the details. 'When do you think he went into the water?'

'He can't tell from the decomposed body. We're estimating it would have been late 1918 or early '19, as no one saw the tank after that time. Superintendent Cobbe is talking to army officials to see if we can get records of the men stationed at Waldenmere Camp. Captain Fortesque is assisting us.'

'You think soldiers were responsible for this?' Elijah paused to light a cigarette. 'Not locals? There was ill feeling in town towards the camp.'

'The tank would have made a noise. The super feels it's more likely to have been an incident that occurred in camp between soldiers.' Ben tapped his pencil on his pad. 'Tank Man's clothes have rotted but a label shows he purchased them from Harry Hall on Oxford Street.'

'An officer?' Elijah exclaimed.

'Who or what is Harry Hall?' I asked.

'They supply uniforms to newly commissioned officers,' Ben replied. 'Judging by the remains of his clothes, he was an infantry officer, but he had no identity tag.'

'Did he have anything on him?' Elijah was scrawling notes in his jotter.

'A compass in the inside pocket of his tunic. It's tarnished and rusty, but there's a distinct emblem on it. We're having it cleaned.' Ben lowered his voice. 'It looks like an eagle with outstretched wings.'

'The Reichsadler?' Elijah's cigarette fell from his fingers. 'You think it's the Imperial Eagle of the German Empire?'

'It's a possibility. The super has asked some experts to take a look.'

'That might explain why he was shot in the back.' Elijah brushed the ash from his desk. 'Someone in camp could have found out he was a German spy?'

'Captain Fortesque is investigating. This must go no further. The military may decide to take the matter out of our hands.'

Elijah lit another cigarette. 'But even if he was a spy, the man must have had some family. Someone who's been missing him?'

'That's why we want you to publish a description of his appearance. See if it brings anyone forward. But don't mention the compass. The body is at the cottage hospital. He's been photographed and we'll have to bury him soon after the post-mortem.'

* * *

'Could Tank Man be connected to General Cheverton's murder?' I gathered up the empty cups from Elijah's desk and tried to wipe the coffee rings from the stained wood.

'I think the answer to that lies at Mill Ponds.' Elijah was making a timeline of events in spidery black writing on his blotter.

'Why?'

'Because I think whoever killed the general was searching for something in that open drawer. The file they were looking for might be linked to our unknown man.'

'You think the general knew something about Tank Man and that's why he was murdered?' I found it hard to believe General Cheverton would hurt anyone. But he had been a soldier all his life and fought in two wars. He must have killed people during that time.

'I don't think the general had anything to do with putting a body in a tank. He was an honourable man. I can't see him allowing anything like that on his watch. But if the murderer was searching for something in his study...' He tapped his pen, spattering black ink all over the area I'd just wiped.

I scrubbed at the stained desk. 'How can an officer go missing and no one notices?'

'Because it was wartime. Hundreds of men went missing.'

'Not in Walden.'

'True.' His eyes narrowed. 'Is Mrs Akers still staying with you?'

'No. She's moved into Grebe House now. She can't help, anyway. She doesn't know what was in the records.'

'Does she still have a key to Mill Ponds?'

My pulse quickened. 'You want to go back to the general's study?'

Elijah nodded slowly. 'I'd like to take a quick look at the files there.'

'I suppose I could call in at Grebe House on my way home to see how Betty's getting on?' I suggested.

He smiled. 'And I'd be delighted to come to supper with you and Lizzy this evening and you can tell me how you got on.'

* * *

I knocked on the front door of Grebe House and was shown into the drawing room by the butler, Mr Grosvenor.

'Iris, what a delightful surprise.' Mrs Siddons rose from her writing desk.

'I hope you don't mind me dropping in like this. I wondered how Mrs Akers was settling in?'

'Her food is divine. I'll be putting on weight if I'm not careful. Mr Grosvenor will take you to see her. But first, sit down and tell me how you've been getting on with your articles.'

'Juliet and Percy have given me examples of other towns and villages similar to Walden that have suffered as a result of the railways. I'll admit, I found it disheartening. These places were never the same again.' I sank into the sofa. After a day of sitting on a wooden office chair, the soft cushions were luxury. The room also smelt heavenly compared to the smoky old office. Wafts of Mrs Siddons' expensive perfume hung in the air. I noticed that even when relaxing at home, she wore a silver and amethyst pendant over her cream silk blouse.

'Stick with it. I'm gaining sympathy from MPs who have incurred similar problems in their constituencies.'

'The article is with Elijah, but he's preoccupied with Tank Man.'

She pulled a face. 'What a gruesome discovery. To think a body has been hidden in the lake all this time. Sounds like a fight got out of hand and this poor chap ended up the worse for it.'

I nodded. People would be even more horrified if they knew the man had been shot in the back.

'I can't help thinking this isn't going to look good for Aldershot Military Estates,' she said, with a gleam of satisfaction in her eyes.

'It's bound to disrupt Sir Henry's plans,' I replied.

'The longer it delays building work, the better.'

We smiled at each other.

* * *

In the kitchen, I found Betty red-faced and up to her elbows in dough.

'Oh, Miss Iris. I'd hug you, but I don't want to cover you in flour.'

I waited for the door to close behind Mr Grosvenor. 'How's it going? Is Mrs Siddons treating you well?'

'She's kindness itself. You should see my bedroom. And I've got my own sitting room. It's so warm and cosy, not like Mill Ponds.' Betty's expression of pleasure turned to guilt. 'Of course, I miss the general terribly.'

'I'm sure he'd be happy you've found a new home. I'm glad you're settling in.' I studied the room in awe. At great expense, electric wiring had been fitted throughout Grebe House and this was never more evident than in the kitchen. As well as light switches, there were sockets attached to the wall.

'It's taking a bit of getting used to. She's got all sorts of modern contraptions.' Betty gestured around. 'That huge wooden thing is a refrigerating cabinet. It's a far cry from my old kitchen.'

'What on earth is this?' I picked up a strange object that

appeared to be a pair of eggbeaters attached to a metal stand. The exposed motor at the top was blackened.

'Don't touch it, Miss Iris. It's dangerous. You plug it into that socket and the beaters go round. It's called an electric mixer. They use them in America. But if you get the motor wet, it sparks and explodes.' Betty scowled at it. 'Can't see the point myself. All you need is a bit of elbow grease to get a good consistency to your mix.'

I quickly put down the hazardous device and peered up the shaft of a small elevator used to convey trays up to the dining room.

'And the amount of money she spends on food. I've been preparing a feast fit for a king every night.' She began to describe shrimp cocktails, Dover sole and saddle of lamb.

I decided to broach the subject of the keys to Mill Ponds before I was tempted to raid Mrs Siddons' larder. Or her refrigerating cabinet.

'Betty, there's something Elijah and I want to look for in the general's study.'

'Is it to do with this tank business?' She stopped pummelling dough. 'Because I won't have a word said against the general. If he thought any of his men had done anything so despicable to a fellow soldier, he'd have kicked them from here to kingdom come.'

'I'm sure he would have. We were wondering whether there might be a link between the records in his study and the man in the tank. Do you still have the keys to Mill Ponds?'

She shook her head. 'The solicitor came and took them from me.'

'Oh, well. That's an end to it.' I swallowed my disappointment. 'Can you remember when the last cadets left the house?'

She thought for a moment. 'They'd all gone by Christmas 1918. It was just the general and me that day. Not like the camp at the lake. That was another six months before it was cleared out and the men demobbed.'

The door opened and Mr Grosvenor came back in with a tray.

'I'd better leave you to your work.'

Betty leant forward and gave me a floury hug, whispering in my ear, 'There's a key hidden on top of the ledge above the back door that leads to the scullery.'

18

I left Grebe House and walked around the lake to Willow Marsh to find Alice working on a painting of Heron Bay.

'Any news?' she asked.

I was repeating the description of Tank Man that Ben had asked us to publish when George appeared. He was panting. 'The office was closed when I walked by. Did you knock off early?'

'I had to run an errand for Elijah.'

Alice packed up her paintbox and easel and the three of us headed towards the railway station.

The tank jutted out of the mud, surrounded by onlookers. People had come from neighbouring towns to see the grisly spectacle. Ben was chatting to one of the workmen but came over when he spotted us.

'Has anything else been found?' I could see more mud-spattered debris on the lawn of Mill Ponds.

'Nothing of interest,' Ben replied.

'What's going to happen to that thing?' George gestured to the tank.

'It's being moved to Aldershot. The military wants to get it out of the way as soon as possible.'

Reporters were still hovering and photographers snapped pictures of the tank from every possible angle.

'I'm sure they do.' George tossed his cigarette to the ground.

'Father says it was probably some local rogue rather than a soldier.' Alice bit the tip of her thumb.

I thought this highly unlikely. The camp would still have been occupied at the time. Moving the tank must have made considerable noise and taken some skill.

Ben didn't reply. I realised this could become awkward for him, especially if he had to question Colonel Thackeray.

'I must go,' I said. 'Elijah's coming to supper.'

'And I need to get back to work.' Ben smiled apologetically at Alice.

'I may as well catch the six o'clock train. I'll see you tomorrow.' George eyed me suspiciously, then strolled towards the station with Ben.

'Why are you rushing home?' Alice lowered her voice. 'I thought you and George spent time alone together after I left you?'

'Sometimes.' I was reluctant to go into too much detail. 'But Elijah invited himself over tonight.'

'Have you kissed him?'

'Elijah? Most certainly not.'

She snorted with laughter. 'You know very well I mean George.'

'We sometimes—' I stopped at the sight of Percy Baverstock strolling towards us.

'You both look jolly pretty.' He was dressed in a casual, open-necked white shirt with beige trousers and a matching buttoned-up waistcoat. He had a tan leather satchel over one shoulder. 'You've been having all the excitement here, haven't you?'

'We have indeed.' My tone was uninviting.

Alice gave me one of her sideways glances. This was her way of telling me that she thought he looked attractive and that I should be nicer to him.

'Is that it?' He pulled a face at the tank, sounding underwhelmed.

'That's it.' I had to admit it had the appearance of an oversized, rusty toolbox.

'Do they know who the chap is yet?' He pushed his floppy hair back over his brow.

'The police are still working on it,' Alice replied.

'I'm sure with Ben on the case, they'll crack it soon enough. Oh, look, he's over there with that other fella, whose name I've forgotten.' He waved cheerily at Ben and George who were watching us from the station concourse.

Ben gave a half-hearted wave in return. George glared and stomped off to catch his train.

'Shall we walk?' Percy offered an elbow to each of us.

'No. I need to get home.' I had to be careful. Lizzy didn't know how much time I spent at the lake with George. She thought I worked longer hours than I did. With Elijah coming over, I needed to get back before he arrived.

'In that case, allow me to walk you home, Alice. Would you like me to show you some water violets that have bloomed near the old jetty? We haven't seen them there for years.'

'How exciting.' To my surprise, she took the arm he offered.

Percy appeared highly pleased with himself.

'I'll see you tomorrow, Alice.' I noticed Ben watching them from the station, looking none too happy.

* * *

After supper, Elijah announced he wanted to see the tank for himself.

'I'll come with you.'

'There's no need.' He frowned at me. 'Thank you, Mrs Heathcote, that was delicious.'

'A pleasure.' Lizzy began to clear the plates.

'I'd like to come with you,' I insisted, knowing he'd have to give in. I'd told him there was a key at Mill Ponds but hadn't said where it was hidden.

'I can manage.' He rose from his seat.

'But you won't know where to look.' I smirked. He knew very well what I was referring to. 'I won't be long, Lizzy.'

'Make sure you're not.' She regarded us with suspicion.

We went out into the hall.

'This isn't strictly legal,' he hissed. 'Just tell me where the key is.'

'I'll show you. It will be quicker if we search together.'

'Your father will never forgive me if we get arrested,' he muttered, opening the front door.

Chestnut Avenue was deserted, even though it was a fine July evening. We walked to the railway station, where a few people were milling around on the concourse, smoking. The workers had left for the day and the tank sat forlornly in the mud. We paused to examine it, then, checking no one was watching us, hurried up the drive of Mill Ponds.

We headed to the back of the house, navigating the muddy debris scattered across the garden. The faint scent of roses reminded me of the terrible afternoon we'd found General Cheverton.

'I'm not happy about this.' Elijah tried to catch hold of my arm. 'Why don't you wait in the garden?'

'We're here now, so we may as well get on with it. Come on, let's find the key.' At the back door, I stood on tiptoes and ran my hand along the top of the rough wooden frame. I felt something metal and passed a large key down to Elijah.

At first, it wouldn't turn, but with a little pressure, the lock yielded. We entered the scullery, then stumbled through the dim kitchen and along a corridor. All the blinds were drawn and there was a musty odour in the air. The wooden floorboards creaked with every step and despite trying to close the doors quietly, every one banged shut behind us.

Elijah indicated the study door and I took a deep breath as the image of General Cheverton's body flashed into my mind. Whoever shot him was yet to be caught and here we were, back at the scene of the crime.

Hinges screeched as Elijah pushed open the study door. The heavy damask curtains were drawn and the room was in darkness. He stopped to turn on the light and I walked into the back of him. This caused him to stumble and we both fell forward onto the floor.

I scrambled to my feet, hoping I hadn't landed on the patch of bloodstained carpet. I hauled Elijah up.

'The electricity has been cut off.' Breathing heavily, he took out a box of matches and lit one, but managed to drop it on the rug. I quickly stamped on it. He tried again, this time succeeding in lighting an oil lamp. The glow revealed I was standing on the stained carpet where the general's body had lain. I scuttled across the room, vowing never to break into a property with Elijah again.

'What are we looking for?' I glanced around. Nothing appeared to have been moved since Betty had made her tour of the room.

'A clue.' Elijah went over to the filing cabinets. 'This is the one that was unlocked. The open drawer was labelled A to E. Do any of the folders seem as though they've been manhandled? Does one stand out more than the others?'

I examined the contents of the drawer closely. 'No, not really.' I spotted a few names I recognised, including Nathan Cheverton. 'Why don't we take a quick look at Nathan's file?'

Elijah frowned, then removed the folder and took it over to the desk. He quickly read its contents.

I carried on flicking through the drawers of the filing cabinet, looking for anything that appeared out of place. It offered no clues as to what the intruder might have been searching for.

'Well?' I whispered.

'Nothing I didn't already know.' He put the documents back in the folder. 'Have you spotted anything?'

'No.'

He took over and examined each drawer. In the end, he admitted defeat.

'This is hopeless.' Elijah closed the drawers. 'There's no point in checking the contents of every folder when we don't know what they should contain in the first place. Maybe they'd just started to search when they were disturbed, which is why they'd only opened drawer A to E. Let's get out of here before anyone hears us.'

We put everything back as we found it and left the house, managing to make as much noise going out as we had coming in.

'I'm sorry I involved you in that,' Elijah said as we reached the railway station. He paused to light a cigarette. 'It was all in vain, anyway.'

'It was worth a try.' It was nearly dark and I wanted to get home. When I was with George, it was romantic to be by the lake after sunset. With Elijah, it was just eerie. 'Come back and have a brandy. Or are you going to the Duck?'

'I think I'll go and see Horace. I want him to contact Finlay Fortesque. See if intelligence has come up with anything.'

'What are you two doing out here?'

We jumped guiltily at the sound of Ben's voice.

'I wanted to take a look at the tank.' Elijah indicated the mudbanks. 'Iris tells me you haven't found anything else in the lake?'

'I couldn't say in front of the others earlier.' Ben checked to make sure no one was nearby. He lowered his voice. 'We did find something.'

'Near the tank?' I whispered.

He shook his head. 'In the water closest to Mill Ponds.'

'What?' Elijah asked.

'The gun that killed General Cheverton.'

'You found his service revolver?' Elijah's face was grim. 'The Webley Mark IV?'

Ben nodded. 'One shot had been fired. Our ballistics chap confirmed the bullet in the general's body came from the gun.'

19

The old lady clutched her husband's hand, her eyes wet with tears.

'Let's go over to the town hall for a cup of tea.' Police Constable Sid King ushered the couple out of the station house. The London papers had reprinted *The Walden Herald*'s article on the grim discovery inside the tank. As a result, grief-stricken visitors had started to arrive in Walden. Mothers, fathers, sisters and brothers, all coming to see if Tank Man was their relative who'd been reported missing in action.

'How sad.' I'd called in at the station house on my way home from work to see if there had been any new developments. 'Another missing relative?'

Ben nodded. 'War Office letters or telegrams were so brief. Sometimes a commanding officer would write a letter of condolence to the family, giving more details, but usually they just received a telegram saying, "missing in action, presumed dead". More often than not, the War Office didn't have any other information than that.'

Shortly after the war, there had been stories of soldiers turning up alive when their relatives had been told they were dead. Most of the missing men had been held in prisoner of war camps.

Ben and Sid had been interviewing the bewildered relatives before delivering them into the care of the Walden Women's Group at the town hall, where Alice and Mrs Gilbert dished out tea and sympathy. Feelings in town had been running high since the arrival of LSWR's workforce and this new development had caused even more unrest as locals tried to help the grieving visitors.

Ben showed me into the station house office. 'Most of these people have read about Tank Man in the national papers and remembered their relative was once based in Walden. They feel it's their duty to come and see if it's their loved one. Many are hoping it is them, so they'll finally know for certain and have a body to bury.'

'Have you shown them the compass?' I noticed the office was much tidier than usual. I guessed Mrs Gilbert had been around to clear up Ben and Sid's usual clutter and make the place more presentable.

'No. We ask questions about their relative. Last known whereabouts, age, physical details and items they're likely to have had in their pockets. We've been given orders not to show the compass to anyone unless we're certain they can identify Tank Man. So far, no one's told us anything that would fit with the pathologist's description of the body.'

'What about the soldiers based at Waldenmere Camp? Have you talked to any of them?' I glanced at the desk, keen to see the compass for myself.

'A few, but it's not been easy. They're scattered across the country. We've spoken to those living locally and they admit to hurling loads of stuff in the lake. They say they were only following orders. The army didn't have anywhere to store unwanted equipment and told the men to clear out the camp any way they could. They did the easiest thing, which was to throw the rubbish into the water.'

'But a tank? Surely it would be missed?'

'No one's admitted to moving it. This one was a prototype used for training. It was already out of date and probably never fit for battle in the first place. The soldiers seemed to have assumed that someone in authority had arranged for it to be taken away.' Ben opened a drawer of the desk. 'Here, I know you're dying to see it. You may as well take a look before it goes.'

'Goes?' I eagerly took the compass from him. Although tarnished and dented, it was clearly of good quality. A large bird with its wings outstretched was engraved into the silver. Rust obscured some of the features but it was still an exquisitely detailed and highly distinctive etching.

'It's going over to Aldershot for safekeeping. Someone tried to break in here last night. Not sure who'd be daft enough to break into a station house but they jimmied the office window open. We were asleep upstairs although we suspect someone climbed in.'

'Did they take anything?' I was still examining the compass.

'Not much to take. I expect it was just kids daring each other. Some of them think we've got the body of Tank Man in here. Sid's snoring probably scared them off. But we can't risk anyone stealing the compass.'

'What about the tank? Have you found out when it went into the water?'

'No one seems to know for sure. It was probably sometime in November or December 1918. The soldiers we've spoken to say they remember it being stuck in the mud. And then one day, it was gone.'

'Were there many men left in the camp at that time?' I could imagine a cold, muddy army camp was the last place anyone wanted to be as winter set in.

'A fair few and they were getting more rebellious by the day.

Food was sparse and they didn't like the way officers were still ordering them about. Demobbing was a long process.'

'Betty said all the officers had left Mill Ponds by Christmas 1918.'

'That's useful to know. We're not getting much out of the army. They're reluctant to say too much until they know what went on themselves. Captain Fortesque's spoken to Colonel Thackeray, who insists it must have been a disgruntled local, but it would have made a hell of a noise going into the water. It's more likely the men in the camp were involved although so far, no one's admitted to going near the tank. Most said the same as George; they wouldn't get back in it again for a million pounds.' He took the compass from me and returned it to the drawer. 'I think our only hope of finding out who Tank Man is lies with Finlay Fortesque.'

'The army must have noticed they were missing a man, especially an officer. Where are the records kept of the soldiers stationed at Waldenmere Camp? We thought they might have been at Mill Ponds?' I hoped we'd left no trace of our hapless break-in.

'No, Waldenmere Camp was run separately from the Officer Cadet Battalion. The camp records are at Aldershot. We've asked to see them although we're not entirely sure what we're looking for.'

This echoed our fruitless search of the filing cabinets at Mill Ponds. 'Do you think whoever killed this man could have shot General Cheverton?' Elijah's theory that the truth lay at Mill Ponds was starting to seem less plausible. Sir Henry and Nathan Cheverton were still my main suspects.

'The bullet is different. Apart from the revolver being found not far from the tank, there's no apparent connection. Whoever killed the general probably threw it into the lake when they left Mill Ponds. If there's a link between the two, Captain Fortesque is more likely to uncover it than we are.' He frowned. 'And he may choose not to share his findings with us.'

20

I went in search of Alice at the town hall and found Colonel and Mrs Thackeray talking to Mrs Gilbert.

'It must be terribly draining for you, having to deal with all these poor people.' Florence was dressed in a lilac silk suit with matching high-heeled shoes.

By contrast, Mrs Gilbert wore a gingham cotton housedress and brown leather sandals. 'Alice has been a great help. I don't know what I'd have done without her. She seems to know exactly the right thing to say.'

Florence smiled, but the colonel appeared unimpressed.

'What are these people hoping to find?' He seemed perplexed. 'Surely, they must know their relatives are dead?'

Mrs Gilbert shook her head. 'Poor souls just looking for answers but not finding any.'

Alice appeared from the kitchen carrying an empty tray. 'What are you all doing here?'

'Being nosy.' I gazed around the hall.

Florence shot me a reproving look. 'We came to see how you were, darling. You've been here for ages.'

'There's been such a lot to do.' Alice's face was pink and her dress crumpled, though she radiated energy. 'So many visitors with relatives stationed at Waldenmere Camp at one time or another.'

'When did all the soldiers eventually leave the camp, Colonel?' I decided to risk his wrath and take the opportunity to see if I could discover anything.

'Oh, it was well into 1919. These things take time with so many men to demobilise.' Although he wore a plain morning suit, his bearing and manner left you in no doubt that he was a military man.

'Wasn't there a rebellion in camp?' I averted my eyes from Alice's warning glance.

He stiffened. 'Any unrest was soon quashed. It's a gross exaggeration to say there was any sort of rebellion.'

'What about the tank?' I knew I was pushing my luck. 'Did you know it had been dumped in the lake?'

Mrs Gilbert made a hasty retreat to the kitchen while Florence and Alice glared at me.

Colonel Thackeray's fingers twitched as they rested on his wife's arm. 'Admin wasn't as efficient as it could have been. It was assumed it had been picked up and taken back to Aldershot.'

'Really, Iris,' Florence protested. 'You've been in Mr Whittle's company for too long. This is turning into an interrogation. Alice, are you ready to come home now?'

'I'd like to stay and help Mrs Gilbert tidy up. Would that be all right?'

'Of course, darling.' Florence touched Alice's flushed cheek. 'But don't be too late.'

'And don't go wandering off around the lake. I want you to come straight home,' Colonel Thackeray said sternly.

'Yes, Father.'

Alice waited for her parents to leave before turning on me. 'You shouldn't have questioned Father like that. He's not been feeling well.'

'I'm sorry.' I realised I'd been insensitive.

'Mother's right. You've been spending too much time with Elijah.' She began to collect abandoned teacups from around the hall.

'Shall I help you clear up?' I trailed after her, knowing she wouldn't be able to stay angry with me for long.

'You can do the washing up.' She handed me a tray of dirty cups.

In the kitchen, I filled the sink and started to scrub. 'Did you enjoy your walk with Percy? He didn't seem impressed by our tank.'

She grinned. 'I wasn't impressed by his water violets. They weren't terribly exciting. They weren't even violet.'

I laughed. 'Ben has nothing to fear, then?'

'Don't be silly.' She began to stack the cups and saucers in a cupboard and didn't look at me when she whispered, 'I love Ben. I have for years.'

'Oh.' I felt happy and sad for her at the same time.

She was putting the last cup away when Mrs Gilbert popped her head around the door. 'Off with you now. I'm going to lock up.'

We hung up our aprons and went back into the hall to find Ben waiting. Alice blushed.

George was loitering outside, smoking a cigarette. 'Thought you'd be here.' He took a last puff before throwing the butt to the ground. 'Anyone identified Tank Man?'

'Not yet,' Ben replied. 'We're talking to Reverend Childs about a burial.'

'Poor man.' Alice sighed. 'Not even to have his name on a headstone.'

'At least he's out of the tank. I wouldn't have liked that to have been my final resting place.' George strolled by her side, his hands sunk in his jacket pockets. I hoped Colonel Thackeray was safely out of the way. He wouldn't approve of the company Alice was keeping.

'It's dreadful.' Alice shuddered. 'I suppose he must have been involved in a fight and came off worst.'

George frowned. 'Still a nasty trick to pull on a bloke.'

I exchanged a glance with Ben. The fact that Tank Man had been shot in the back hadn't been made public. Superintendent Cobbe wanted to keep it that way. It was just as well. Things were tense enough in town without that information leaking out. Or the suspicion that he could have been a German spy.

Even partially drained, Waldenmere was a glorious mass of silver water glistening in the July sunshine. Normally, we'd have lingered at Heron Bay, but Alice kept checking her watch. I indicated to Ben and George that we needed to keep moving.

All was quiet at the building site, though it appeared there had been some new excavations. I turned to Ben. 'They've started work again?'

'Once we'd searched the site, there was no reason to stop them. Superintendent Cobbe gave them permission to go back.'

My former exasperation at Sir Henry's invincibility returned. 'Did you find anything else?'

He shook his head.

'You'd think they'd show some respect for what's happened,' Alice said in disgust.

'It's not the railway company's fault,' George retorted. 'If anyone's, it's the army's.'

Alice's lip trembled and I could see George regretted his words.

Ben glowered at him. 'We can't blame anyone until we know the facts. The superintendent has a meeting with Captain Fortesque. If there is a link between what happened to General Cheverton and Tank Man, Military Intelligence is our best hope.'

'Where's the tank now?' I asked.

'It's been taken to Aldershot.' Ben looked at Alice. 'I'm afraid I've got to go. I need to make a call at the railway station, then head back to town.'

'I have to get home anyway,' Alice replied.

'Are you catching the next train?' I asked George.

He shook his head. 'I'll walk you both home and come back for the later one.'

We left Ben at the station and continued along the lake path. George fell into step with Alice, trying to win back her favour after his remark about the army. He succeeded, of course. Soon, she was laughing at his imitation of Councillor Mansbridge and Mrs Siddons fighting over the last biscuit at a council meeting. I glanced back and saw Ben standing by the station, watching them.

We said goodbye to Alice at the old jetty and watched as she made her way up the slope to Sand Hills Hall.

'Poor kid.' George took my hand when she'd disappeared from view.

'Kid? She's the same age as me,' I said. 'Do you think I'm a kid?'

'No.' He pulled me close and kissed me hard on the lips to prove his point.

I laughed and pushed him away, checking no one had seen.

'I feel sorry for her.' He pulled me back towards him. 'What's the point of being pretty and well off if you're stuck in that hall all the time?'

'I know. I wish Florence would let her grow up. She never gets to go anywhere or do anything. She puts all her energies into painting and the Women's Group. And her father won't entertain any suitors.'

'Slim pickings for a girl like Alice around here. Anyway, I thought you considered marriage some kind of slavery?'

'It doesn't have to be. I think Alice would enjoy marriage and raising a family. With the right man. At least it would be an escape from her father.'

'But you don't consider yourself that sort of girl?'

'Not if it means being told what to do by someone else. According to law, you become your husband's possession. I could never be that. What about you? Do you want to get married?'

'Maybe one day. For now, I just want to get out of here. Travel, see the world a bit.' He looked thoughtful. 'If I did marry, I wouldn't want to *possess* my wife. I'd just want someone to enjoy things with, someone who'd go places with me.'

'I suppose that's what I'd want, too. Come on, let's go to our bench.'

We walked in companionable silence. The trees were in full leaf, creating a green archway over the footpath. Our bench was even more densely hidden and we had to push through branches to get to it. The lake was barely visible through the foliage of surrounding oaks.

George put his arm around me and I rested my head on his shoulder, enjoying his familiar scent.

'What happened to your mother?'

His question took me by surprise. 'She died when I was fourteen.' I closed my eyes, trying to capture her image in my head. I hated that my memories of her were starting to fade.

'I'm sorry.' He pulled me closer. 'My dad died of Spanish influenza right at the end of the war. I didn't get home until about a month afterwards. Came back and both he and Reg were gone.'

'That must have been rough for your mother.'

'She was always the strong one. She tried to keep going after Reg was killed, for my aunt's sake, but she was devastated. He was like a second son to her, more like my brother than my cousin.' His voice cracked. 'Then Dad went.'

I wrapped my arms around him.

'Nearly every family on our road lost someone. If it wasn't the war, it was influenza.' He squeezed me tightly. 'How did your mother die?'

The question hung in the air for a few moments before I could answer. 'It's complicated.'

I knew he expected more but it was difficult to explain. He didn't say anything but grazed my hair with his lips.

'She was a member of the WSPU.'

He looked down at me blankly.

'The Women's Social and Political Union. She was a suffragette.'

'Oh, right,' he said hesitantly.

'Sometimes, she broke the law. She was sent to prison twice.' I swallowed. 'When she was in prison, she'd go on hunger strike and they'd force feed her. She became very weak.'

'Christ.' He held me tighter.

'Her last big protest killed her. She broke into the House of Commons and caused some damage. On the way out, she ended up in the Thames.' I gulped. 'She was pulled out and taken to hospital but her body couldn't take any more.'

'Bloody hell.'

I could sense he was struggling to find appropriate words. But what was there to say? I turned and placed my lips on his to end the conversation.

21

'My father isn't happy about me being seen with Ben and George.' With a delicate hand, Alice dabbed her brush on the canvas. She was adding the finishing touches to her watercolour of Heron Bay.

'Does that mean you won't meet us in the evenings any more?' My anger flared. Was her father never going to allow her any pleasure? And why didn't Florence intervene?

'No. I've told him we're just friends and there's no harm in it.' She continued to paint with deft, confident strokes.

'Good for you.' This was a promising first step in standing up to her father, though I worried about the repercussions.

She stopped painting. 'But Ben isn't just a friend.'

'Ah.' I thought back to Florence's words at the garden party, about how Ben couldn't make Alice happy because she would feel too disloyal to her father.

'I want to talk to Father about him but I'm not sure how Ben would feel about that.'

'He's obviously crazy about you. It's just that...' I watched a pair of swans leading their cygnets across Waldenmere.

'It's impossible, isn't it?' She gave a helpless smile. 'What should I do?'

'Talk to Ben. Tell him how you feel. I know he feels the same. What I don't know is what he intends to do about it.' I paused. 'Be honest with him about what your father has said.'

'I'm not sure...' She faltered. 'I don't want him to feel obligated towards me. Or insulted.'

'I'm sure he'll understand the situation.' I tried to sound reassuring, but in truth, I didn't think this would end well. I suspected Ben was aware it had been Colonel Thackeray who'd scuppered his chances of becoming a captain when he was at Mill Ponds. He knew full well what he was up against.

'Miss Thackeray, Miss Woodmore,' said a soft voice. We turned to find Horace Laffaye raising his hat to us.

'Mr Laffaye, how are you?'

'I'm very well, thank you, Miss Thackeray. You're looking as lovely as ever.'

I smiled, noting he wasn't about to throw any compliments in my direction. But Alice did look beautiful in her sky-blue summer dress with her red hair pinned under a simple straw hat.

Horace inclined his head towards the easel. 'May I look at your painting?'

'Of course.' She stepped aside.

He leant in to inspect it. 'Charming, absolutely charming. You have a real eye.'

'Thank you, Mr Laffaye.' She blushed. 'I'm so pleased you like it. Praise, indeed, coming from such a talented artist as yourself. I'm sure it's not up to the standard of your own work.'

'Oh, I dabble. Just for fun, you know.' He waggled a finger at her. 'Now, you have real talent.'

'Your paintings are wonderful, Mr Laffaye. You're too modest.'

'You are kind to say so, Miss Thackeray.' He smiled with pleasure.

I was starting to wonder how long this appreciation of each other's art would continue when he turned to me.

'Miss Woodmore, will you be seeing Mr Whittle today?' he asked.

'I'm on my way to the office now, Mr Laffaye.' I'd spent far too long chatting with Alice.

'Perhaps I could prevail upon you to give him this.' He handed me a roll of thick paper tied securely with a red ribbon. 'Could you tell him I'm still working on the other matter he enquired about?'

'Of course.'

With that, he raised his hat and continued on his walk.

'I wonder what that's all about?' Alice eyed the mysterious roll of paper.

'I'm not sure. It occurred to me that Horace could be our anonymous cartoonist.' I ran my fingers over the ribbon. If it had been loose, I'd have been tempted to undo it but it was so neatly secured, I knew I'd never be able to re-tie it again without Elijah knowing I'd taken a peek.

'Oh.' Alice considered this. 'You could be right. I've seen some of his work. He can certainly draw.'

'The picture of Mrs Siddons as Boadicea? And Sir Henry as Marie Antoinette?'

'Yes,' she laughed. 'That would be his sense of humour.'

'He and Elijah are always trying to come up with ideas to increase *The Walden Herald's* circulation. And the cartoons have become popular.'

She nodded. 'I can see him using his newspaper to make a point. He likes to exert his influence where he can.'

Horace Laffaye enjoyed the quiet rhythm of life in Walden and kept himself informed of everything that went on in town. I wondered how much he'd known about what went on at Waldenmere Camp.

'How did Horace cope with the army camp on his doorstep? He must have hated it.'

'He shut up Heron Bay Lodge for long periods and went away. When he was in Walden, he was always tutting.'

'Tutting?'

'Whenever I met him, he'd be making these funny little "tut, tut, tut" noises under his breath. I think the war was a major inconvenience to him.'

I laughed. 'Now he has Sir Henry spoiling his little corner of Hampshire.'

'I wonder if he'll start tutting again once the hotel has been built?'

'He might shut up Heron Bay Lodge and go away again.' That was what Elijah feared. 'I'd better get this mysterious missive to the office.'

I turned to go when I heard someone call my name. Juliet Rendall was striding along the footpath towards us.

'Iris, I was hoping to catch you. Good morning, Miss Thackeray.' She glanced at Alice's painting, then leant in to scrutinise it more closely. 'You've captured the essence of the lake beautifully. Do you exhibit your work?'

'Oh, no.' Alice looked startled. 'I'm not good enough for that.'

'You are.' Juliet cast a critical eye over the canvas. 'If we could reprint this alongside an article on Waldenmere, it could make all the difference. People would see the natural beauty that's being destroyed.'

'That's an excellent idea.' I could visualise it. My words next to Alice's painting. 'A picture like this could make a big impact.'

'Would you be willing to let the society reprint your work?' Juliet asked.

'I'd be delighted.' Alice was clearly thrilled at the prospect. 'It would be wonderful if I could help your cause.'

'How kind.' Juliet beamed. 'It's so heartening to know people do want to support us.'

'I must go.' I glanced at my watch. 'I'm already late.'

'May I walk with you?' Juliet asked. 'There's something I'd like to discuss.'

'Of course. See you later, Alice.'

Juliet fell into step with me and we headed towards the town. 'One of our members has drafted an article comparing what will become of Waldenmere if the hotel goes ahead with what could happen if it's managed as a nature reserve.'

'That sounds like it might capture attention.'

'The problem is, it's far too long and written in academic terms.' Juliet pulled a sheaf of documents from her battered leather case. 'I was hoping you'd be able to pick out the relevant facts and condense them into something more appealing. I like the way you portray the personal side of a story. I suppose that's what I need you to do in this case. It will help us reach a wider audience.'

I was flattered by her words. Few people complimented me on my work, least of all Elijah, but I was beginning to feel more confident in my style of writing.

* * *

'You're late.'

'I saw Mr Laffaye on my way. He asked me to give you this.' I handed Elijah the rolled-up paper. 'He said he's still working on the other matter you enquired about.'

I waited for him to untie the ribbon and unroll it, but he placed it in his drawer without looking.

'Can I spend some time working on an article for Juliet?'

'If it will keep you quiet. Shut the door on your way out.'

His mood didn't improve and the door of his den stayed closed for most of the day. When I poked my head in to say I was going home, he just grunted in reply. I was glad to find George waiting outside.

'You look like you could do with cheering up,' he observed.

I pulled a face. 'Elijah's been in a foul mood all day. I could have done with his help with a difficult article, but he's barely said a word to me.'

George finished his cigarette and we began to stroll down Queens Road.

'What have you done to upset him?'

'Nothing. He just gets like this sometimes.' I knew the war had left Elijah with his own demons, even if I wasn't sure what they were. I guessed he was also fretting over Horace.

'Forget about him. Let's go and see what's happening at our favourite building site.'

'Not this evening. I'm going home.'

'Why?' He looked disappointed.

'I want Ben and Alice to spend some time alone together.'

'Ah.' He thought for a moment. 'Is that such a good idea?'

'Alice's father has started asking questions about the time she spends with us.'

We dawdled alongside Grebe Stream. I noticed George had slowed his pace, but I suspected it was to prolong our walk rather than because his leg was hurting.

'Surely she's allowed some friends?' he said.

'Not male ones.'

'Then is it wise for her to be seen alone with Ben? I wouldn't want to be in his shoes if her father found out. And from what you've said, he might take it out on Alice.'

'But she can't stay shut up in the hall forever.' I thought of her determined expression that morning. 'She's finally started to stand up for herself but she needs to know how Ben feels before she talks to her father about him.'

George sighed. 'He's in love with her but he knows better than to do anything about it. Ben's a decent bloke. And a sensible one. He's not in the same class as a colonel's daughter.'

'They could run away together?' I wasn't sure this was a good idea, though I was afraid that if Alice didn't act soon, the moment could be lost forever.

He shook his head. 'Do Ben and Alice strike you as the types who'd run away? Up sticks and leave their families behind?'

'No,' I admitted.

'That's the kind of thing you and I might do.' He gave me a wicked grin.

I laughed.

His expression became serious. 'You know I said I was saving up, so I could travel? I might just have enough. I could be leaving here soon.'

My heart sank but I kept my voice light. I'd known this couldn't last. 'Really? I didn't think the council paid that well?'

'It's not a huge amount but I don't need much. You could come with me.'

I smiled. 'I wish I could.'

'You said you wanted to live your life your own way, enjoy every experience, even if it meant disapproval.'

'I do. But there's my father and Lizzy. And Alice. Even Elijah.'

We dallied at the end of Chestnut Avenue, though for different reasons. George didn't want our walk to end while I was hesitating over what I was about to say. A reckless impulse was doing battle with sensible caution.

He sunk his hands into his pockets. 'I'll see you tomorrow then?'

'I don't want you to go.'

'I don't want to leave you.' He stared at the ground. 'But I don't want to stay here.'

The reckless impulse won. 'I mean, I don't want you to go now. I've got the house to myself tonight.'

His head shot up.

'Lizzy's staying with a friend in London.' I flushed at his shocked expression. 'We'd have to be careful.'

'Of course,' he stammered.

'I mean, we can't be seen going in together.' My cheeks were burning. 'I'll go in as normal. You wait here for a bit and then go around to the back of the house. I'll let you in through the kitchen door.'

'Your dad's definitely abroad, isn't he?'

'He's still in Germany.' His sudden wariness amused me and made me feel bolder, but my nerves returned with a vengeance when I entered the house. Peering into the hall mirror, I patted my face with powder and tidied my hair. I went into the kitchen and realised there were still dishes in the sink that I hadn't cleaned that morning. I turned on the tap and then turned it off again, deciding it wasn't the time to do the washing up.

All was silent and I began to wonder if George had changed his mind. Perhaps he'd taken fright and gone to catch his train. I'd never be able to face him again if he had.

I felt a jolt of relief combined with panic when I heard a light tap on the back door.

For a moment, we stood staring at each other. I had no idea what to do next and wondered if I should invite him into the drawing room for a drink. Why hadn't I thought of having a drink before he arrived? A brandy to settle my nerves.

Then he pulled me towards him. We kissed and my hands

instinctively moved along the contours of his back and up to his neck. My anxiety disappeared as our bodies drew closer.

'Iris,' he whispered, 'are you sure about this?'

'Yes.'

'I...' He paused. 'My leg. It's badly scarred.'

I took his hand and led him into the hallway. We stopped to kiss again and then tumbled our way up the stairs.

22

I turned onto my side. I'd have to wake George soon. It would be safer for him to leave the house in darkness rather than stay until morning but I was still relishing the thrill of lying next to him. The hours we'd spent together had been even better than I'd imagined.

A wave of satisfaction washed over me. I'd broken the rules and it felt good. I knew I'd shocked him with my sudden invitation but I didn't regret it. What I'd done was an assertion of how I wanted to live my life, free from the restrictions polite society enforced on women.

I stroked George's tousled hair, then traced my finger along the scar that ran down his thigh. He woke and pulled me towards him. I breathed in the sandalwood scent of his skin, feeling more tempted than ever to go away with him.

A sudden noise from downstairs made us both sit upright. Someone was hammering on the front door. We looked at each other in panic, then George jumped out of bed and scrambled around for his clothes.

'What time is it?' I grabbed my cotton nightdress from the floor and pulled it over my head.

He grappled for his watch. 'Quarter past ten. Who can it be?'

'I don't know. Lizzy must have come back early and forgotten her key.'

'What should I do?' he whispered.

'Stay here and keep quiet.' I took my dressing gown off the hook on the door and wrapped it around me. 'I'll go down and see who it is.'

'Be careful.' George watched me from the top of the stairs.

Another loud bang on the door increased my panic.

'Who is it?' I called.

'Ben.'

I let out a long breath. George was lurking in the shadows halfway up the stairs.

'Stay there while I talk to him,' I whispered. He took a few steps back into the darkness and I opened the front door.

Ben burst in. 'Have you seen Alice? Is she here?'

'No. No,' I stammered, alarmed by the expression on his face. 'Why would Alice be here?'

'Her father says she's missing. She didn't come home for dinner.' He looked towards the kitchen door as though he expected her to emerge. 'I thought she might be with you.'

'She's not here, Ben.' I stared at him. 'Perhaps she went into town? Was there a meeting of the Women's Group?'

'No.' He shook his head. 'Mother's at home. There wasn't a meeting this evening.'

'When was she last seen?'

'I left her at about a quarter to eight.' He rubbed his face. 'We'd been talking by the lake. She said her parents expected her home for dinner by eight o'clock.'

'It's only been a couple of hours. She had a lot on her mind when I spoke to her earlier.' I was trying to reassure myself as much as Ben. This was out of character for Alice.

'Earlier?' He pounced on the word. 'What time was that?'

'Earlier this morning.'

He deflated. 'I thought you meant this evening.'

'I'm sure there's nothing to worry about.' I placed a hand on his arm. 'Perhaps she's still out walking?'

'It got dark at about half-past eight. Haven't you seen her at all this evening?' He sounded desperate.

'No, I haven't. I, er... I came straight home after work. I was tired.'

Ben didn't seem to notice the slight creak from the staircase.

'I'd better go. Sid's waiting. He said that if I didn't find Alice here, he'd organise a search party to look for her around the lake.'

'I'll get dressed and come with you.'

'No. Stay here in case she turns up. I'll let you know when we find her.'

'Please do,' I begged. 'I won't sleep until I hear from you.'

Ben nodded. As soon as I closed the door, George appeared behind me, pushing his shirt into his trousers.

'Alice is missing.' With Ben gone, I let my anxiety show.

'I heard.' He put his hand on my shoulder. 'Perhaps she's decided to stay out late to teach her father a lesson.'

I shook my head. 'Alice wouldn't do that.'

'No, probably not,' he conceded. 'Maybe she's fallen over and twisted her ankle, or something like that?'

'Ben and Sid are going to search Waldenmere for her.'

'I'll join them. I'll tell them I ran into someone who told me she was missing.'

'I want to come with you.'

'You can't. We mustn't be seen together at this time of night. You should stay here in case she comes looking for you. I promise I'll get word to you when we find her.'

I followed him into the kitchen. He paused by the back door, leaning forward to kiss me. He held my face for a few moments and seemed about to say something, then changed his mind.

I locked the door after him, went upstairs to dress and then returned to the kitchen to make cocoa. My eyes constantly drifted to the clock on the wall.

After half an hour, I gave up. Rummaging around in the kitchen drawers, I found an old torch. Grabbing my jacket from the hatstand in the hall, I headed out.

Chestnut Avenue was dimly lit by streetlamps but when I reached the footpath that circled the lake, I was in total darkness. I switched on the torch, feeling exhilarated at entering a world so different by night. Hearing an owl hoot, I wished Juliet or Percy was with me. They'd be able to identify the strange noises coming from the undergrowth.

I had to decide which way to go. I could reach Sand Hills Hall by turning right and taking the path to Heron Bay Lodge and Grebe House or going left and passing Walden Railway Station and Mill Ponds. Our recent walks had gravitated towards the railway station to see how work was progressing, so I went left.

I walked briskly, keeping the torch light fixed on the ground. The footpath was uneven and tree roots jutted out of the earth. Alice knew the lake paths well, but she could easily have tripped if she'd been distracted.

Passing where the tank had been submerged, I shivered, wondering whether we'd ever find out who Tank Man was. The footpath veered right towards the slope up to Sand Hills Hall. I felt sure I'd get there only to find Alice safely back home and apologising for the fuss she'd caused. But I could hear voices and make out torchlights ahead. I quickened my pace, seeing the outline of figures in the distance by the old jetty.

I drew closer and saw that a few men seemed to be standing at a distance from two dark shadows hunched under the jetty. The shadows grew more distinct and I recognised Ben in his uniform. He was kneeling in the mud, leaning over something. To my horror, I realised the other strange shape was Colonel Thackeray. He was on his knees, hunched over, with his head in his hands.

I walked forward in a daze. George suddenly came rushing towards me.

'What's happened?' A tremor ran through my body.

'You shouldn't have come. I'll walk you home.' He wrapped his arm around my shoulders and tried to pull me away. I resisted. I could see Ben and the colonel crouched over someone lying in the shallow water. I stumbled forward, recognising the sky-blue summer dress from earlier that morning.

'No.' It came out in a low wail.

Alice's long, red hair was wet and matted with mud. It fell loosely around her face, strands sticking to her white skin.

'No.' I wailed again, gripping George's shirt. 'Is she...'

'I'm sorry,' he whispered hoarsely. 'She's dead.'

23

'I loved her,' Ben muttered.

'I know you did.' I reached out to take his hand, tears rolling down my face.

I couldn't remember how I'd got home. I had a vague recollection of George dragging me away from the jetty.

It was past midnight when Ben had knocked once again on the front door. George had guided him into the kitchen and poured him a glass of the brandy he'd found in my father's drinks cabinet.

We'd sat for hours, drinking, crying, trying to make sense of it until the light of dawn seeped through the window.

'I told her I wanted to marry her.'

'When?' I looked at him, startled.

'This evening. She...' He tried to stifle a sob. 'She wanted to talk to her father about me.'

I nodded. 'She needed to know how you felt first.'

'I should have told her before,' he sobbed, 'but I thought it was hopeless. The colonel stopped me from becoming a captain when I was at Mill Ponds. I knew he would never stand for me seeing Alice. I wanted to stay away from her, but... I just couldn't.'

'Who found her?' I couldn't keep the image of Alice's lifeless body from my mind.

'Colonel Thackeray. We heard him shout. When we got to him, he was kneeling over her, weeping.' Ben's voice shook.

I felt my chest tighten. The thought of Alice lying in the mud under the jetty was unbearable.

'It's my fault.' Ben stared into his empty brandy glass. 'I should have walked her to the hall, not left her by the jetty.'

Guilt washed over me. Why hadn't I met Alice that night instead of leaving her alone? Why had I been so reckless? 'It's my fault. I should have been with her.'

'Stop blaming yourselves.' George stood by the stove, boiling the kettle. He came over and put his arm around my shoulder. 'Did she drown? I don't understand how it happened?'

'Superintendent Cobbe is arranging for a pathologist to examine...' Ben gave up before he had to say the words.

George poured him another slug of brandy.

'Did you go to the lake?' Ben suddenly looked up at him. 'Before the search, I mean.'

'No, he didn't.' I cut in before George could answer. 'I told him I wanted to give you and Alice some time alone together.'

'Where did you go?' Ben stared at George.

'Just out walking.' George went back over to the stove. 'I'm planning to go away soon. I wanted some time to think about how I'm going to tell my mother.'

'Did you go to the Duck?' Ben's eyes followed George's every movement.

'No. I didn't feel like a drink.' George's hand shook as he poured boiling water into the teapot.

I wanted to say something, to defend him, but I couldn't speak. How could I admit to Ben that we'd been upstairs in my bed while Alice was lying dead?

'How did you know we were searching for her?' Ben wasn't going to let it go.

'Some bloke told me when I was walking back to the station.' George placed the teapot on the table.

We lapsed into silence. The quiet was broken by the sound of the front door opening. A moment later, Lizzy entered the kitchen.

'Something terrible has happened.' Without warning, my voice turned into a wail.

'I know. I was on the paper train. I heard as soon as I got to the station.' She took me in her arms and stroked my hair. I sobbed into her chest.

'Thank you for looking after Iris,' I heard her say in a firm but shaky voice. 'I know you've all had a terrible shock but it's time for you to leave. I can take care of her now.'

'Yes, of course.' George went over to Ben. 'Come on, Ben, I'll walk you home.'

Unsteadily, Ben got to his feet. George took his elbow and guided him out of the back door. I watched them go, my eyes meeting George's for a split second. My pain and confusion were mirrored in his face.

'Go upstairs and I'll bring you up some cocoa. You need to get some sleep.' Lizzy wiped her eyes as she pushed me out of the door.

In a daze, I climbed the stairs and fell wearily onto my bed. Catching the faint scent of George's cologne, I buried my face in my pillow and wept.

* * *

'We need to call on the Thackerays to offer our condolences.' Lizzy placed a boiled egg and a slice of toast in front of me. 'Eat this. You're going to need all your strength.'

The sight of food made me feel nauseous, as did the thought of facing Colonel Thackeray and Florence, but I knew she was right. It had been days since Alice's death; I wasn't sure how many.

The lake glistened under the glare of the August sun but the only thing I could see was Alice. She was in my head, day and night. My beloved Alice lying alone in the mud. At night, I dreamt I was holding her body in the water, trying to wipe the dirt from her sleeping face. I wanted to make her as beautiful and alive as she'd been on that last morning.

Lizzy and I neared the old jetty and I felt my stomach lurch. The structure had taken on a sinister identity in my mind, though in the bright sunshine, it looked harmless.

Our tears began to flow when we saw the flowers. Everyone in Walden must have come to pay their respects. Bouquets, wreaths and sprigs covered the ground and single roses floated in the water. It was some time before we could speak.

Eventually, we clung to each other and made our way up the slope. Sand Hills Hall seemed enveloped in a shroud of sadness despite the glorious weather. Holly, the Thackerays' maid, showed us in, her eyes red and swollen. Bear, Alice's spaniel, came scampering towards us. He waited expectantly on the doorstep for someone else and Holly had to push him back into the house so she could close the door.

Florence was seated in the drawing room. Her face, always pale, looked translucent, with blue veins showing around her eyes. 'How kind of you to come.' She reached out to me. 'I'm afraid Charles isn't fit for company. He's shut himself away in his study.'

'I'm sorry.' I took Florence's outstretched hands and she pulled me onto the sofa beside her. Bear lay despondently at my feet, watching the door.

'We won't stay long, Mrs Thackeray. We had to come and offer our condolences. Alice was so very dear to us.' Lizzy was fighting back tears. She perched on the edge of an armchair and dabbed her eyes with a handkerchief.

Holly set a tea tray down on the table and left us.

'Mrs Heathcote, would you be so kind as to pour?' Florence murmured. 'I'm afraid my hands tend to shake. I'm so terribly clumsy.'

'Of course, Mrs Thackeray.' Lizzy took her time arranging the cups and saucers and stirring the pot.

Florence held my hand. 'When did you last see Alice?'

'That morning.' My voice came out in a whisper. I cleared my throat. 'The morning it happened. I was on my way to work. She was finishing her painting of Heron Bay.'

'You didn't see her that evening?'

'No, I went straight home.' My face flushed. 'I wish I hadn't.'

'I'm not sure what time she went out. Or if she came back and went out again.'

'Why would she have gone back out again?' Though I suspected the reason. Colonel Thackeray's temper.

'My husband and I argued that evening. We were in the drawing room with the French doors open. I was afraid Alice might have overhead. I thought I saw her in the garden though I might have been mistaken.'

I wondered if the argument had been about Ben. Could Alice have heard what was said?

Florence continued. 'What did you talk about that morning? Was she upset? Her father had spoken to her rather sternly about being seen out with young men. He told her she shouldn't walk by the lake of an evening.' Her lips trembled. 'Alice disagreed with him. It was only the second time she'd done that. He didn't like it.'

'When was the first time?' I'd never known Alice to stand up to her father before.

'It was when you came back to live in Walden. He told her not to see you any more. Said you were disreputable. Your mother being a suffragette.' She gave me a sad smile. 'But Alice stood her ground and refused to give you up.'

The sob burst out of me before I knew it was there. I hid my face in my hands until I could breathe again. Lizzy handed me a cup of tea and I managed a tiny sip of sweet hot liquid.

'Was she upset when you saw her that morning?' Florence gripped my hand again. 'I need to understand what happened.'

'She wasn't upset. In fact, she seemed happy. We were laughing about...' My mind went blank. I couldn't remember what we'd been laughing about. 'Mr Laffaye had admired her painting. So had Juliet Rendall. She was pleased when Juliet said we should use her picture to illustrate my article.'

'Did she say anything about Ben Gilbert?' Florence tried to sound casual but there was a hint of desperation in her voice. 'Had they planned to meet that evening?'

'I'm not sure.' I didn't blame Florence for searching for answers but it felt like I was betraying Alice's trust by sharing her confidences. And my heart ached for Ben. I wanted to say how much he loved Alice, how he would never harm her, but common sense told me I could end up making things worse for him. 'I'm so sorry I let her down. I should have been with her. She said I was more worldly than she was. I was glad she was still innocent but what if one of those workmen tried to take advantage of her? Perhaps they pushed her into the water? I should have been there to look after her.'

'You're no more able to look after yourself than Alice was.' Lizzy brushed a tear away and glared at me. 'Remember that and don't go gadding about on your own.'

* * *

After days of doing nothing but think about Alice, I decided to do something practical. I took the long route into town rather than walking by the lake.

'You don't need to be here. Go home.' Elijah got up and came out to my desk.

'I want to write Alice's obituary.' I couldn't stop the tears from pricking my eyelids. 'I want people to know how kind and sweet and good she was.'

'I think they know that already,' he said gruffly. He went over to the gas ring in the corner to heat some coffee.

'What's going on?' My voice was hoarse. 'Why is this happening in Walden?'

'I don't know.' He ran his fingers through his sparse grey hair, his face as crumpled as his suit.

'Do you think one of the railway workers could have hurt Alice? I saw the way they looked at her.'

'Maybe.' He put a mug of coffee on my desk. 'Start on Alice's obituary. I'll have a read when you've finished.'

I put a sheet of paper into my typewriter and stared at it but the words wouldn't come. Minutes or hours might have passed. Elijah occasionally glanced in my direction but didn't say anything. I sat listening to the sound of the old railway clock on the wall and the printing presses below.

I was roused from my stupor by the noise of footsteps on the stairs. Ben's pale face peered around the door.

'What is it? Is it about Alice?' For some reason, I felt panic rising in me.

'I shouldn't be here.' He clung to the door frame. 'But I knew you'd want to know.'

Elijah rose from his desk. 'Come in, Ben.'

But Ben seemed rooted to the spot. 'I'm not on duty. I'm not allowed to work on the case.'

I poured him a mug of coffee while Elijah dragged him into his den and pushed him into a chair.

Ben slumped forward, staring at the floor. 'Sid told me the pathologist found marks on Alice's throat. Someone held her under the water.'

24

Elijah went to the filing cabinet and fished out a whisky bottle and a couple of glasses. He poured a measure in each and handed them to Ben and me before adding a healthy slug to his coffee.

I brought the glass to my lips, but my throat was too constricted to attempt to swallow. Instead, I inhaled the strong woody aroma. 'Were there any other marks on her?' I asked hoarsely.

'No. She was fully clothed. The pathologist said there were no signs she'd been touched underneath.' Ben looked nauseous. 'But her lungs were filled with water.'

I felt conflicting emotions. I'd been torturing myself with thoughts of what could have happened. I'd envisioned one of Sir Henry's men, perhaps drunk, trying to take advantage of her. 'I don't understand. Why would someone kill Alice?'

Ben rocked forwards in his chair. 'When I find them, I'm going to kill them.'

Elijah pulled out a large white handkerchief and wiped his eyes. 'Who was the last person to see her?' he asked gruffly.

'Me. We... we talked,' Ben stammered. 'After she finished painting that morning, she went home to have lunch with her parents. She spent the afternoon writing letters and the maid said she took her afternoon tea at about four o'clock. No one seems sure what time she went out. It would vary, depending on whether she was planning to paint. I saw her by Mill Ponds at six-thirty and we walked for a bit. She said she had to be home for dinner with her parents at eight. I left her at the old jetty at about a quarter to. I had to get back into town.'

'Did you see her go up the hill?' I asked.

He shook his head, tears filling his eyes.

Elijah's face was lined with concern. 'Have you been suspended?'

'No.' Ben gulped his whisky and grimaced. 'I can carry out my usual duties in town but I can't be involved with the investigation. I've told Superintendent Cobbe about my relationship with Alice.'

'Colonel Thackeray found her?' Elijah topped up Ben's whisky.

'We went out with torches. But we were looking along the pathways.' Ben's hand shook as he picked up the glass. 'I don't know what made him go over to the marsh by the jetty.'

'Presumably, whoever killed her would have been wet? Covered in mud?' Elijah picked up his pen and made a few notes on his jotter.

Ben nodded. 'My trousers were soaked and so were the colonel's when we tried to revive her.'

'Could it have something to do with Tank Man?' It occurred to me that Alice was one of the few people who'd been close to Waldenmere Camp throughout the war. 'Perhaps she saw something?'

Ben rubbed his unshaven chin. 'Wouldn't she have told us if she had?'

'I don't mean recently but at the time the tank went into the water. Something she didn't realise the significance of until now?'

'Did she mention anything when you last saw her?' Elijah asked.

I shook my head, tears threatening once more. The realisation I'd never speak to Alice again was still sinking in.

'This all started with General Cheverton's death at Mill Ponds.' Elijah drummed his pen on his desk. 'How in God's name did it lead to this?'

* * *

On the surface, life in Walden carried on as usual, but you could sense the underlying sorrow.

Superintendent Cobbe and his officers had become a familiar presence, using the town hall as their headquarters to conduct interviews. Sir Henry's workmen had all been questioned and hostility towards LSWR was growing by the day. Rumours had spread that Sir Henry's men would refuse to return to Waldenmere once permission was given for work to start again. They were saying the project was cursed and more deaths would follow.

I'd told the police I was at home at the time of Alice's death, omitting to say George had been with me. I was racked with guilt and desperately wanted to talk to him but we'd had no opportunity to be alone together. Elijah had taken it upon himself to walk me home from the office each evening and George had wisely stopped waiting by the printworks.

The situation was unbearable and I felt suffocated. My anxiety increased when I received a message from Superintendent Cobbe asking me to call in at the town hall for a chat.

'Would you like me to come with you?' Elijah asked. I shook my head. This would be bad enough without his presence.

* * *

Inside the town hall, I was immediately reminded of Alice. When she was here, she'd felt like she had a job and was part of something. Working with the Walden Women's Group had given her a sense of purpose.

I thought of the afternoon we'd washed up in the kitchen and she'd confessed her love for Ben. How I wished I could turn the clock back to that day.

Superintendent Cobbe was alone, sitting at a desk in the corner. He beckoned me over. Feeling self-conscious, I sat down in front of him. He was a tall, broad-shouldered man with a kindly face. When he spoke, his manner was gentle, but there was an underlying steeliness about him.

'Thank you for coming so promptly, Miss Woodmore. I know you've already spoken to PC King, but there are a few questions I'd like to ask you, if I may?'

'Of course.'

'You'd known Alice Thackeray for a number of years, is that correct?'

'We met at school when we were eleven and became friends. When I was thirteen, my family moved to London. We wrote to each other and occasionally met. Then my father bought our house on Chestnut Avenue and I moved back to Walden last year.'

'And you and Miss Thackeray picked up your friendship as before?'

'It was as though I'd never been away. Except that I had. I'd missed out on so much. I think she was lonely during the war, mostly confined to Sand Hills Hall. Though she had her work with the Walden Women's Group to keep her occupied.'

'And did she have any boyfriends during that time? I'm aware of her relationship with PC Gilbert.'

I shook my head. 'The only person she ever told me she liked was Ben. She even wanted to talk to her father about him but she knew that Colonel Thackeray was unlikely to approve of the match.'

'Was she upset by this?'

'More resigned than anything. She loved her father dearly, but... but it was difficult.'

'If Colonel Thackeray found out his daughter was seeing someone he disapproved of, how do you think he'd react?'

'I don't know.' This was something I'd been turning over in my head.

'Did he sometimes shout at Miss Thackeray?'

'He would shout. I never heard him shout directly at Alice.' I wanted to be as factual as possible.

'Was she afraid of her father?'

'She didn't like it when he lost his temper.'

'Was he violent?'

'He occasionally broke things.' It felt disloyal to Alice to speak badly of the colonel.

'Do you think he was ever violent towards Alice?'

'I don't think so.' It was true. I'd been scared he might lash out at Alice in a fit of temper but I didn't believe him capable of murdering her. Or did I simply not want to believe that? My thoughts on the matter were muddled.

'When did you last see Miss Thackeray?'

'On the morning of the day she died. She was painting a view of Heron Bay. I chatted with her on my way to work.'

'Did she say anything unusual or seem disturbed in any way?'

'She mentioned that her father wasn't happy about her being seen out with male friends.'

'I believe you and she were in the habit of walking by the lake of an evening, often going to the construction site. PC Gilbert and Mr George Hale would sometimes join you?'

I nodded. My palms grew sweaty. Was George under suspicion? I needed to find a way to speak to him soon.

'Yet you didn't meet her the night she was killed?'

'I wish I had.'

'Why didn't you?'

'I wanted her to spend time alone with Ben. She intended to talk to her father about him.' I was trying to stick to the truth as closely as possible.

'And what did you do that evening instead?'

'I bumped into George Hale at about six o'clock. We chatted for a while, I mentioned my plan to him and then I went home.'

'Who was present at home that evening?'

'No one.' I stared into my lap.

'Was that usual?'

'Generally, Mrs Heathcote, our housekeeper, is there, but she sometimes stays in London with a friend. My father is away at present.'

'Is your father often away?'

'His work takes him abroad quite frequently.'

'I see.' The superintendent leaned back in his chair and studied me. 'What made you go looking for Miss Thackeray that night? I believe you turned up at the jetty at around eleven o'clock?'

'Ben had called earlier, searching for Alice. He said he'd tell me when she was found but I couldn't wait. I wanted to know what was going on.'

'And when you reached the jetty, Mr Hale was already there?'

'That's right.' I was becoming hotter and more uncomfortable by the minute.

'And he walked you back home?'

'He could see I was distressed. He took me back to Chestnut Avenue. Ben turned up about an hour later.'

'Was Mr Hale friends with Miss Thackeray too?'

'The four of us had become friends.' I guessed what was coming next.

'Miss Thackeray was a very pretty girl. She must have had lots of admirers?'

'More than she probably realised. She was very modest.' Had Alice been aware of how some men looked at her? She never appeared to notice. I hated the thought that she might have been blind to the danger she'd faced that night.

'May I ask you a personal question?' He folded his arms and tilted his head to one side as he scrutinised me.

I didn't like the sound of this.

Without waiting for me to reply, he asked, 'Did you ever feel jealous of her?'

I smiled. The question came as a relief. 'Of course not. Why would I be jealous?'

'Perhaps you felt Mr Hale was paying her too much attention?'

'George liked Alice, but not in that way. He felt sorry for her because of... well, because of Colonel Thackeray.'

'And what about Mr Baverstock?'

'Percy?' I hadn't anticipated this.

'Yes. Did he like Alice?'

'No. Well, yes. Of course, he *liked* Alice – everyone did – but he didn't know her that well.'

'Mr Baverstock is a friend of yours, I believe? You introduced them. Is that correct?'

'Yes.'

'Mr Baverstock has recently been spending a lot of time at Waldenmere, along with Mrs Juliet Rendall. I've read some of your articles on the work they do.'

I nodded. My mouth was dry.

'Miss Thackeray often painted by the lake. She and Mr Baverstock must have run into each other on occasion.'

'I suppose so.' I had no idea what else to say. It hadn't occurred to me before, but Alice had gone willingly with Percy to see the water violets, which was unusual for her. Perhaps they'd chatted together more than I'd realised.

'This gave you no cause for concern?'

'Why would I be concerned?'

'I don't know. Perhaps you felt Mr Baverstock was paying too much attention to Miss Thackeray. You may have regretted introducing them?'

'Percy is just... Percy.' I ran out of words. He was flirtatious, but he was also kind. I had no idea how to explain this to Superintendent Cobbe. 'I didn't regret introducing them. Percy is fun. It was good for Alice to mix with people of her own age. She'd been cooped up in the hall for too long with only her parents for company.'

'You never harboured any ill feelings towards Miss Thackeray?'

'It wasn't possible to harbour ill feelings towards her.' I looked at him directly. 'If you'd known her, you'd understand. Everyone loved her.'

'That could be a cause for jealousy.'

I shook my head. I took a moment to gather my thoughts and emotions. 'Alice was beautiful and accomplished. She could really paint; she never knew how talented she was. She was sweet and kind – she didn't have to try - she just was. It was in her nature. I often wished I could be more like her.' I tried to keep my voice steady. 'But I was never jealous. I loved her and I'm going to miss her.'

'Thank you for your time, Miss Woodmore.' The superintendent rose from his chair. 'I appreciate this is difficult for you. I'll let you get back to work now but I may need to speak to you again.'

I nodded and quickly left the hall, wiping my eyes.

25

'Are you going to work again today?' Lizzy picked up my plate containing the remains of half-eaten toast.

I nodded. Work was the only thing that distracted me from thinking about Alice. Even sitting at the kitchen table was a reminder of how she used to join us for breakfast, glad to escape from the hall.

'Mrs Siddons has summoned us to attend a meeting at the council offices.' I drank the tea Lizzy put in front of me, even though she'd put far too much sugar in it.

'You don't have to go. Elijah's quite capable of taking his own notes for once.'

'I want to go.'

'That's where your friend George works, isn't it?' She took a wet cloth from the sink and wiped the table.

I nodded, caught off guard by the question. I'd been thinking about how I could get a message to him.

'Would you like to invite him to supper one day?' She kept on wiping the table, not meeting my eye.

I appreciated the offer but the thought of sitting down with

George under Lizzy's watchful gaze and not being able to touch him or talk privately wasn't an appealing prospect.

'Not now. Perhaps another time.'

She nodded.

* * *

For once, Elijah and I fell into step as we walked along the high street to the council offices. I'd lost my usual vigour, so we strolled side by side like an old married couple.

George came down the staircase to greet us, his face solemn. I didn't know how I could speak to him with Elijah sticking close to my side but as I followed him up the stairs, George mouthed the word 'portrait' to me.

He guided us to the antechamber before going into the meeting room to check if they were ready for us. I went to the portrait of Alderman Redvers Tolfree and saw a small piece of paper tucked behind the bottom corner of the frame. George returned to show us in and while Elijah stubbed out his cigarette, I pulled the note free and shoved it into my pocket. George saw and smiled.

Seated around the mahogany table were Mrs Siddons, Councillor Mansbridge and, to my surprise, Sir Henry Ballard. I stiffened at the sight of him.

As expected, it was Mrs Siddons who took charge of proceedings. 'Thank you for coming. As you'll appreciate, the terrible events of the last weeks have cast a dark shadow over Walden.' She was dressed more sombrely than usual in a plain black suit. 'Feelings are running high and people are venting their anger towards the construction site. Sir Henry is giving the police his full cooperation while they investigate Miss Thackeray's tragic murder.'

'I have daughters of my own, you know.' Sir Henry was wearing a dark suit and cravat, his usual ebullience replaced by subdued gravity. 'I've sent my deepest condolences to the Thackerays. This is a terrible, terrible tragedy and my heart goes out to them.'

I remembered the photograph of two young girls on his desk and a little of my hostility towards him melted.

'If I find any man in my employ had anything to do with this vile act. Let's just say, they'll wish they'd never been born.' Sir Henry's eyes flashed with anger.

'Quite.' Mrs Siddons continued without emotion. 'I think we're all of the same mind. Our priority is to support Superintendent Cobbe and his officers in whatever way we can. All this hostility towards Sir Henry and his workers isn't helping the police do their job.'

Councillor Mansbridge cleared his throat. 'None of us could have foreseen this terrible sequence of events when work started at Waldenmere and until we know the facts, it would be unfair to cast blame.'

'Far be it for me to tell you what to print in your newspaper, Mr Whittle.' Mrs Siddons was clearly about to tell Elijah what she'd like him to print. 'But a more conciliatory tone towards Sir Henry and LSWR may be appropriate at this time given the situation we find ourselves in.'

An uncomfortable silence followed. I suspected the cartoon of Sir Henry in wig and makeup as Marie Antoinette was flashing through all our minds. For the first time since Alice's death, I almost smiled.

Mrs Siddons coughed. 'What I mean is, it may help to calm feelings in the town and ease pressure on Superintendent Cobbe's men if they don't have to deal with any more heated altercations.'

Elijah inclined his head in agreement. 'Do you still intend to build the hotel?'

'I'm not sure. I've suspended work for the present time. No matter what the cost, there will be a respectful pause before we decide on our next steps.' Sir Henry frowned and shook his head. 'So much bad luck with this project.'

'Bad luck?' My former hostility returned with a vengeance. How dare he talk about cost and dismiss Alice's murder as another piece of back luck?

'Er, what I mean to say is...' Sir Henry trailed off. 'Things could have gone better.'

I ignored the pressure of Elijah's hand on my arm, unable to contain the rage that had been simmering since Alice's death.

'You started all this. You probably had General Cheverton murdered to get your hands on Mill Ponds,' I shouted. 'None of this would have happened if it hadn't been for your bloody hotel.'

'That's enough, Iris.' Elijah stood. 'I'm sorry, Sir Henry. Miss Woodmore is naturally upset by the death of her friend.'

There was a hasty scraping back of chairs. I was vaguely aware of Mrs Siddons' look of concern and the men's embarrassed faces as Elijah dragged me out of the door.

* * *

Elijah and I talked little that day and after work, he walked me home in silence. I wanted to get rid of him, but he insisted on coming in, saying he needed a private word with Lizzy.

I waited for the kitchen door to close behind him, then slipped out of the front door.

I'd been avoiding the lake, but in his note, George had asked me to meet him at our bench. I sat under the shade of the oak tree, feeling uncomfortably hot and not just because of the weather. Embarrassment at my outburst was mingled with anger, guilt and grief. I wanted to wade into the stream, lie in the cool water and let it wash over me. Or wash me away.

'Iris.' George's arms were around me.

I buried my head in the crook of his neck. 'I feel so guilty.'

'You can't blame yourself. It's not your fault.'

'We should have met her that night, not left her alone.'

'God knows I wish we had.' His eyes were wet. 'But she should have been safe. She's lived by Waldenmere all her life, for goodness sake.'

'Who could have done this? Why Alice?'

'I don't know, but if I get my hands on them...' I felt his grip on me tighten.

'When are you going away?' I suddenly realised how alone I felt without Alice. The thought of George going was unbearable.

'I can't leave now. Not without knowing what happened.' His face creased with anxiety. 'If I go, people will think I had something to do with Alice's death. You're the only one who knows it can't have been me.'

'Have the police questioned you?'

'Superintendent Cobbe came to my house.'

'Your house? Why didn't he interview you at the town hall?'

'I came home to find him in the kitchen with my mother. He asked her if I'd come home that night and gone back out again and if she'd noticed any mud on my clothes or shoes. Then he questioned me.'

'Oh, God, your poor mother.' I couldn't bear the thought of causing more pain to this woman who'd suffered so much already. 'What did you tell him?'

'That I chatted with you by the lake for a while, then decided to go for a long walk. I said I'd taken the path alongside the canal and lost track of time and when I realised it was getting late, I headed back to the station. I told him I'd passed a bloke on the way who'd said they were looking for Alice.' He paused. 'I'm not sure he believed me. He wanted to know why I hadn't gone to the Duck for a drink, as I often go there.'

'If he questions you again, I'll tell him you were with me.'

He squeezed me tightly. 'Thank you. I hope it won't come to that but I admit I'm scared.'

I sighed. 'I may have to tell him to prove my innocence. Superintendent Cobbe questioned me, too.'

His head jolted back. 'That's ridiculous. They can't possibly think you had anything to do with it.'

'He suggested I was jealous of Alice. That I felt you or Percy had been paying her too much attention.'

'Oh, God, this is madness.'

'It's a nightmare. I wish I could wake up from it and find Alice still alive.'

He frowned. 'What about that Percy bloke? I saw him flirting with her.'

'Percy flirts with everyone. He's harmless.'

He said nothing and I put my head in my hands. Everyone was becoming a suspect. Ben was suspicious of George and George wanted to turn Percy into some sort of fiend.

'Why did I have to be so rebellious that night?' My voice cracked. 'I'm so selfish.'

'It's my fault. I should never have...' He rubbed his eyes. 'I'm sorry I got you into this mess.'

'But why did Alice have to suffer? Why her?' I knew I was pleading for an answer he couldn't give.

'During the war, I gave up trying to figure out why some people live and others die. Why did I come home and not Reg?'

We sat in silence, my head resting on his shoulder. Eventually, I roused myself. 'I must go. Lizzy told me not to go walking alone.' I didn't want to move but I had to get back. I was in enough trouble already.

'She's right. It was stupid of me to ask you to meet me here, but I didn't know where else we could be alone. While this lunatic's out there, you've got to be careful.' He kissed me softly on the lips and held my face close to his. 'I wish I could look after you. Be with you.'

We stood up and held each other for a long time before slowly walking to Chestnut Avenue. At the front door, I turned to find him watching me from the end of the road. I wanted to run back to him. Instead, I took a deep breath and went inside.

'Iris, where have you been? I was getting worried.' My father rushed towards me, his arms outstretched.

26

'A hotel at Waldenmere? It's madness.' Father stood by the water's edge, shielding his eyes from the sun.

'I would have said more in my letters, but I wasn't sure you'd get them. You were moving about so much.'

'Things were chaotic over there and I ended up staying longer than I intended to.' He put his arm around me. 'I'm sorry. I wish I'd been here with you when all this was going on.'

I'd heard this many times before. My father always became immersed in whatever he was working on. Then each time he returned, he'd be surprised to find things had changed in his absence. I'd also begun to suspect some of his vagueness around where he was staying was because he had a woman in his life. He was only forty-six and had been widowed for seven years. It was probable he had formed a relationship. But like so much else, he kept it from me.

He strode over to inspect the debris still strewn across the garden of Mill Ponds and I noticed passers-by glance at him. He was tall with an intense demeanour that attracted attention.

'How long were you at Mill Ponds during the war?' In 1916 he'd been recruited into the Intelligence Corp because of his contacts in overseas news agencies. He'd drafted in Elijah to help him with an assignment, which I think involved devising ways to channel information to their contacts in occupied territories. All I knew for certain was that they'd attended a briefing at Mill Ponds before ending up somewhere in France.

'Not long. It was strange to find myself back in Walden, but good to be able to walk by the lake again. I decided then we should return here once the war was over.'

'Did you have much to do with General Cheverton or Colonel Thackeray?'

'Thackeray was kept busy training raw recruits. I spent some time with the general. By then, he was more of a strategist, too old for front-line duties, but he still went out of his way to help soldiers going into battle, irrespective of their rank.'

'Unlike Colonel Thackeray?'

'I can't say I liked the man's methods, but it was wartime; there weren't many alternatives.' He breathed deeply. 'I can't bear to think of what he and Florence must be going through.'

'Will you come with me to Alice's funeral?'

'Of course I will.'

* * *

When we returned home, Elijah was seated in the drawing room. I listened in silence while he and Father discussed events in Walden.

'I spoke to Superintendent Cobbe earlier.' Elijah turned to me. 'They're drawing a blank when it comes to Sir Henry's men. They're all giving each other alibis for the night Alice was killed.'

'If it's not one of them, it must be linked to Tank Man. Alice was at Sand Hills Hall for the duration of the war. She would have seen a lot of what went on in the camp at that time.'

'It's plausible.' He took the drink Father offered him. 'She never said anything to you? You must have talked about the tank?'

'We all chatted about it.' I instantly regretted using the word 'all'. I didn't want to mention George to my father. 'Alice and I talked about it a lot but she was as mystified as anyone. It could have been something that only made sense to her later.'

Elijah sipped his whisky. 'Did you mention this theory when Superintendent Cobbe interviewed you?'

'I didn't think about it at the time.'

'The police interviewed you?' Father had been leaning against the mantelpiece. He came and sat next to me. 'Why didn't you tell me? What did they ask you?'

'They wanted to know about Alice, how she'd been when I talked to her last and if she was upset about anything.'

Elijah tried to reassure him. 'As Alice's closest friend, it's not surprising they wanted to speak to Iris. Superintendent Cobbe's a decent chap. I didn't have any worries on that score.'

Father nodded. 'I'm sorry I wasn't here to accompany you.'

'Elijah would have come, but I didn't want him to.' I averted my eyes from my father's. 'I felt I was betraying Alice's trust. I had to tell the superintendent about our private conversations.'

Elijah knew I'd been questioned about George and I was grateful to him for not mentioning it, but as the investigation into Alice's murder continued, things were bound to come out. I felt a sense of hopelessness at the way events were unfolding.

* * *

My feeling of being carried along by an unstoppable force intensified on the day of Alice's funeral. It seemed like the whole of Walden had turned out to pay their respects. People lined the road up to St Martha's Church and tears welled in my eyes as I caught snippets of their conversations, '...such a sweet girl...', '...always a kind word for everyone...', '...no airs or graces...'

In spite of my tears, I almost smiled when I caught sight of Horace Laffaye strolling side by side with Mrs Siddons, his neighbour. For once, Horace was wearing a dark suit and cravat while Mrs Siddons was dressed in black silk with jet jewellery. They made an unlikely, though extremely well-dressed, couple. I remembered what I'd been laughing about with Alice on the morning before she died. We'd suspected Horace had been the one to draw the cartoon of Mrs Siddons as Boadicea. I experienced a sharp stab of pain at the thought of never being able to laugh with her again.

I entered St Martha's Church holding Father's hand, with Elijah walking behind us. The Walden Women's Group had filled every available vessel with flowers and the scent of sweet peas hung in the air.

George was standing on his own at the back. We exchanged a brief but intense look. If the police were to question either of us again, we'd have to tell them we'd been together that night. I felt the familiar sense of shame creep over me at the thought of my father finding out.

Then the door opened and Alice's coffin was carried into the church. I dug my nails into my palms, hating myself for caring about my stupid reputation when she was lying in a wooden box.

The service seemed to go on forever and I felt suffocated with guilt and grief. When we finally walked out into the churchyard, I took large gulps of air.

As Alice's coffin was lowered into the ground, there were sobs from many of the mourners. Even Reverend Childs seemed to struggle with his reading. I turned away to look towards my mother's grave and noticed a freshly dug mound of earth nearby. It was marked with a simple, unadorned cross and I guessed it must be where Tank Man had ended up.

My eyes searched the sea of faces but there was no sign of George. It was kind of him to come to pay his respects, though wise not to linger in case his presence was observed by Colonel Thackeray. Ben was standing with his parents. His father seemed uncomfortable in his black suit and kept tugging at his tie.

The mourners began to disperse and Ben approached the Thackerays to offer his condolences. Colonel Thackeray nodded stiffly and walked away but Florence leant forward and whispered something in Ben's ear before she followed her husband.

Ben couldn't hold back his tears and his mother took his arm and led him away. Elijah went up to him and suggested a pint at the Duck. Father and I trailed behind them out of the churchyard. Our ordeal wasn't over yet. We'd been invited to attend a small private gathering back at Sand Hills Hall.

At the hall, Florence had put a selection of Alice's watercolours on show. I thought how embarrassed Alice would have been by this, even though the paintings were exquisite. I could tell the guests were surprised by their quality.

I was admiring a delicate watercolour of a wren, thinking how impressed Juliet Rendall would be by Alice's detailed depictions of birds and flowers, when Florence touched my arm.

'Come with me. There's something I want to show you.'

Propped up on an easel in the drawing room was the painting of Heron Bay that Alice had been working on.

'It's wonderful. I didn't know she'd finished it.' I examined the detailed brushwork. It was probably Alice's best piece. 'She was so talented.'

'I kept telling her she was too modest.' Florence's eyes swam with tears. 'My clever, beautiful daughter. God knows she didn't deserve this.'

We stood in silence, mesmerised by the painting.

'You'll miss her, won't you?' Florence whispered.

Still unable to speak, I nodded. She picked up the picture, wrapped it in a linen cloth and handed it to me.

'I can't take it,' I gasped.

'She planned to give it to you. She knew how much you hated the thought of Waldenmere changing. She wanted to capture it for you as it is now.'

I brushed away my tears and took the painting. 'She was kind to me from the first day we met. I'm not sure I always deserved it.'

Florence was about to reply when Colonel Thackeray marched into the room, followed by my father.

'Iris.' The colonel stood directly in front of me. 'I want you to tell us everything you know about George Hale.'

27

'Who is George Hale?' Father came and stood beside me.

Bear, who'd been dozing on the rug, whimpered and ran from the room. I wanted to go with him.

I turned away from Colonel Thackeray and addressed my father. 'He's a friend of mine. When Alice and I used to stroll around the lake in the evening, George and Ben Gilbert would sometimes join us. When work started on the hotel, the four of us used to go to the site to see what was happening.'

'What do you know about the background of this George fellow?' The colonel took a step back but still barked at me.

'He lives in Basingstoke and works as a clerk for Councillor Mansbridge in Walden's council offices.' I felt humiliated by this interrogation. 'After he was injured during the war and couldn't return to the front line, he worked for General Bartlett for a time.'

'And you allow your daughter to go about in public with this class of person?' Colonel Thackeray said to my father.

'Iris is old enough to choose her own friends. This George Hale sounds perfectly respectable to me.' Father's manner was cool and measured in contrast to the colonel's heated agitation.

'I do not consider him to be suitable company for my daughter.' He stopped abruptly, appearing to remember he no longer had a daughter.

I could sense the underlying anguish in the colonel's temper and adopted my father's calm demeanour. 'There was no harm in it. We would just walk by the lake and chat. Alice used to enjoy it.'

Florence stifled a sob.

'But look at what it led to.' Sweat was forming on the colonel's brow. 'I've been speaking to Superintendent Cobbe and told him Ben Gilbert must be removed from duty.'

'He's done nothing wrong.' I was dismayed at the repercussions this could have for Ben's career.

'He became too attached to Alice. He should be arrested and interrogated.' Despite his words, Colonel Thackeray's anger seemed to be dissolving into a kind of bewildered sorrow.

I shook my head. 'Ben would never have hurt her.'

Florence, who'd sunk into a chair at the side of the room, revived somewhat at this. 'I don't know about George Hale, but I don't believe Ben Gilbert could have harmed Alice.'

'And neither did George. He was fond of her. As a friend.' I hated that no matter what I said, there was the implication of something improper about George's relationship with Alice.

'I know you think George liked you best, but...' Florence hesitated, 'maybe he liked Alice more than you realised?'

I stared at the pattern on the oriental rug, feeling the walls closing in on me. I had to get out of there.

When I didn't answer, Florence continued. 'If she refused him, perhaps he lost his temper and...' She buried her face in her hands.

I cleared my throat but my words still came out in a croak. 'Neither Ben nor George had anything to do with Alice's death.' I picked up the painting and walked out of the room.

* * *

I scrambled down the slope, falling in my haste, but I needed to get away from Sand Hills Hall. I could hear my father calling, so I left the footpath and stumbled into the rough ground of Willow Marsh, avoiding looking in the direction of the old jetty.

Water started to seep into my best shoes but I didn't care. Passing a gorse bush, I closed my hand over its spikes, crushing the coconut-scented yellow flowers. Ignoring the pain and blood that smeared my palm, I kept walking, wanting to cry out in frustration but unable to make a sound. I fell to the ground, still clutching the painting of Heron Bay.

A rustling noise brought me back to the present. It grew louder and seemed to be made by something larger than a fox or squirrel. A knot of apprehension formed. I was sitting close to the spot where someone had murdered Alice.

Fear washed over me when a tall figure emerged from a dense grove of willows.

'Iris,' Percy knelt by my side, 'are you hurt?'

I sat up, clutching the painting. Juliet appeared behind him, holding a pair of field glasses.

'Are you all right?' She crouched beside me. 'Have you hurt your hand?'

'It's nothing.' I blinked back tears.

'You're bleeding.' She pulled a handkerchief from her pocket and gently wrapped it around my hand. 'Come and sit over here where it's drier.'

With Percy's help, I managed to navigate my way over to a grassy patch. They were both wearing wellington boots while I squelched in my leather shoes.

'Have you been at Sand Hills Hall?' Percy sat next to me, his long legs sticking out in front.

I nodded.

'I'm so sorry about Alice.' He looked at Juliet. 'We both are.'

Juliet knelt in front of me. 'Is that one of her paintings?'

'It's the view of Heron Bay she was working on.' I carefully opened the linen wrap to show her. 'Her mother gave it to me.'

She sighed. 'It's beautiful.'

'Mrs Thackeray has put all of Alice's pictures on display. You would love her drawings of birds and flowers. They're so delicate and precise.'

'I'm sure I would. Her work reminded me of a biologist and painter called Marianne North.'

Percy nodded in agreement.

'Alice was thrilled when you suggested her picture should accompany my writing.' I longed to go back to that morning and make things happen differently. Alice would still be here and we'd sit together by the lake and plan a series of illustrated articles.

'The two of you would have made a formidable team.' Juliet leant back on the grass, weariness showing on her face. 'It's such a tragedy.'

'Won't your father be wondering where you are?' Percy asked gently. 'I saw you with him at the funeral.'

'You were there?'

He nodded. 'Outside the church. We both were. We wanted to pay our respects.'

'She was much loved.' Juliet swept back her long, dark hair. 'It was humbling to see.'

'We had our wellingtons and field equipment in the back of Juliet's car, so we came here afterwards to check on the water violets. We saw you all going up to Sand Hills Hall.' Percy sighed. 'Her poor parents.'

'Was it dreadful being there? Is that why you left?' Juliet was trying to wipe the mud from my skirt. 'Funerals are difficult to cope with.'

'It was all too much. Colonel Thackeray's angry and making accusations. I had to get away.' I clung to Alice's picture with my clean hand.

'Have the police made any progress?' Percy's usually open, sunny face was tense and pinched.

My stomach formed a knot. 'Did they question you?'

'I've spent a lot of time here recently.' He nodded towards the jetty. 'And I saw Alice on occasion. They made all sorts of insinuations.'

'You weren't here that night, though, were you.' I didn't meet his eyes. I said it as a statement, but it was a question. And he probably knew it.

'I'd been here that afternoon, but no, not then.' He locked eyes with Juliet and she reached over to squeeze his hand.

'He was with me at my cottage in Odiham. We had supper together. It was all perfectly innocent, of course, but now I'm considered to be a woman of dubious morals.' She gave a short laugh.

The irony wasn't lost on me. She'd done the right thing; despite the damage it had done to her reputation.

'Come on.' Percy stood and reached down to help me up. 'We'll walk you home. Your father will be wondering where you are.'

'I can go on my own.'

Juliet started to gather their belongings. 'I think we've all had enough for one day. My car's parked near your house. We should get back.'

I let Percy help me to my feet. I didn't want to go home but there was no point in putting it off any longer. On the way, Juliet and Percy pointed out various plants that hadn't been seen growing at Waldenmere for years and a badger's den that I must have passed dozens of times without noticing. I found their presence calming and by the time I reached home, I knew what I had to do next.

* * *

'Iris,' Ben was bleary-eyed and unshaven, 'you're up early.'

'Can I talk to you in private?' I'd called at the station house first thing, banking on Sid still being asleep.

'Sid's gone to the town hall already. The superintendent ordered everyone to be there by seven.'

'But not you?' I followed him into the parlour, dismayed by his appearance. I was used to seeing him smartly turned out in his police uniform, with shining shoes and neatly combed hair. He was wearing a greying vest and a pair of old trousers. 'Have you been removed from duty?'

'Not yet, but I'm aware of the finger-pointing.' His lips were dry and cracked.

'Florence Thackeray doesn't believe you had anything to do with Alice's death.'

'I didn't think she did.' He still looked relieved. 'She was kind to me at the funeral. She told me she knew how I felt about Alice and that she'd cared for me too.'

'It's the colonel who's throwing around accusations. He's in a terrible state.'

'The super's asked me to keep out of his way but to continue with my rounds. He feels it will be reassuring for people to see me following my usual routine.'

'God knows the town needs all the normality it can get right now.' I wondered if Walden would be considered worthy of its own police station after such a spate of violence. The new hotel might bring even more crime in its wake.

'He wants me to keep an eye out for any unusual behaviour and listen to local gossip. Who's saying what about whom. I can imagine there's been plenty of speculation.'

I told him what Colonel and Florence Thackeray had said after the funeral.

He bit his dry lips. 'I know you like George but are you sure he didn't have feelings for Alice? He always seemed to go out of his way to make her laugh. Perhaps something happened...'

'No.'

'He doesn't have a strong alibi for that evening. He says he was out walking and planned to go to the pub before last orders, then changed his mind and went to catch his train.' Ben spread his hands in a hopeless gesture. 'And he's vague about who told him we were searching for her. What are we supposed to think? Perhaps he liked Alice more than he let on. He might have tried it on with her and things got out of hand.'

'Do you believe that?'

'I like George but how well do we know him? I'm sorry but we've got to consider the possibility. We owe it to Alice.'

I took a deep breath. 'I should have told you the truth before. George was with me.'

'What do you mean?' He rubbed at his unshaven chin in confusion.

'When you came to tell me Alice was missing, George was upstairs. We'd been alone together at my house that evening. Lizzy was staying with a friend in London. You were there when she came back the next morning.' I hoped I'd made it as clear as I needed to.

'Oh.' The expression on his face made me want to run from the room. He walked into the kitchen and turned on the tap. I watched him splash water into his eyes.

'What time did you meet George that night?' He came back into the parlour, rubbing his face with a cloth.

'About six, like we told you. George met me from work. He thought we were going to Waldenmere as usual. I told him I wanted you and Alice to have some time alone to talk. Then I invited him back to my house. We were together all evening. When you called, George went after you so he could help in the search for her.'

'You're not saying this to protect him?'

'I loved Alice too much for that.'

I could tell by his dazed expression he wasn't sure what to do. Perhaps even what to think. I'd embarrassed him.

He cleared his throat. 'Sid tells me George isn't a strong suspect. His clothes and shoes were the same ones he'd been wearing all day and they were clean when he turned up to help with the search. Whoever killed Alice would have had mud on theirs.'

'Thank goodness,' I breathed.

'They'll look into the possibility he somehow managed to clean himself up before then. If the super does decide to investigate George or you any further, you'll have to tell him what you've told me.'

I nodded. 'I will. It's not fair to George. Or Alice. I need Superintendent Cobbe to find out who killed her.'

28

Horace Laffaye's garden was a riot of colour, with dahlias filling every inch of neatly cut borders. The inside of the house was as pristine as the outside.

We'd been invited to afternoon tea and as Elijah and I passed through a reception room decorated in the palest of greens, a few framed illustrations caught my eye. I didn't have time to stop for closer inspection, but the style looked familiar. Where had I seen the artist before? Then it came to me. The cartoons in *The Walden Herald*. The thought that I must tell Alice rapidly collided with the realisation that I couldn't.

A smartly dressed young man showed us up to the wide veranda that overlooked Waldenmere. Horace was seated beside a tall man with a neat moustache, who I recognised from General Cheverton's funeral. Captain Finlay Fortesque.

Greetings were made and tea was served. Horace also poured each of the men a small glass of clear liqueur that smelt of oranges. I was tempted to point out that I'd not been offered this particular refreshment but decided against it. For one, I didn't want to draw too much attention to myself and risk being excluded from future meetings. Also, I wasn't sure what the liquid was. It would be embarrassing to ask for a glass and start choking if it tasted foul.

'As you know, Captain Fortesque is with Military Intelligence. I called on him to assist after the death of General Cheverton. None of us could have imagined at that time what was to follow.' Horace appeared almost tearful. 'The worst of which is the despicable murder of dear Miss Thackeray.'

Elijah leant towards Finlay. 'May I ask you a few questions? Do you mind if Iris takes notes?'

'Ask away and I'll answer if I can.' Finlay sipped his liqueur. He was of indeterminate age with an inscrutable face.

I reached into my bag for my notepad and pen. My hand was visibly shaking but I wouldn't give in to emotion as I had at the meeting with Sir Henry.

'This must be hard for you, my dear.' Horace gently squeezed my arm. 'But I know you're desperate to find out what happened to your friend. That's why I asked you to accompany Mr Whittle.'

Tears threatened, but I wasn't going to let them fall.

'This all started at Mill Ponds with the death of General Cheverton.' Elijah hadn't deviated from this opinion. 'Someone was looking for something and the general disturbed them. Can you tell me what was kept there?'

'Records of the Officer Cadet Battalion based at Mill Ponds between 1916 and 1918. The documents should have been moved.' Finlay shrugged. 'But they're short of space at Aldershot, so they were left there for the time being.'

'What about the records of the men based at Waldenmere Camp?' Elijah asked.

'They're kept at Aldershot. They were never at Mill Ponds.'

Elijah looked disappointed. 'I thought our intruder might have been trying to find out who drove the tank into the water or was looking for a record of someone who went missing at that time. When was the camp finally cleared out?'

'Not until June '19. Demobbing took time. The men were getting restless and mutinous.'

'What were the mutinies about?' I asked.

'Mainly food. Rations were poor for the lower orders. Money was scarce. And some soldiers felt they were being treated unfairly by commanding officers. They didn't like being told to clear out the camp. Hence, army equipment ending up in the lake.'

It didn't sound like a rebellion that would escalate to murder.

'If Tank Man were a commanding officer, surely he'd have been reported missing?' Elijah said.

'That's why it's such a mystery. There was hostility towards the officers, but no real violence. The petty rebellions petered out as the men were gradually demobbed. Everyone wanted to get the camp closed as soon as possible. I've found no reports of anyone going missing, officers or lower ranks.'

'Could you get a list of who was left in the camp when the tank went into the water?' Elijah lit a cigarette and Horace pushed an ashtray towards him.

'The police have asked the same question. There's a reluctance to release that information. We all want the matter cleared up, but...' Finlay hesitated, 'I can't deny there's concern over what a formal investigation might uncover.'

'And what do you think it's likely to reveal?' Horace poured more tea.

'Nothing sinister. Just general inefficiencies. Plenty went on during and after the war that isn't public knowledge.' Finlay stroked his moustache. 'But Tank Man is an odd one. We'd like to find out how he came to be there, especially if it turns out to be a civilian matter rather than a military one.'

'You think that's a possibility?' Elijah appeared sceptical.

'We can but hope.' Finlay's sigh indicated he knew this was unlikely. 'I'll see if I can get hold of any of the men who were left in camp. They might be more willing to speak to me than they would to the police.'

'Is it a coincidence that Military Estates decided to sell the lake before all this came out?' Elijah asked.

'I don't think there's a connection,' Finlay said. 'No one I've spoken to seems to have the slightest knowledge of how, why, or when the man, or the tank, went missing. Selling Waldenmere has been on the cards since the camp cleared out. It was never ideal for military training purposes, too close to the town.'

'What made them sell now?' I asked.

'Money. The war was expensive. There was no point holding off any longer. Colonel Thackeray and General Cheverton presented their plan for a convalescent home and that was bandied around for a while. In fact, it came close to being agreed upon. But when the money men worked out how much it would cost to run, Aldershot decided to cut its losses and sell.'

'But why LSWR?' My tone was bitter. I couldn't help thinking Alice would still be alive if Waldenmere hadn't been sold to them.

'Because Sir Henry Ballard can be very persuasive.' Finlay pursed his lips.

'Are you saying he paid senior officers?' Elijah waved his cigarette, dropping ash on the table. Horace took his napkin and carefully swept it into the ashtray.

Finlay nodded. 'That's part of it. But it was the risk of losing the deal and being left with no other offers on the table that swung it. If they turned down Sir Henry, they could have been stuck with a lake they no longer needed.'

'But there was another offer on the table if they'd waited.' My frustration at the army's haste resurfaced. 'Mrs Siddons told me she'd secured funds. It was just taking time for the money to come through from central government.'

'Aldershot Military Estates knew it would be better for their reputation if they sold Waldenmere to the council, but they got word that the money wasn't going to materialise. They were told Mrs Siddons had exaggerated her influence within the Cabinet and any funding was a work of fiction.' Finlay seemed to be enjoying delivering his tale in tiny morsels. I wondered what else was to come.

'But why would they believe Sir Henry?' Elijah asked.

'They didn't. They believed what was coming from Walden Council.' Finlay smiled at our looks of astonishment.

'You're teasing us, Finlay.' Horace tutted. 'Tell us what you mean?'

'A council official told them there was no money to buy Waldenmere.' Finlay took a sip of liqueur and sat back. 'Walden Council and LSWR were the only potential buyers. With the council out of the picture, they snapped up Sir Henry's offer.'

'Pray tell us, who within the council gave them this information?' Horace demanded.

'Councillor William Mansbridge.' Finlay was clearly pleased with the effect he was having on his audience. We all appeared suitably shocked.

'What an odious man,' Horace spluttered. 'To betray the town like that. Despicable behaviour. I'll see he loses his seat on the council.'

Elijah's eyes narrowed. 'How do you know it was him?'

'When Mr Laffaye asked me to find out what was going on, I started to make enquiries. It didn't take long to follow the trail back to Mansbridge. His clerk, George Hale, had been feeding information to a chap on our side.'

I felt as though I'd been punched in the stomach.

'And you believe Mansbridge and Hale were being paid by Sir Henry?' Elijah avoided looking at me.

Finlay nodded. 'Ever since it was first suggested that Waldenmere might be for sale, Sir Henry's been greasing the palms of anyone who could facilitate the deal. It wasn't just the council fellows on the receiving end of backhanders. A few of our chaps were financially encouraged to push the paperwork through at top speed.' He glanced at my notepad. 'This is in the strictest confidence, of course. There's nothing on record to back this up.'

I nodded, keeping my expression blank. I'd already stopped taking notes. The extent of George's deception was beginning to sink in and I let the hurt wash over me.

29

After a fitful night, I woke feeling betrayed, angry and ready for confrontation. When Elijah went out at lunchtime, I used the telephone to ring the council offices on the pretext of having to ascertain information for the newspaper. I was put through to George and arranged to meet him at our bench that evening.

Elijah walked me home after work and tried to steer the conversation in the direction of what we'd learned from Finlay, but I evaded his attempts to discuss it. My feelings were too raw. I took my time at the front door, waiting until he was out of sight, then headed to the lake.

George rose from our bench when he saw me. 'I've missed you.' He smiled, pulling me close. Despite myself, I wanted to wrap my arms around him and breathe in his familiar smell but I took a step back and pushed him away.

'What's happened?' His expression changed.

'I told Ben you were with me the night Alice died.'

'Thank you.' Relief showed in his eyes. 'Will he tell Superintendent Cobbe?'

'He doesn't think you're a serious suspect. If that changes, I'll tell the superintendent myself.'

'Hopefully, they'll catch the bastard soon and you won't have to. It's Ben I feel sorry for. Poor bloke's heartbroken and he has to put up with all these ridiculous rumours about him and Alice.'

'He wasn't as sympathetic towards you. He even wondered if you liked Alice more than you let on. Made advances towards her.' I wanted to lash out and was rewarded by the flash of hurt in his eyes.

'Did he? I suppose I can't blame him; his head's all over the place. It's the uncertainty that gets to people. They start imagining all sorts. At least he knows now I had nothing to do with it.'

'He's not the first person to have suggested it. That you liked Alice more than me.' I didn't know why I was taking this route. It was some form of punishment for both of us.

'You know that's not true, don't you?' He tried to pull me towards him again, but I resisted.

'I thought I did.' I sat on the bench, suddenly feeling overwhelmed by tiredness.

'Why would you doubt it?' He sat next to me and took my hand.

I pulled it away. His warm touch made me yearn to forget his cold betrayal. 'Why *did* you start waiting for me after work?'

'What do you mean?' He became wary.

'I mean, you only became friends with me because you thought I'd be useful to you – that I'd tell you anything I knew about the sale of Waldenmere. You wanted to know what gossip I picked up at work and what we were going to publish in *The Walden Herald*.'

I saw his confusion and uncertainty over what to say next in case his words incriminated him. I turned away. 'You acted as a messenger for Mansbridge and you took Sir Henry's money.'

In the silence that followed, I stared at the glistening silver water in the distance. I'd never have believed my beloved lake could be the cause of so much pain.

'It's true.' His voice was little more than a whisper. 'I took Sir Henry's money. And, yes, to begin with, I thought I'd get to know you because you worked for the paper. Mansbridge wanted me to tell him what was going on around town. But then...'

'But then what?' I hissed.

He held my gaze. 'I got to know you. I wanted to see you all the time.'

I remembered the evening I'd first met George. I was walking home by the lake and he was a few yards behind me, on his way to the railway station. He caught up with me and joked that he didn't want me to think he was the sort of chap who made a habit of following women home. After that, it hadn't seemed odd to keep running into him as we both finished work at around the same time. Then he started to wait for me outside the printworks so we could walk together.

He stared at his shoes. 'The railway company was always going to have the most money. It would have happened anyway. The council couldn't compete.'

'They could have if they'd been given the chance, but you and Mansbridge made sure Mrs Siddons didn't have enough time.' I stood up.

'I'm sorry.' He jumped up to follow me. 'I'm not proud of what I did. I had no idea all this would happen. Or that I'd end up feeling like this about you.'

I swung around. 'Why did you do it?'

'For the money,' he mumbled. 'Sir Henry was throwing it around and I thought I might as well take some of it. He was paying Mansbridge and Mansbridge needed a messenger.'

'Did you want money so badly you shot General Cheverton?

Did you remove that obstacle for Sir Henry?' I wanted to lash out and hurt him again.

He gasped. 'Of course not. You know I could never do anything like that.'

'Do I? I don't know what you're capable of. Why is money so important to you?'

'Because I want to get out of here. I can't settle, not since the war. Mansbridge made it sound easy. I thought passing on a bit of information wasn't such a big deal. I know you love Waldenmere, but someone's going to buy it, so why not LSWR?'

'Because they'll destroy it,' I shouted.

'It's going to happen one day. If not them, some other big company will buy the land and build houses on it.' He looked pleadingly at me, but his words infuriated me even more.

'That's why there needs to be a law to protect it. That's what we're fighting for.'

'That's what you and that bloody Percy are fighting for. No one else gives a damn about that sort of thing.'

'They will when they realise what's at stake and what they'll lose. That's why we're trying to make them understand.' I wanted to slap him. Instead, I carried on walking.

'That's just your excuse for seeing him.' He moved in front of me, forcing me to stop. 'Admit it. You still like him.'

'I made my feelings clear to you the night we...' I gave up and closed my eyes, trying to stop the spinning in my head.

'I'm sorry,' he whispered. 'It's all such a mess. If I'd known any of this was going to happen, I would never have done it.'

'You could have told me before.' Before accepting my invitation to come home with me, is what I meant.

'I nearly did. That night we were together. But then Alice...'

'Leave me alone.' I shoved him out of the way and started walking, my anger replaced by weariness and grief.

He trailed after me. 'I'm truly sorry for everything that's happened. It goes round and round in my head. Would Alice still be alive if Sir Henry hadn't bought the lake? I don't know what to think any more. I'm not going anywhere till they've caught the bastard and I know you're safe.'

I didn't reply. We reached the end of Chestnut Avenue and he grabbed my hand.

'I know what I did was wrong and this will sound like an excuse, but things like a lake don't seem important when you've been to war, seen men die and don't know why you're still alive.' With that, he dropped my hand and walked away.

* * *

I crept out of the house early the following morning. After a warm and dry July and August, September was more unsettled. I stood by the lake, watching drops of rain form ringlets on the water. The more I stared, the more mesmerised I became by the repetition of circles.

I shook off my inertia and started to walk to Grebe House. I owed it to Mrs Siddons to tell her how she'd been betrayed.

Knocking on the front door, I realised it was much too early for a social call, but Mr Grosvenor answered without showing any surprise at my damp appearance. He asked me to wait in the hall and a moment later, Mrs Siddons appeared wearing an alarming red silk paisley dressing gown.

She showed me into the drawing room and handed me a cup of tea. 'This is a pleasant surprise, my dear. Drink this. It will warm you up.'

'Councillor Mansbridge was working against you.' I sank into the red velvet cushions. I couldn't be bothered with small talk.

'How do you know?' She sipped her tea.

'You don't seem surprised?' I wrapped my hands around the cup to warm them.

'I've suspected it for a while,' she said calmly, 'but I haven't been able to pin anything on him. I know he talks behind my back and uses his influence for personal gain. That's not unusual in politics.'

'He was being paid by Sir Henry to sabotage the council's plans to buy Waldenmere. He told Aldershot Military Estates there would be no offer from the council.' I watched her mouth form a tight line.

'Did he indeed.' Her voice was low. 'Can you prove it?'

I shook my head.

'Where did you get this information?'

'I can't say.'

'You're friends with George Hale, aren't you? If he told you, I can make sure his job is secure and see he suffers no repercussions from Mansbridge.'

I gave a short, bitter laugh. 'George was being paid by Sir Henry to do the legwork. He acted as a messenger between Mansbridge and Military Estates. He told them you were exaggerating your influence with the government and that you hadn't got the funding. As there were no other offers on the table, or so they thought, they did the deal with LSWR.'

'I see.' Outwardly, she was her usual composed self, but I saw the glint of steel in her eyes.

It was a good job George was planning to leave because I knew Mrs Siddons well enough to know his time at the council was about to end.

'The person who told us is in the military.' I felt I owed her some kind of explanation. 'One of Mr Laffaye's contacts.'

She nodded her understanding.

'He suspects it wasn't just Mansbridge taking backhanders. It's likely a few army officials were too.'

She was silent for a few moments. 'Have you spoken to George Hale about this?'

I nodded. 'I had to hear the truth from him.'

'You must feel betrayed?' she said softly.

'I feel angry. And stupid. I thought he liked me. All the time, he was just trying to find out what was going on at the paper.' Tears threatened, but I wasn't going to waste them on George. Alice is the only person I'd cry for.

'He's a foolish young man and not just for taking Sir Henry's money. What does he plan to do now?'

'Travel, see the world, but he won't go until the police find out who killed Alice.'

'If I were him, I'd start packing my bags. It won't be wise for him to be seen in Walden.'

'Why not?'

'Because you're going to expose him and William Mansbridge in the paper.'

'Am I?'

'Yes, my dear. I think it's time for some creative journalism.'

The rain had cleared by the time I left Grebe House and the sun was trying to break through the clouds. Usually, Waldenmere was quiet at this time of day, but I could hear the sound of children's laughter coming from Heron Bay. Horace was leaning against his garden gate, smiling.

Juliet and Percy were wading into the lake, surrounded by a dozen young children. Discarded shoes and socks lay on the sand. Small boys had their trousers rolled up to their knees while little girls gingerly held their skirts aloft. They were all waving nets around in the water. Miss Millicent Nightingale had wisely decided to stay on dry land and watch from a distance.

I strolled over to her. 'What's going on?'

'Mrs Rendall and Mr Baverstock are showing the children the different types of creatures that live in the water. Biology is a subject best studied outside the classroom, although I'm bound to have a few soggy pupils by the end of the lesson.'

'With Percy in charge, I think that's highly likely.'

She laughed. 'I decided it was worth the risk. He's marvellous with the children and Mrs Rendall has an encyclopaedic knowledge of natural history. They're wonderful together. The children learn more from them than they do from any books.'

In the water, Juliet and Percy laughed and held each other up as children clung to their legs. It made me wonder if their supper together had been as innocent as Juliet had professed.

'Perhaps you'd like to join our group?'

'Sorry?' I realised Miss Nightingale had been talking to me.

'The Walden Natural History Group. It was Mr Baverstock's idea. He and Mrs Rendall are going to help me set it up. We have lots of local interest.'

'I'd be delighted.' I felt a flicker of energy returning. It was time to get back to the article I'd promised Juliet.

I called over to her. 'I'm working on that article we talked about, but I need some information on the history of the society.'

'I've got some old newsletters and stuff at University College in Reading. I'll pick them up for you this afternoon,' Juliet shouted. 'Actually, why don't you come with us? I can collect you from your office.'

I waved and nodded. George had been wrong when he said no one was interested in that kind of stuff. Perhaps we could salvage something worthwhile from Sir Henry's destructive plans.

30

I dumped my bag on my desk and strode into Elijah's den.

'I've been to see Mrs Siddons and told her what Mansbridge and George did. I didn't say where the information came from.'

He smiled. 'Good for you. That will make life at the council offices interesting.'

'She wants us to expose Mansbridge in the paper.' I explained her idea. 'Can we do it?'

'Horace made a similar suggestion. It doesn't surprise me about Mansbridge. I'd heard rumours he was corrupt, took the odd backhander, that sort of thing. Never anything you could prove.' He leant back in his chair. 'I'm sorry about George, though. I know you liked him.'

I didn't reply.

'All the time, I thought I was getting information from him in the Duck and he was seeing what he could get out of me.' He eyed me warily through the smog of his cigarette.

I appreciated his tact. 'My only comfort is there wasn't much we could have told him that would have made any difference.'

'True.' He took a long drag and exhaled a stream of smoke. 'All this doesn't bring us any closer to finding our murderer. Or murderers. Though, it does give Mansbridge a motive for wanting General Cheverton dead. He needed to pave the way for Sir Henry to buy Waldenmere.' His expression changed. 'But he wouldn't have had anything to gain by killing Alice.'

I knew what was coming next.

'Are you sure George can't have been involved?' He shuffled the papers on his desk, not looking at me. 'He lied to you about—'

I stopped him. 'I know he had nothing to do with Alice's murder.' I didn't elaborate. Elijah knew Lizzy had been away on the night Alice died and he was no fool.

I changed the subject. 'I'm going to try to finish the article I said I'd write for Juliet. Sir Henry isn't going to put his plans on hold forever.' I was aware of a sense of things starting to get back to normal. I wasn't sure I liked it. It felt disloyal to Alice to think anything could be normal again, but what choice was there but to carry on? 'Can I go with Percy and Juliet to University College in Reading this afternoon?'

'All right. But let's get this story on Mansbridge done first. And we need to leave room for the cartoon that's going to appear alongside it.'

I raised an eyebrow.

'A picture paints a thousand words,' he said, smiling.

I was intrigued and slightly apprehensive of what Horace would come up with.

* * *

It took a long time to craft an article that was subtle enough to implicate William Mansbridge in corruption without going so far as to name him. Elijah was finally satisfied after several rewrites but decided to call on Horace and ask him to check the final draft. He didn't want to risk an accusation of libel.

I'd managed to put together a first draft of my article for Juliet when I heard the toot of a horn and went into Elijah's den to look out of the window. Percy was leaning out of the passenger door of Juliet's motor car, waving up at me. I went back to my desk, scooped up my notes and locked up the office.

Percy was full of enthusiasm for 'the splendid' Miss Nightingale and their plans for the Walden Natural History Group. I listened to his chatter with half an ear, enjoying the feeling of being away from Walden. It only took half an hour to reach the University College and I was sorry the journey had been so short.

We entered a large red-brick building and followed Juliet through a labyrinth of green-tiled corridors. 'You obviously know your way around,' I commented.

'My father worked here for many years,' she said. 'He was a professor of botany.' She stopped outside an office and tapped on the open door.

'Juliet.' A thin, bespectacled man stood up from behind a desk.

'Hello, Frank. This is my friend, Iris Woodmore. She works for *The Walden Herald*. She's been helping us with the Waldenmere case. And you know Percy.'

'I've heard what's been happening over there.' Frank shook his head. 'I can't imagine what your father would say.'

'I miss having him or Rob to talk to.' Juliet sighed. 'Especially with everything moving at such speed. I just don't know what more we can do.'

'Your father would be proud of what you are doing. Have you come to collect his things?'

Juliet nodded. Frank patted her arm and led us along more green-tiled corridors to another office. The room was bare, apart from some photographs, framed certificates and a pile of boxes stacked on a desk.

'I've packed up all his papers for you. I'll leave you to sort through his personal items.'

'Thank you, Frank. That's kind of you.'

I stood by the door, feeling uncomfortable. I hadn't realised the purpose of the visit was to collect Juliet's late father's possessions. Percy seemed unperturbed and began to rummage through the boxes.

Juliet picked up a photograph and handed it to me.

'These are the founding members of the society. That's my brother, Robert, and next to him is my husband, Peter.'

I examined the photograph, wondering how many other young men in the group had lost their lives. Juliet was the only woman in the picture.

'Here they are.' Percy took a bundle tied with string from one of the boxes and handed it to Juliet.

'I knew Father would have kept them.' She untied the string and began to flick through the papers. 'These are old society newsletters. I thought they might be useful to you. Why don't you sit down and have a read through while I sort through the rest of my father's things?'

I sat at the desk and examined the newsletters, starting with the earliest ones. Something about them seemed familiar, but I couldn't immediately think what it was.

'Remember this?' Juliet picked up another photo and showed it to Percy. 'The 1914 Christmas Ball at the museum?'

'Good grief, I look drunk.' He pushed his hair out of his eyes and squinted at the photo.

'You were drunk. You ended up falling in the fountain.'

'So I did. It was freezing. Sobered me up.' Percy picked up one of the boxes Frank had packed. 'I'll take these out to the car.'

I'd expected to find the newsletters dull but I quickly became absorbed by the story of the society and how it had fared over the years. It was evident Juliet's husband and brother hadn't been the only members lost in the war. And despite numerous setbacks, this small band of people never wavered in their fight to create nature reserves. In almost impossible circumstances, they'd somehow managed to keep going.

Juliet finished packing the last of her father's belongings while Percy took the boxes to the car. I was tying up the bundle of newsletters when my brain suddenly made the connection and I realised what it was that looked familiar. It was so silly it almost made me laugh out loud. My amusement turned to dismay when I fully understood the repercussions of what I'd discovered.

I picked up the first newsletter, which showed the photograph of the founding members on its front cover. 'Was your husband or brother ever stationed at Walden? At Mill Ponds or Waldenmere Camp?'

'Yes, my brother, Rob, was. He became an officer,' Juliet said with pride. 'He trained at Mill Ponds. He was a second lieutenant and then became lieutenant.'

'What happened to him?'

'Missing in action in France. Right at the end of the war.'

Percy shot me a warning glance and I knew I couldn't trespass any further.

'Would it be possible for me to borrow a few of these newsletters?' I asked.

'By all means. I have my own copies at home.' Juliet gazed around the empty office. 'You two go ahead. I'd like to spend a few moments alone. Then I'll go and say goodbye to Frank.'

Percy picked up the last box and I followed him out into the corridor. He glanced back at Juliet and they exchanged a sad but intimate smile. I felt like I was intruding on their private moment.

Outside, I helped Percy shift the boxes around the car so we could get the last one in.

'How's the article coming along?' he asked.

'Now I have these newsletters, I can finish it today. We plan to publish in this week's edition.'

'That soon?'

I nodded. I'd suggested to Elijah that we hold it back until after we'd gone to print with the exposure of William Mansbridge – that article would gain the most attention – but Elijah thought we should take advantage of the additional interest it was likely to generate. I didn't want to explain this to Percy. He'd only gloat and tell me he'd known that George was wrong for me.

'Excellent.' Percy beamed. 'It won't be long before Sir Henry tries to start things up again and we need to do whatever we can to slow him down.'

Percy kept up his usual chatter on the way back although I barely heard a word. If what I suspected was correct, it would offer a potential clue as to who Tank Man might be, but I needed more information. And the only place I was likely to find it was Mill Ponds.

* * *

After dinner that evening, I said I was going up to my room to work on an article. When I crept downstairs at a quarter to nine, I could hear Father listening to music in his study. I suspected Lizzy was sewing in the kitchen. I pulled on my jacket, slipped a torch into my pocket and carefully opened the front door.

The night of Alice's death had prepared me for the sudden plunge into darkness once I left Chestnut Avenue. I switched on the torch to illuminate the tree-lined lake path, then dropped it in fright when something brushed against my leg. I had the impulse to turn and run back home. Instead, I fumbled on the ground and picked up the torch. Its shaft of light was reflected in a pair of bright green eyes. Startled, I waited for the fox to move, but it held its ground. When I strode forward, it darted away into the undergrowth.

I quickened my pace until I got to the railway station. All was quiet and I was glad of the concourse lights. It was only a short distance to Mill Ponds and I was relieved I didn't have to go as far as the old jetty. The memory of Alice's pale, deathly face was always with me.

I slipped through the gates of Mill Ponds, noticing the garden and driveway had been cleared of debris. Sir Henry must have ordered his men to clean up the mess. I could see no sign of new excavations.

At the back of the house, my anxiety increased. As frightening as it had been to walk alone by the lake in the dark, the prospect of going into the empty house was far worse. Reaching up, I ran my fingers along the wooden doorframe. My thumb caught on a splinter and I winced. I couldn't find the key and felt a moment of relief. Then I touched something metal.

Dread returned. Part of me hoped the lock had been changed but it opened more smoothly than it had last time. I dashed through the scullery into the kitchen. The sour smell of meals cooked long ago hung in the air. I followed the route I'd taken with Elijah, my heart jumping with every groan of the ancient floorboards.

The study door made a screeching sound as I pushed it open. Torchlight illuminated the bloodstained carpet. My imagination conjured up a vision of an ashen-faced General Cheverton rising from the dead, billows of pipe smoke circling his shock of grey hair.

I had to quell the panic that was rising in me. Whoever killed the general and Alice was still out there.

I took a few deep breaths. It wouldn't take long to check the files and then I'd go straight home. I didn't bother lighting an oil lamp, deciding torchlight would be sufficient for what I had to do. Opening the filing cabinet drawer marked A to E, I flipped through the folders until I came to the name I was looking for. Elmes.

I removed the file and took it over to the desk. When I opened it, I was stunned to find it was empty.

I returned to the cabinet to see if any papers had fallen out. There was nothing. I checked the folders before and after but couldn't see any documents with the name Elmes. In despair, I checked every file under E. Then I flicked through every folder in the drawer. I even went back to the desk and examined the empty folder again.

I pulled open the drawers of the other filing cabinets, but it would take all night to check every single name from A to Z. It was hopeless.

Resigned to the fact that it had been another futile search, I put all the folders back where I'd found them and closed the cabinets. All I wanted to do was to get home as fast as possible.

Then I heard a soft tap on the window.

31

It came again. Someone was outside, tapping on the French doors. I crouched low behind the desk and tried to steady my breathing while I decided what to do. The telephone on the general's desk might still be connected. Could I reach it without making a sound? If I sat in silence, the person might go away. Or if they suspected an intruder, they might go and fetch Ben. It would be a relief to see his solid figure appear.

The tapping came again and I tried to stay calm.

'Iris.'

It was unmistakable. Someone had said my name. It was a male voice. Could it be Ben? I waited, not willing to come out of my hiding place yet.

'Iris,' the voice hissed again.

I was silent.

'It's Percy.'

I would have sworn out loud if my throat hadn't been so constricted. I tried to stand, but my knees didn't seem to be working. I steadied myself on the desk and hauled myself up. Drawing the curtains, I still found it a shock to see Percy's pale face pressed to the glass.

I unlocked the doors. 'You idiot. You always do this to me.'

'It's an annoying habit of mine, isn't it?'

'Very annoying. How the hell did you know I was here?'

'I saw you go by. I was near the station jetty watching bats.'

'At this time of night?' I demanded.

'That's when bats come out,' he said apologetically. 'I had supper with Juliet and then she dropped me at the station. My train isn't due for a while, so I thought I'd see if I could spot any Daubenton's bats. They catch insects just above the surface of the water. Small flies and that sort of thing.'

'Now isn't the time for a natural history lesson. You scared me half to death.' My legs were starting to come back to life. 'Let's get out of here now.'

'What are you doing in there?'

'Looking for something.'

'You're not meeting someone?' He stayed on the patio but peered in through the door.

'Who would I be meeting?'

'That chap you seem to like.' He tried to sound casual. 'George, is it?'

'I wouldn't be meeting him here.' I shone the torch onto the bloodstained rug.

Percy's eyes followed the light. 'Bloody hell. Is that where...?' He gave a nervous laugh. 'Not the most romantic spot, is it?'

'Stay here.' I locked the door, pulled the curtain in place and made my way back through the house.

Percy was waiting on the driveway, shifting from foot to foot. 'What were you doing in there?'

'I'll tell you as we walk.' I set off at a brisk pace, anxious to get home before my father or Lizzy missed me. 'I was looking through the army records. Did you know Robert Elmes?'

'Juliet's brother?' He stumbled after me.

'Yes.' I switched on the torch and pointed it at the path.

'Not well. I joined the society in 1914. It had been going a couple of years by then and we met at meetings. Nice chap. Why were you asking about him earlier?'

'Juliet said he was reported missing in action. Presumably, he was never found?'

'No. It was tragic. It was in one of the last battles in France in November 1918. Why? What's going on?'

'I can't tell you yet. I need to speak to the police first.' My hand was cold and I couldn't hold the torch steady. Percy took it from me and directed the light onto the path.

'You don't think he's still alive, do you? Not after all this time? She used to believe he was.'

I stopped. 'What do you mean?'

'Juliet. She thought he was still alive, living in France some-where. Do you think he is?' He pointed the torch in my face.

My eyes were drawn towards the mudbank. 'No, I think he's dead.'

Percy swung the torch to where the tank had been found. Moonlight was reflected on the still black water. 'Not Tank Man?'

I fell against him and managed to steady myself. I grabbed his hand and pointed the torch back onto the path.

'It's just something that I came across.' I wished I hadn't mentioned Robert Elmes' name until I was more certain. 'I could be completely wrong.'

We walked towards the railway station, where a train was pulling in.

'I don't want you to mention this to Juliet. Not until you know for sure,' Percy said.

'Why did she think he was still in France?'

'She was confused.' He hesitated. 'She didn't want to believe he was dead. It's taken her a long time to accept it. Raking it up won't help her recovery. She's been through a lot.'

I thought recovery was an odd word to use – not one I'd associate with the calm and contained Juliet, but I didn't question him. I'd already said too much and just wanted to get home. I pulled my jacket around me, feeling cold, tired and despondent.

I held out my hand to take the torch back. 'You'd better catch your train.'

'I'm not leaving you here. Not after what's happened.' His voice changed. 'How are you coping? Without Alice. I know you loved her.'

I couldn't speak.

'Come on, let's get you home.' He linked his arm through mine.

'You and Juliet have become close, haven't you?' It was a personal question, but it diverted us from a subject too painful to talk about.

'I, er, well, yes.' Percy being tongue-tied was a first. 'Do you mind?'

'Of course not.'

'It just sort of happened. You know how it is.'

'Yes, I know how it is.' We reached the end of Chestnut Avenue and I took the torch back. 'Thanks for walking me home. Don't come any nearer to the house in case my father sees us. I sneaked out and I'm going to have to sneak back in again.'

He chortled. 'That doesn't surprise me. Go on. I'll wait here until I see you go in.'

I hurried up the road and waved at Percy before I slipped in through the front door. The hallway was in darkness. Placing my jacket on the hook, I started up the stairs. My foot was on the first step when I heard my father's low voice.

'Iris, where have you been?' He was standing by the door of his study, watching me.

'I needed some fresh air. I was getting in a muddle with my article and thought a walk would clear my head.' I didn't look at him.

'Please don't go out on your own at night. I don't want to restrict you, but you must understand how worried I am after what happened to Alice.'

I didn't reply.

'Were you meeting George Hale?'

'No, I wasn't meeting George.'

'Are you still seeing him?' He hesitated. 'I feel you're keeping things from me. You seem to talk to Elijah more than you do to me.'

'I've spent more time with him recently, I suppose.' I saw him stiffen. I'd hit the intended target.

'Yes, of course.' He shifted uncomfortably. 'I missed out on a lot while I was away.'

This was undoubtedly true and I had no intention of telling him what he had missed. When he returned from his travels, he never shared much with me about what he'd been up to. Why should I tell him what I'd been doing?

* * *

'I think I know who Tank Man is.' I put the photograph of the compass down on Elijah's desk. Next to it, I placed an SPNR newsletter.

Elijah squinted. 'What am I looking at?'

'This picture of an eagle.' I pointed to the top right-hand corner of the newsletter. 'It's the emblem of the society. It's the same design as the bird on the compass.'

He ran a nicotine-stained finger over the two pictures,

comparing the intricate detail of the overlapping rows of feathers. Then he followed the curve of the bird's tail.

He gave a low whistle. 'They're the same.'

I felt a surge of relief. I'd begun to doubt myself, thinking I was seeing clues where there weren't any.

Elijah started to laugh. 'All this time, we've been thinking it's the Reichsadler and it's the emblem of a nature society.'

I smiled. 'I know. I thought it was funny until I realised who it could be.'

He stopped laughing and gestured to the newsletter with the photograph of the society founders on the cover. 'Which one?'

'This man here, Robert Elmes. He's Juliet Rendall's brother.' I pointed to the front row of a group of eight people. 'He fits Tank Man's description. Tall, sandy hair, the right age.'

'Is he missing?'

'Missing in action, presumed dead. He was supposed to have been involved in one of the last battles of the war in France in November 1918.'

'Is there any reason to believe that isn't the case?' He lit a cigarette and stared hard at the young man in the photo.

'For some reason, Juliet had doubts to begin with. She thought he was still alive and living in France.' I paused, wondering if I could avoid telling him about my nocturnal visit. I decided I'd have to come clean. 'Robert Elmes' file is missing from Mill Ponds.'

Elijah's head shot up. 'How do you know?'

'I went back there last night. I found his folder, but it was empty. Someone has removed all the documents.'

'Iris.' He groaned in exasperation. 'What possessed you? Does your father know?'

I shook my head. 'I had to do it. I wanted to tell you, but you would've stopped me.'

'Of course I would have stopped you,' he snapped. 'How could you be so stupid? Someone out there murdered Alice. Do I really need to remind you of that?'

I winced but stood my ground. 'Alice is why I did it. I have to find out what happened to her – and this might help.'

'You should have come to me.' He brandished the newsletter at me. 'I would have gone to get the file for you if you'd told me what you suspected.'

I smiled at his acknowledgement that he would have sneaked into Mill Ponds again too and was touched that he would have done so based purely on my suspicions.

'What should I do now?' I asked.

He picked up the photograph of the compass and the newsletter and stood up. 'We're going to see Superintendent Cobbe. And we will not be mentioning any visits to Mill Ponds.'

32

'Our experts have confirmed the society's eagle emblem is identical to the engraving.'

A few days later, Elijah and I had been summoned back to the town hall. We stood awkwardly in front of Superintendent Cobbe's desk like a pair of schoolchildren sent to the headmaster's office.

'I interviewed Mrs Rendall and showed her the compass,' the superintendent continued. 'She confirmed it belonged to her brother, Robert Elmes. She had it engraved and gave it to him as a Christmas present in 1914.'

'So much for the Reichsadler,' Elijah commented.

Superintendent Cobbe smiled. 'Yes, I think we can rule out the spy theory.'

'Did Mrs Rendall say why her brother might have been in Walden?' I wondered if Robert Elmes had just been in the wrong place at the wrong time. His love of Waldenmere could have prompted him to visit the lake and he might have got caught up in hostilities at the camp. 'Presumably, his training would have finished years before?'

'She confirmed her brother spent time at Mill Ponds when he

was in the Officer Cadet Battalion, although there was no reason for him to have returned there or visited the camp. Mrs Rendall said he had keys to her cottage in Odiham and would usually stay there if he was in the area.'

'How did she find out he was missing?' Elijah asked.

'Mrs Rendall showed us the telegram her parents received from the War Office saying Robert was missing, presumed dead in northern France in November 1918.' Superintendent Cobbe frowned. 'Unfortunately, there wasn't a letter from a commanding officer or anything like that.'

'What happens now?' I was worried that the events I'd set in motion might affect Juliet badly.

'We've asked Military Intelligence for further help with our investigation.' The superintendent coughed. 'Robert Elmes' records appear to be missing.'

'That in itself is significant. Were they kept at Mill Ponds?' Elijah asked innocently.

'They were.' The superintendent eyed us warily. 'I'd appreciate it if you didn't disclose this information or the identity of the man. I can't comment further until I've spoken with Captain Fortesque. He's trying to find out if there are copies of the records.'

Elijah nodded. 'Of course.'

'There must be a link between Robert Elmes' death and General Cheverton's murder. The person who killed the general must have taken those records?'

'Thank you, Miss Woodmore,' the superintendent said drily. 'It's certainly something we'll look into.'

Elijah took my arm. 'Thank you for keeping us up to date, Superintendent. We'll leave you to your work.'

Back at the office, Elijah spent most of the afternoon napping at his desk. When it was time to go home, I considered sneaking out without waking him, but I couldn't face any more nagging about walking alone.

My dilemma was resolved by the sound of footsteps on the stairs. Ben's head peered around the door. 'Are you finished for the day?'

This roused Elijah. He lifted his drooping head and peered at the clock. 'It's time you were going home. You should've told me it was so late.' He got up unsteadily.

I rolled my eyes at Ben.

'That's why I stopped by,' Ben said. 'To walk Iris home.'

Elijah grunted in acknowledgement and gratefully sat down again. I gathered my belongings and took my jacket from the hatstand. We could hear snoring before we reached the bottom of the stairs.

'You've heard about Tank Man?' I asked.

Ben nodded. 'Sid told me. Do you think there's a connection with Alice?'

'She was at Sand Hills Hall throughout the war. She must have been aware of some of what went on at Mill Ponds and Waldenmere Camp. Perhaps she knew something about Robert Elmes. Or someone presumed she did.'

'That's what I was thinking.'

'We need to find out why Robert Elmes was here in Walden instead of France, but I've no idea where to begin.'

'Sid said Superintendent Cobbe got the impression Mrs Rendall was holding something back when he spoke to her. Something she wasn't saying about her brother.'

'She's protective of his memory. I'll try to talk to her.' The problem was Percy was protective of Juliet. It would be difficult to question her with him around.

* * *

Percy was sitting on the steps when I arrived. I'd sent him a note asking if I could take up his invitation to visit the Natural History Museum. My father had made no objection to my trip to London after Elijah commented that it was probably safer in the city these days than it was in Walden.

'How's Juliet?'

'Not too bad.' He ran his fingers through his hair. 'I persuaded her to do some cataloguing of the botanical artwork collection. It's a task I find soothing.'

The glassy eyes of stuffed animals and birds followed me as I trailed after Percy through long, empty halls. The museum was closed and the sound of our shoes clicking on the tiled floor echoed through the vast rooms.

Percy showed me into a magnificent gallery with a high domed ceiling. The walls were hung with artwork depicting every type of flora and fauna.

'Iris.' Juliet was standing by a mahogany table covered in watercolours. Her long dark hair was tousled and her eyes were red. 'I've picked out some special paintings to show you.'

I walked over to the table and saw she'd put together a collection of pictures of Waldenmere. I felt a lump in my throat, wishing Alice was with me. 'These are beautiful.'

'Some famous artists have painted the lake over the years, or the flowers around it.' Percy gestured to a collection of small pictures hung in a cluster on the wall. 'Marianne North is believed to have painted all these at Waldenmere.'

I studied the pictures for a long time. The colours and detail were astonishing. I could see why Percy had encouraged Juliet to work there. It was hypnotic to be surrounded by so much exquisite artwork. The reverential way the paintings were displayed added to the calming atmosphere.

'I wanted to say how sorry I am about what's happened.' I spoke softly, reluctant to disturb the mood of the cathedral-like gallery. But I was there for a reason.

'Superintendent Cobbe told me you were instrumental in helping them to identify my brother. I'm grateful to you for that.' She stared down at the paintings, tears in her eyes.

'It must have come as a shock to you.'

'I don't know what to think. Someone shot Robert in the back. Did you know that?' Her anguish was painful to hear.

Percy put an arm around her shoulder. 'It's unbelievable. I don't understand how it could have happened.'

'Can you think of anyone who would have wanted to harm him?'

She shook her head. 'He was the sweetest, kindest person. He didn't have enemies. I can't believe anyone would do that to him. And then to hide his body in the tank. So cruel.'

'When did you last hear from him?'

'We met here at the museum one afternoon in October 1918. He'd been given two weeks' leave and I had a few days off before I had to return to my nursing unit. He'd finished his training at Mill Ponds long before that, so I can't understand why he would have gone back to Walden.' She took the handkerchief Percy offered and wiped her eyes. 'He was supposed to have returned to France.'

'It must have been hard not knowing what happened to him.'

'At least now I know for sure he's gone. For a long time, I hoped that it had been a mistake. That he was alive and living in France somewhere.'

'Why did you think that?' It seemed a strange idea to have clung to.

She didn't answer immediately. 'We met once in Marne, south of Paris. Neither of us knew the other was there. I was nursing in one of the camps by the river when he came in with a wounded soldier. We managed to spend some time together and he told me how much he hated it. Hated the futile waste of lives. "We're all the same," he said. "Us and the Germans. We're killing each other because of a few men's monstrous egos." He should have been a conscientious objector.'

Percy stiffened at this.

'I understand how you feel, darling.' She patted his arm. 'But that was our upbringing. We were taught it was wrong to kill any living thing. Rob did his duty, but it was against everything he believed. He wanted to resign his commission and become a conscripted private. At least then he wouldn't be responsible for sending men into battle, but they wouldn't let him.'

I was confused. 'If he hated it there, why did you think he might still be in France?'

'He'd written and spoken of a woman he'd been seeing. He didn't tell me her name, but said they planned to be together after the war. When he was reported missing, I thought she might contact me, but I never heard from her. I wondered if she might be French. I liked to imagine him hidden away somewhere in the French countryside with her.'

Percy glared at me. 'Perhaps now's not the time to be asking these questions.'

'I've never told anyone this. I can't bear people thinking badly of Rob.' Juliet wiped her eyes. 'But the thing is, I always suspected he might have deserted.'

33

Elijah chuckled as he examined the latest edition of *The Walden Herald*. I'd felt uneasy all afternoon.

On the front page was our subtly worded article implying someone within Walden Council had been responsible for sabotaging the council's efforts to buy Waldenmere. The accompanying cartoon depicted an easily recognisable Councillor Mansbridge counting out thirty pieces of silver, helped by a dark-haired young man.

My uneasiness grew at the sound of heavy footsteps coming up the stairs. A moment later, the door to the outer office swung open. William Mansbridge marched towards us, waving a copy of the paper.

'What the hell do you think you're doing? What proof do you have there was anything underhand in my dealings with Sir Henry?'

'What dealings would those be?' Elijah leant back and lit a cigarette. 'Did you have dealings with Sir Henry? I thought all Walden Council's negotiations were with Aldershot Military Estates?'

William Mansbridge was a big man whose size would intimidate many, but Elijah seemed unperturbed. In fact, I was sure he was enjoying himself.

'That's what I mean. All my dealings were with the army. So, why does this article suggest I took money from Sir Henry?' Mansbridge spat the words across the desk.

'The article doesn't mention you. It reports on the rumours that have been circulating that someone in the council deliberately sabotaged Mrs Siddons' efforts to buy Waldenmere.'

'Well, it wasn't me,' Mansbridge growled. 'And you can't print these lies.'

'I haven't printed any lies. I've simply reported facts.' Elijah puffed contentedly on his cigarette.

'What about this ridiculous cartoon? Is this supposed to be me?' He wiggled a thick finger at the corpulent frame in the picture. I had to suppress a smile. The image was a good likeness.

Elijah made a show of peering at the front page. 'I think it's supposed to be a humorous illustration of corruption. I'm not sure it's supposed to portray anyone in particular.'

'Who drew it?' Mansbridge demanded.

'I'm afraid I can't say. The artist wishes to remain anonymous.'

'And who's been spreading these malicious rumours you claim to have heard?'

'You'll appreciate as a journalist, I'm not always able to reveal where my information comes from. It would be unethical to do so.' Elijah delivered these lines as though he were a member of the local amateur dramatic society.

'Be very careful.' Mansbridge brandished the paper in his face. 'I won't stand for any more lies. If you print another word against me, I'll sue.' He swept out, slamming the office door behind him.

'The protest of a guilty man?' Elijah sat back in satisfaction.

'I wonder. This publicly highlights the fact that he had a motive for killing General Cheverton. Someone might have seen him around Mill Ponds that afternoon but thought nothing of it. Now it might look more suspicious.' It was unlikely, but Mansbridge had just shown he had a temper.

'It's possible.' He gave a sardonic smile. 'Do you think George will be our next visitor?'

I shook my head. I didn't think George would attempt to deny it or make a scene. He wouldn't want to draw attention to himself. But how would he feel when he read the article and saw the cartoon? As much as I tried to banish all thoughts of him, he kept creeping back into my mind.

I jumped in alarm when the office door crashed open again.

'Elijah, you in there?' Nathan Cheverton leant heavily against my desk. His shock of grey-brown hair was standing on end and he was breathing heavily.

'Nathan, what on earth are you doing here?' Elijah took his arm and tried to guide him into a chair.

'Want to pay my respect to the Thackerays.' He stumbled but stayed upright, clinging to Elijah. 'Terrible thing happened.'

'Yes, of course. Are you staying at Mill Ponds?' Elijah turned to me and nodded towards the coffee pot.

'No, don't want to go there,' Nathan slurred. 'Terrible about the girl, sweet thing. Good painter, too. Felt I ought to go and see the Thackerays. Don't like him much, but poor Florence. Dreadful business.'

I suddenly remembered Alice's story about Nathan hugging her before he went to France.

'How long have you been in Walden?' I handed him a cup of black coffee and he peered at me, seeming confused by the question.

'You remember Iris Woodmore, my assistant?' Elijah prompted.

'Oh yes, that's right. Thomas's girl.' Nathan leant forward and scrutinised me, his breath thick with alcohol. 'Not as pretty as her, but no matter. I can still see her.'

'Alice?' I wanted to step back from him but stayed where I was, trying to hold his train of thought. 'You can still see her?'

'Here in my head. I know the exact shade of red to use for her hair.'

'Do you?' I said encouragingly. 'Have you painted her?'

'She didn't want me to.' He sounded petulant, then tapped his head. 'But she's in here.'

'Have you been back in Walden long?' I needed to know if he'd been anywhere near Waldenmere on the night she was killed.

'Been staying at Wildmay, but couldn't stick it there any more. At the Duck now. Ted Cox is putting me up. Fine fellow. Some others have been a bit rude. Guess I'm not popular with the locals.' He stuck out his lower lip like a naughty schoolboy.

'A lot has happened in Walden since Sir Henry's men started work. None of it good,' Elijah said dryly.

'I heard.' He raised bleary eyes. 'The chap in the tank. Think he may have been one of mine. I lost a few, you see.'

Elijah and I stared at each other in astonishment.

'What do you mean, you lost a few?' Elijah offered him a cigarette.

'Couldn't account for 'em all. Not sure where they all went. Wanted to write to the families of each of them. Tell them what happened.' He peered at me again as though willing me to understand something he didn't understand himself.

'I'm sure you did.' I tried to reassure him. 'It must have been confusing.'

'I wasn't sure what did happen to some of 'em. One minute they were there.' He waved his arm in the air. 'The next, gone. Need you to help me.'

'Help you to do what?' Elijah asked.

'See the chap, the one in the tank. Check if he's one of mine. Thought you'd be able to tell me what's what and who I should speak to. That kind of thing.' Nathan's eyes were glazing over.

'Why don't we go to the Duck first so you can rest a bit?' Elijah helped him to his feet, but Nathan leant against the hatstand. I managed to catch it before it toppled. 'Tomorrow, we can talk to the police.'

'Good thinking. Knew you'd know what to do. Must look after my men. It's my duty, you know.'

Elijah took him by the arm, struggling under Nathan's weight. As he led him out of the office door, he mouthed over his shoulder, 'Go and see Cobbe and tell him about this.'

I locked up the office and went over to the town hall. To my surprise, Ben was alone with the superintendent. They seemed to be having an intense conversation and I coughed to alert them to my presence.

'Miss Woodmore. Come in.' Superintendent Cobbe beckoned me over.

I took the chair next to Ben's and told them about Nathan Cheverton's sudden appearance and his drunken ramblings. 'Perhaps Nathan knew Robert Elmes?' I suggested.

'It's possible.' Ben looked thoughtful. 'They could have been at Mill Ponds at the same time.'

The hall was draughty and I pulled my cardigan around me. 'There's something else you should know that Alice told me. It may not be relevant.'

'Anything you can tell me about Miss Thackeray will be helpful.'

'During the war, Nathan Cheverton often visited Sand Hills Hall. Once, before he was due to go over to France, he was alone with Alice in the drawing room and suddenly hugged her.' As I said it, I realised it didn't sound particularly remarkable, but I saw Ben's jaw tighten.

'Were they close?' The superintendent picked up his pen and wrote something in his notebook.

'No, not like that. They would paint together sometimes, but they weren't close friends. The hug took Alice by surprise. He wrapped his arms around her and held her tightly. She couldn't move.' I blinked. An unwelcome vision of a mysterious figure putting their hands around Alice's neck flitted across my mind.

'Was she upset by this?' Superintendent Cobbe seemed to be taking it seriously. 'Did she tell anyone about it at the time?'

'She was embarrassed more than anything. She didn't think Nathan meant her any harm. She thought he wanted to hug someone before he went off to fight. She decided not to mention it in case it caused bad feelings between her father and General Cheverton. Nathan suddenly appearing in the office this afternoon made me think of it.' I tried to banish the image of a tall, clumsy Nathan trying to pull Alice towards him. 'After General Cheverton's funeral, he called Alice a beautiful girl and said he wanted to paint her. He was obviously keen on her. And today, he said he'd asked her to sit for him, but she'd said no. He said he could still paint her as she was in his head.'

Ben's jaw clenched tighter.

'Do we know how long Mr Cheverton has been in Walden?' Superintendent Cobbe asked.

'I'm not sure. He's been at Wildmay Manor – he's had treatment there in the past – but he said he'd had enough of it and was staying at the Drunken Duck. He could have gone to Waldenmere that night and—'

The superintendent held up his hand. 'Let's not jump to conclusions until we've found out more about Mr Cheverton's whereabouts. I'll speak to him in the morning. It sounds like he's not in a fit state to go anywhere today.'

I nodded and went to go, but then stopped. 'We had another visitor to the office before Nathan arrived.'

'Yes?' He paused, pen in mid-air.

'Councillor Mansbridge. I don't know if you've seen the latest edition of *The Walden Herald*?'

The superintendent's lips twitched. 'I have.'

'He was rather upset by our article.'

'I can imagine.'

'It led me to wonder how far he went to help Sir Henry get Waldenmere. General Cheverton's murder, for instance.'

'Indeed.' He gave a half smile. 'Thank you for sharing your thoughts with us.' He turned to Ben. 'We've finished here for today, PC Gilbert. Please walk Miss Woodmore home.'

'Yes, sir.'

Ben and I avoided the lake path and walked down the high street. It was getting dark and the streetlamps were being lit. How could it be September already? Where had the summer gone? I remembered a story I'd once read by H. G. Wells about a man who'd invented a machine that allowed him to travel back in time. I wished such a machine existed and I could travel back a few months.

'I saw the article. The rumour is George was in on it. Is it true?' Ben asked.

'He acted as a messenger for Mansbridge. They were both being paid by Sir Henry.' I focussed on the flickering lamps that lined the road.

'Have you spoken to him about it?'

'Yes. He admitted it.'

'What does he plan to do? I can't imagine Mrs Siddons will tolerate him at the council offices after this.'

'He was planning to go abroad anyway. Now he has the money.' I tried not to sound bitter but didn't succeed. 'He says he won't go until Alice's killer is caught and that he's worried for my safety. He's probably just worried about what people will think if he disappears suddenly.' I glanced at Ben. 'He did say he was sorry for what he did.'

'How do you feel about him?'

'I don't have any feelings. Except for grief. And guilt.'

'I know how that feels,' he replied with fervour.

'I'm not sure he regrets taking Sir Henry's money, but I believed him when he said how sorry he was for everything that's happened.' I rubbed my eyes. I felt exhausted, but my mind wouldn't stop conjuring up different scenarios of who might have murdered Alice. Especially since Nathan had reappeared. 'Is George still a suspect?'

'I don't think the super's ruled anyone out, including me. In his view, it's most likely to be a male admirer. And now he can add Nathan Cheverton to his list.'

'What about a connection between Alice's murder and Robert Elmes?'

'Captain Fortesque hasn't come up with anything. Elmes could have been a spy, but there's nothing to suggest it. It's more likely he was a deserter.'

'Juliet spoke to you?'

He nodded. 'She went to see Superintendent Cobbe and told him what she'd suspected when she heard Robert was missing.'

We reached home and Ben stared at the front door. He seemed transfixed by it.

'Come in and have supper with us.'

He shook his head. 'I can't. I keep thinking if only she'd been inside with you when I came looking for her.'

My feelings of guilt escalated. 'It's my fault. I should have been with her. I was the one who was reckless that night and Alice paid the price for it.'

'I didn't mean that. I'm not blaming you. It's my fault. I should have acted sooner. Taken her away from him.' His voice had a hard edge to it that I hadn't heard before.

'Her father?'

'Why didn't I?' His despair was more than I could bear.

I wrapped my arms around him and held him tightly for a moment. I heard a muffled sob, then he pulled back and strode away.

Stepping inside, I was overcome with grief. Alice had been happy when she was here. And loved. I hope she knew how loved she was.

When Ben had rapped on the front door that night, he'd hoped she was safe behind it with me, but she was lying dead in cold, black mud. She didn't deserve that.

Before I could stop myself, sobs wracked my body and I fell down at the foot of the stairs. My father and Lizzy rushed out to me.

'Shush, love. I know it hurts.' Lizzy cradled me in her arms. 'It will get better.'

But I knew the image of Alice in the mud would be with me for the rest of my life and I wasn't sure if I could cope with it.

34

The following morning, I decided to pay a visit to Wildmay Manor. I'd woken with the impulse to do something, anything, to find out who murdered Alice. Was the answer staring me in the face in the ungainly form of Nathan Cheverton? Had he known Robert Elmes? He'd been at Wildmay when the general was murdered. Was it too much of a coincidence that he'd been back there on the night Alice died?

I stopped off at the station house to check on Ben and to ask to borrow his bicycle. He opened the door wearing an old jumper and a pair of corduroy trousers worn at the knees. He hadn't shaved.

'Wait while I put on my uniform. I'll come with you,' he said when I told him where I was going.

'You can't. Superintendent Cobbe will find out when he goes there to interview the staff about Nathan Cheverton's alibi.'

He rubbed his eyes. 'I don't care. How are you going to get them to talk to you?'

'I thought I'd say *The Walden Herald* plans to publish an article on the work they're doing. I'm not going to ask them about Nathan.

I just want to have a snoop around the place. Can I borrow your bicycle?'

'You can borrow Sid's. He'll be stuck at the town hall all day.' He opened the door wider to let me in. 'Wait here while I get changed. I won't come in with you, I'll stay by the gate to the manor.'

I decided not to bother arguing with him.

Ben set off at speed on his bicycle while I lagged behind, familiarising myself with the strange workings of Sid's bike. I wasn't the most competent cyclist, but after a nervous start, I began to enjoy the thrill of pedalling faster and speeding along winding country lanes. I felt lighter than I had in weeks.

We dismounted at the gates and sat on the grass to examine Wildmay Manor. It was an ornate mansion built in a French style and surrounded by landscaped gardens. I left Ben with the bicycles and walked down a long gravel driveway towards an imposing pair of oak doors framed by four tall pillars. I was steeling myself to lift the iron knocker when the doors swung open and a woman in a nurse's uniform appeared.

'Hello.' She looked taken aback. 'What are you doing here?'

'I'm from *The Walden Herald*. We're planning to write a feature on the work the hospital does. I believe my editor sent you the details?'

'I don't know anything about that. It's probably Dr Outen's doing.' She shook her head in exasperation. 'I'll show you to his office.'

The interior of Wildmay Manor was as impressive as the exterior, with sturdy mahogany furniture and elaborate wall hangings. The only thing that spoilt the illusion of being in a luxurious country house was the strong smell of carbolic soap.

The nurse stopped outside a door labelled Dr Outen and rapped three times. A voice called for her to enter.

'Dr Outen, this lady is from *The Walden Herald*.'

'Ah, yes, thank you, Matron.' The short, balding man behind the desk seemed anxious and nodded. With this, Matron strode off down the corridor.

I stepped inside the office. 'My name's Iris Woodmore. My editor contacted you about the article we're planning to write on your pioneering work.' I hoped flattery would help.

Dr Outen peered at me through round, wire-rimmed spectacles. 'Did he?' His desk was overflowing with piles of documents and he glanced down at the mess. 'You're probably right.'

'I won't take up much of your time. I already know a little about the work you're doing here.'

'Then you'll be aware of the controversy surrounding it?'

'That's why we want to cover it. With so many soldiers returning to their families suffering from nervous and mental shock, my editor feels it's a subject that will interest our readers.'

He nodded. 'How much do you know of the matter?'

'I believe physicians who study psychology use the word shell shock to describe war neurosis. While people know hospitals like yours treat mental diseases and shell-shock, they don't fully understand your methods. By increasing their knowledge on the matter, they might become more receptive to your work.' I was warming to my theme, thinking it was a topic that would interest our readers. I'd managed to convince myself with my lies if no one else.

'Precisely. We do need to educate.' Dr Outen came out from behind his desk. 'During the war, soldiers were treated harshly. Displays of emotion were thought to be cowardly. Did you know that some shell-shocked soldiers were charged with desertion, cowardice, or insubordination? Some were even shot.'

'My father has written about such cases. He's also a journalist.'

'Woodmore, did you say your name was? Is your father Thomas Woodmore?'

I nodded. My story was going down better than expected.

'I've read some of his articles. Excellent work. Excellent.' He was positively bouncing with enthusiasm.

'Perhaps you could explain how you treat your patients?'

'I'd be delighted, Miss Woodmore. We use various methods, such as hypnosis, massage and dietary regimes. All of these can help a patient's recovery, although what they need most is to be able to rest and recuperate in peaceful surroundings.'

'It's beautiful here.'

'Let me give you a tour. I won't be able to take you into any of the wards, but I can show you some of our recreational facilities. We encourage our patients to participate in outdoor activities, like gardening and farming. We have livestock here and the men find it comforting to tend to the animals. Caring for a living thing helps them regain their sense of purpose.'

I followed him out of his office into the entrance hall and back through the vast oak doors.

He ushered me across the driveway around to the side of the house. 'As well as the landscaped gardens, we have a kitchen garden that supplies all our fresh produce.'

The grounds were well tended, with neat lawns and borders crammed with flowers and herbs. I caught a glimpse of a well-stocked kitchen garden before Dr Outen was on the move again. I scurried after him and suddenly entered a farmyard.

I looked back, experiencing a strange sensation of things not being quite as they seemed. It was disconcerting to walk a hundred yards out of a formal garden that had the appearance of a London park into a farmyard full of animals.

Dr Outen stopped to greet a young man tending to a brown mare. The man stammered a reply, averting his eyes. The scar on his cheek made me think of George and I felt a twinge of guilt. Had George seen *The Walden Herald*'s article?

I pushed him from my mind and scuttled after Dr Outen, who, I was discovering, could walk at great speed.

'Stammering and disconnected speech are common symptoms among our patients. Many still relive their wartime experiences. Simon prefers the company of animals to people.' Dr Outen stopped by a pigsty, where a row of piglets suckled on a huge sow. 'And who can blame him?'

I gazed around the farmyard. It looked like any other, but what was different was the level of care the men gave to the animals. These weren't farmers preparing livestock for slaughter.

'We also have a studio where patients are encouraged to undertake creative pursuits such as pottery and painting.'

I tensed. 'May I see the studio?'

'Let me check first.' He strode over to a large barn and peered through the door. 'No one here. Come and have a look.'

From the outside, the barn didn't appear to be any different from the others, but again, all was not what it seemed. Inside, it was fully furnished and stocked with easels and canvasses.

I walked around, examining the artwork on display. Stacks of pictures were leaning against the wall. At the front of one of the stacks, I recognised a painting in the distinct brushwork of Nathan Cheverton.

'I'm familiar with the work of this artist. Mr Cheverton?'

'Yes, you're right. As you can see, Nathan is one of our most prolific painters.'

'May I take a look?' I was itching to see what Nathan had been working on.

'I'm afraid not. Our artists value their privacy.'

'Of course.' I took a step back. 'Is Mr Cheverton still with you?'

'I believe he's left.' He opened the barn door and gestured for me to go first. 'He's a voluntary patient and can come and go as he wishes.'

I glanced back at the stack of paintings.

'There's Matron.' He waved her over. 'She'll know for sure.'

Matron came over, wearing the same exasperated expression as earlier. She confirmed that Nathan had left Wildmay some days before.

'I'm afraid that's all I can show you, Miss Woodmore.'

'Thank you so much for your time, Dr Outen. It's been fascinating.'

'Why don't I show Miss Woodmore the ladies' garden?' Matron's lips twitched and Dr Outen stiffened.

I was intrigued. 'The ladies' garden? You treat female patients?'

'We do. But I'd rather you didn't mention that in your article.' Dr Outen frowned. He took off his wire-rimmed glasses and cleaned them with a handkerchief.

'Why not?' My fictitious article was becoming more enticing by the minute.

'We try to keep the ladies out of sight as much as possible. We don't want the men to think they're suffering from the same nervous afflictions as the women. These are brave soldiers who fought for their country. We want them to regain pride in themselves.'

My eyes narrowed. I'd warmed to Dr Outen, but I was quickly revising my opinion of him. 'Are these women suffering from the same mental afflictions as the men?'

'Mostly, yes. They all spent time on the front line as nurses and ambulance drivers. Matron will show you their garden. I must get on.' He bowed formally. 'I look forward to seeing your article, Miss Woodmore.'

I thanked him again and followed Matron out of the farmyard, across undulating lawns, until we reached a wooden door set into a rough flint wall. She took a heavy set of iron keys from her pocket.

Once again, the transition from one scene to another was

disconcerting. This private, walled garden was less formal than the ornate one the men had been working on. The flow of the borders was softer, the flowers and herbs mixed casually. The overall impression was of peace and harmony.

'You're shocked by Dr Outen's attitude?' Matron gave a small smile. 'I'm afraid it's common in the medical profession.'

'Surely it's about the cause of the affliction rather than the sex of the person suffering from it?'

Only two ladies were in the garden. One was kneeling at the front of an overgrown border, delicately pulling weeds from a tangle of flowers. Another was sitting on the patio, staring into the distance. Occasionally, she raised a white handkerchief to watery eyes.

'I agree. These are women who served on the battlefields. In their way, they're soldiers too. It's hardly surprising they're suffering in the same manner.'

'Did you know Mrs Juliet Rendall?' When Dr Outen mentioned these women had served on the front line as nurses and ambulance drivers, I remembered Juliet saying she'd spent time at Wildmay Manor.

'Yes, Juliet was typical of the type of woman we see here. She spent years nursing casualties and, of course, she suffered her own losses. Sadly, it's a combination we see all too often in men and women. They reach a certain point where they can no longer cope.'

'I must admit, I was surprised when Juliet told me she'd been here. She always seems so strong.' I didn't say I'd assumed Juliet had been there in a nursing capacity.

'There's no shame in seeking treatment. These aren't women of a nervous disposition. Quite the contrary, they tend to be extremely capable women who have pushed themselves too hard.'

'Yes, of course.'

Matron continued. 'These women have suffered because of

what they gave for their country. Mrs Rendall was grief-stricken. The loss of her husband and then her brother were too much for her. She struggled to come to terms with her brother's death, wanting to believe he was still alive.'

I nodded. 'Wouldn't it be beneficial for male and female patients to mix?' I wondered if Juliet could have come across Nathan Cheverton while she was there.

'Dr Outen thinks not. Perhaps he's right. These ladies need their solitude.' Matron turned and led me away. 'I think we've disturbed them enough for today.'

I followed her into the house and she led me back to the entrance hall.

'Although I disagree with Dr Outen on the need for secrecy around the women's ward, I admire his work. He's achieved excellent results with the patients in his care.' She unlocked the oak doors and showed me out.

I thanked her for her time and walked slowly down the stone steps. Glancing back to check no one was watching from the windows, I nipped across the lawn and headed towards the farm. Nodding to Simon as I passed, I walked confidently over to the studio barn. Fortunately, it was still empty.

Nathan's paintings were stacked against the wall and I gently pulled each one forward to look at the next. Many were similar to the one he'd given Elijah, messy and frantic depictions of war with mud, blood and barbed wire. By contrast, others were peaceful studies of the hills and streams surrounding Wildmay Manor. It seemed Dr Outen's treatments were beginning to have a calming effect on Nathan.

I came to a landscape that was clearly Waldenmere. It was a charming painting. He'd captured the serene, sometimes eerie quality of the lake at dawn. Another showed Grebe Stream as it wound its way down to Heron Bay. In the distance, you could see the gables of Grebe House. Nathan Cheverton had obviously spent a lot of time painting at Waldenmere.

Noises outside jolted me back to the present. I knew I had to leave, but I couldn't resist peeking at the remaining two paintings.

One was a rather abstract depiction of Heron Bay that made use of a wide palette of colours, but it was the flash of red that made me gasp. On the shoreline was a young woman in a white dress, her red hair loose around her shoulders, as Alice's had been when her body was found. My hands became clammy.

I removed the two paintings from the back of the stack. Alice was in both. In one, she was lying on the shore, her white dress pulled up to her thighs, with bare legs and feet in the water. In the other, she was laid out like a corpse resting on a bed of bronze bracken with blue flowers clutched in her hand.

I pushed the stack of paintings back against the wall and ran from the barn, glad Ben hadn't been with me to see them. I'd have to tell him and Superintendent Cobbe what I'd found.

35

'Did your brother know Nathan Cheverton?'

I perched next to Juliet and Percy on the banks of Grebe Stream.

'Yes, he did. Why?' Juliet asked in surprise.

'If they trained together at Mill Ponds, perhaps Robert came back to Walden to see him?'

She shook her head. 'They trained at the same time, but I'm not sure how close they were. Rob never mentioned Nathan to me. I only found out later.'

'Nathan often paints at Waldenmere. I thought they might have become friends because of that.'

'Possibly,' Juliet conceded. 'I've seen some of his paintings. They would have interested Rob.'

'Where did you see them? I saw them when I visited Wildmay Manor yesterday.'

Percy handed me his field glasses. 'If you keep talking, we'll never see a kingfisher.'

We sat in silence, watching the branches sway above the flow of water. After a while, we were rewarded with a flash of blue. I peered through the glasses at the distinctive orange and turquoise plumage. The kingfisher was perched on an overhanging branch, studying the water below. Suddenly, it dived, emerging with a silver fish in its beak, then disappeared behind leafy cover to devour its prey.

'What a beautiful bird.' I handed the field glasses back to Percy. 'I sometimes see them on my walks. Usually just a flash of blue, then they're gone.'

'This is a good place to watch for them,' Juliet said. 'They nest in banks. But they're very territorial. They'll chase off their own fledglings rather than share their patch.'

'They nest on the ground?'

'Many birds do.' She was quiet for a moment and then finally replied to my earlier question. 'I saw Nathan's paintings when I was at Wildmay Manor.'

'Is that where you met him?' I knew I had to tread carefully.

She nodded. 'I went out walking one day and came across him painting. We started chatting. That's when he told me he'd known Rob. I felt sorry for him. I wondered if Rob would have ended up there too if he'd survived.'

'Were you there long? At Wildmay, I mean?'

'Only a few weeks.' She shifted her position to face me. 'Did you visit the women's ward?'

'Just the walled garden.' I glanced at Percy.

She smiled. 'It's all right. Percy knows I was a patient there. He was a huge support to me at the time. He kept things going at the museum until I was ready to come back.' She took his hand and squeezed it.

'I hadn't realised they took women patients until Matron told me.'

'It's a well-kept secret. Dr Outen thinks his male patients would be ashamed if people thought they had a woman's "nervous disposition", the implication being they're some sort of fainting female. The women's ward is tucked away where no one can see it.'

'Bloody stupid,' Percy muttered.

'I'm afraid I've been guilty of letting people believe I was a nurse there rather than a patient,' Juliet confessed. 'We should be more honest about it. Perhaps more women would seek help if we were.'

'You believed your brother was still alive then, didn't you?' It was interesting that Juliet had sensed something was wrong about Robert's death. I could see how this would have tormented her. Sadly, being proved right nearly three years later was hardly a comfort.

'It all got too much for me. Losing Peter, my husband, and then Rob. I'd seen the chaos of the battlefields. I wanted to believe Rob had run away and was living quietly somewhere in the French countryside. I told myself that he couldn't contact us for fear of reprisals from the army.'

'Did you try to investigate what happened to him?'

'I talked to the War Office, but they couldn't help me. They told me he was a casualty of war, like thousands of others. I didn't mention my suspicion that he may have deserted. It would have distressed my parents too much. They chose to believe Rob died a hero.'

'Juliet went through hell,' Percy muttered. 'And all along...'

And all along, her brother was lying dead in a tank. I could understand Percy's protectiveness of Juliet and admired the way he'd supported her all this time.

'I tortured myself with the thought that I should be searching for him, although I didn't know where to begin. In my heart, I knew that if he were alive, he would have made contact with me. By the time I left Wildmay, I'd come to terms with his death. And now this.' She made a strangled noise that was almost a wail. 'I should have tried harder.'

I wondered what would have happened if Juliet had persisted in trying to find him. Would his body have been discovered sooner? I doubted it. It was more likely she'd have been dismissed as a grief-stricken, neurotic woman.

Percy placed his field glasses on the bank and put his arm around her. 'What are the police doing? Has Ben told you anything?'

I shook my head. 'I think Superintendent Cobbe hopes Military Intelligence will supply him with some answers.'

'Someone in authority must have covered this up.' Juliet's mouth set into a hard line. 'There's no other explanation.'

I exchanged a glance with Percy. It was difficult to come to any other conclusion.

'Has Superintendent Cobbe checked on Nathan Cheverton's whereabouts for the night of Alice's murder?' I pounced on Ben as soon as he entered the office. 'Has he taken the paintings away? Surely, they're evidence?'

'Give the man some coffee before you interrogate him,' Elijah called. 'And bring me one, too.'

I headed into his den, armed with the coffee pot.

Ben scratched his unshaven chin. 'The superintendent wasn't impressed by our visit to Wildmay Manor.'

'Neither was I.' Elijah glared at me.

'I'm planning to write an article about the work they do there.' I was stopped by his withering look. 'But we can talk about that another time.'

Ben sat down and stretched out his legs. 'He and Sid talked to the staff at the manor. They confirmed he was staying there that day. He got back late, after midnight and was drunk.'

'Where did Nathan say he'd been?' I refilled Elijah's mug and poured a cup for Ben.

'According to Sid, it was hopeless. He hasn't got a clue what day of the week it is, let alone where he was on a particular night. It was impossible to get a coherent answer out of him.'

'But he could have been at Waldenmere? Did they ask about the paintings?'

It was fortunate Nathan hadn't been around when I'd told Ben about the pictures of Alice. His face still showed the disgust he felt. 'Superintendent Cobbe has seen them.'

'And has he questioned Nathan about them?' I asked.

'Cheverton doesn't deny painting them. He said he did them from memory as she wouldn't pose for him.' His voice was heavy with loathing. 'He says he doesn't think he was at Waldenmere that night. He thinks he was drinking in a pub and not out painting.'

I sipped my coffee, wondering whether Nathan's vagueness was an act. 'Juliet said Nathan knew her brother. They trained at Mill Ponds at the same time and it sounds like neither was suited to military life. They may have become friends. Perhaps Robert confided in Nathan about his plan to desert? They could have argued over that and Alice witnessed something.'

'The super isn't convinced Cheverton is capable of that degree of violence.' Ben rubbed his eyes, clearly not knowing what to think.

'I agree. I don't think it was Nathan,' Elijah said.

'It's obvious he's traumatised from his wartime experiences. Who knows what that could lead him to do? He may not even remember his actions, especially if he was drunk at the time.' I was sympathetic to Nathan's suffering, but it didn't mean he wasn't a murderer.

'He's not been ruled out, though there's nothing to put him at the scene. The super feels that with his disorganised mind, Cheverton would have left clues behind. And the staff at Wildmay say that when he returned, he was dishevelled but his clothes were clean. There was no mud on his trousers or shoes.'

'Maybe he's not as disorganised as he seems.' I was frustrated. 'Robert Elmes, General Cheverton and Alice. Whatever or whoever the link is, it must be a military one. Nathan knew them all.'

'I'll speak to Horace.' Elijah ran his pen along the timeline of events he'd scribbled across his blotter. 'See if Finlay Fortesque has come up with anything.'

* * *

'I've been doing some digging on Robert Elmes since you told me his file was missing.' Finlay scrutinised me with cool blue eyes and I sank down in my chair. 'And I've had all the records removed from Mill Ponds. We don't want to risk another intrusion.'

I hadn't thought about the repercussions of what I'd done. Or the trouble I could be in with the military.

'If the records hadn't been left there in the first place, perhaps none of this would have happened.' Horace patted my arm, much to my embarrassment. Elijah and I were seated once again on his veranda. A tumbler of whisky sat in front of each of the men while I'd been given a glass of lemonade.

'Point taken,' Finlay said dryly. 'Anyway, I've managed to find a copy of Elmes' records. And, more importantly, the report that was issued to the War Office to inform them he was missing.'

Finlay took out a tiny notebook from his blazer pocket, attached to which was an equally tiny pencil on a piece of string. He carefully turned the pages. 'The dates don't add up. Robert Elmes was supposed to be in France by the first of November. His old unit disbanded on the thirty-first of October. Records show that on this date, Elmes asked to resign his commission. He was told that he had to join his new unit immediately, but he went missing in action before he could. Yet it seems unlikely he would have been killed in action if he hadn't yet joined the new unit.'

'I must say, Finlay, I'm astonished an officer can be mislaid so easily.' Horace sipped his whisky. 'Surely someone would have noticed his disappearance. His commanding officer, for instance?'

'There seems to have been a presumption that he'd joined his new unit as arranged. After he was reported missing in action, another lieutenant was put in charge of that unit and no one raised any concerns. This was the tail end of the war and plans were constantly changing.'

'When do you think he was killed?' Elijah asked.

'Late October or early November 1918. Robert Elmes was on two weeks' leave until the end of October. Mrs Rendall confirms she met up with him in London during that time.' Finlay traced his tiny pencil down the pages.

'But when was he put in the tank?' I asked.

'I would guess at the time of the murder,' Finlay replied. 'The alternative would have been to bury the body or weigh it down with stones and sink it in the lake. Whoever killed him must have banked on no one going near the tank in the short term.'

'Who reported Elmes missing and when?' Elijah lit a cigarette.

'A communication was sent to the War Office saying Robert Elmes went missing in action during the battle at Sambre on 4 November 1918.'

'One of the last battles of the war.' Horace tilted his head towards Finlay. 'And who was the author of this communication?'

Finlay stroked his moustache with a glint in his eye. We watched him expectantly.

'Colonel Charles Thackeray.'

36

Horace inhaled sharply.

Elijah swore under his breath. 'Are you saying Colonel Thack-eray shot Robert Elmes in the back sometime in November 1918?'

I winced at these words. 'Just because Colonel Thackeray's name is on the report doesn't mean he had anything to do with the murder.' I didn't know why I was defending the colonel. I guessed it was because I knew it was what Alice would have done.

'It looks pretty damning, I'm afraid.' Finlay picked up his glass and downed the remaining whisky in one gulp.

'But why?' Horace spread his hands in disbelief. 'Why would he shoot him?'

We all looked at Finlay.

He shrugged. 'No idea.'

'Finlay, you disappoint us.' Horace sounded aggrieved.

'I can't find anything to link the two men apart from the fact that their paths would have crossed at Mill Ponds. Elmes' file documents his progress from new recruit to second lieutenant and then lieutenant. There's no indication of any problems with him until he asked to resign his commission when his old unit disbanded.'

'Juliet suspected her brother was considering deserting. She felt he should never have joined up and it might have been better for him to have been a conscientious objector.'

'Is that reason enough for the colonel to shoot him?' Elijah seemed doubtful. 'Why not report him?'

'Tensions may have been running high?' Finlay tapped the side of his glass with his pencil. 'It's a tricky situation. We plan to question Colonel Thackeray, but we have to tread carefully, given the circumstances.'

'The circumstances of his being a colonel or the fact that he's just lost a beloved daughter?' Horace reached for the whisky bottle and topped up the men's glasses.

'Both,' Finlay replied.

'What about General Cheverton?' Elijah asked. 'Why kill him?'

'It's possible the general suspected something wasn't right about Elmes' disappearance,' Finlay replied.

'But,' I took a deep breath, 'Alice?'

Finlay was silent for a moment, then said, 'Did Miss Thackeray confide in you about her relationship with her father?'

'It was a difficult subject,' I muttered. 'Alice was protective of him.'

'But you've known the Thackerays for a long time. Was there anything that caused you concern?' Elijah asked gently.

'Was she afraid of him?' Finlay was more direct.

I remembered Ben saying he should have taken Alice away from her father. 'She was scared of his temper – he would smash ornaments when he was angry – but I don't believe he was ever violent towards her.' I decided to voice my suspicions. 'I'm not so sure about Florence. Mrs Thackeray, I mean.'

'You think he may have been physically aggressive towards his wife?' Finlay asked.

'I don't know. I suppose I suspected it,' I admitted.

'Did Miss Thackeray ever row with her father?' Finlay clearly wasn't going to stop questioning me until he knew everything. 'Can you think of anything that may have caused him to lose his temper with her?'

'I, well, I believe he may have been unhappy about Alice's friendship with PC Gilbert.' I felt I was betraying Alice with every word and my instinct was still to protect the colonel. But what if he had killed her?

'Did he know about it?' Elijah asked.

'Alice was planning to talk to him about Ben.'

'I see.' Finlay drew out the words. 'And when did she tell you this?'

'That morning. The morning of the day she died.'

In the silence that followed, I thought of what Ben had said about asking Alice to marry him. Had Colonel Thackeray found out or seen them together?

I took a sip of lemonade and cleared my throat. 'What happens now?'

'I've arranged a meeting with Superintendent Cobbe to share my findings. For the moment, this goes no further. Tell no one of the conversation we've just had.' It was a command rather than a request. 'I'll be in touch soon. I may have a lead on how the tank got into the water.'

'Thank you, Finlay.' Elijah rose. 'We're grateful for all you've done. Come on, Iris, let's get back to the office.'

My knees felt weak as I stood up. I had no idea what to make of these revelations.

* * *

The next day, Ben peered around the office door. His eyes were bloodshot. 'Can we talk?'

I nodded. 'Elijah's not here.'

'I know.' He came in and sat on the edge of my desk. 'I saw him at the town hall with Superintendent Cobbe.'

Finlay had been true to his word and shared Robert Elmes' records with the police. The superintendent had telephoned Elijah and asked him to call in at the town hall. I'd wanted to go too, but to my annoyance, the superintendent had made it clear he wanted to talk to Elijah alone.

'Do you think Colonel Thackeray killed Alice?' Ben's knuckles were white as he gripped the side of my desk.

'You've heard what Finlay found out?'

He nodded. 'Sid told me.'

'I would never have believed it of him, but...' I didn't know what I believed any more.

'His clothes were dry and clean when he reported her missing.' Ben leant towards me and I could smell sweat on his rumpled shirt. 'But I suppose he could have gone back to the hall and changed. It was sometime after dinner that he reported her missing.'

'But why would he?' I hated to ask – but Ben must realise the reason could be because of him.

He didn't answer immediately. When he did, his voice was choked with emotion. 'We kissed that night. Under the jetty. He might have seen us. Do you think that's what happened?' Ben's eyes pleaded for an answer and I could sense his desperation.

'I don't know.' My confusion was mirrored in his face. I thought of Colonel Thackeray's temper. He was a controlling man who liked to get his own way. The usually docile Alice defying him so blatantly might have sent him over the edge.

After Ben left, I sat staring at the clock until Elijah returned.

'What did the superintendent say?' I watched him struggle out of his suit jacket.

'Finlay's told him about Thackeray. The pair of them have agreed they need more evidence before they question him. Cobbe wants to make sure that we keep our mouths shut until he says otherwise.' He fixed me with a hard stare. 'And that you don't do anything foolish, dangerous, or illegal. Leave the detective work to him was his message.'

I ignored this last bit. 'Does he think the colonel killed Alice?' It was what Ben had asked and I knew we were both going around in circles. But it was such an incomprehensible idea. What made it so hard to accept was the thought of the pain and bewilderment Alice would have felt if her father had turned on her.

'No. Cobbe still thinks it's more likely Alice was killed by an admirer. Finlay disagrees. As much as he'd like it not to be a military matter, he feels there's too much evidence pointing towards Thackeray.'

'What do you think?' I was driving myself mad, speculating over what could have happened. I wanted Elijah to tell me the idea of Alice being murdered by her father was preposterous. I wanted a different culprit from the one staring us in the face.

'The man had a temper.'

'But he never took it out on Alice.'

'Are you sure?'

'No. I'm not.' I buried my head in my hands, ashamed to admit that I couldn't be certain Colonel Thackeray had never hurt his daughter, my best friend.

Elijah put his hand on my shoulder. 'I think you have to face up to the fact that it's possible. She could have witnessed something to do with Robert Elmes, or they could have argued over her relationship with Ben. Either of those things would have triggered a strong reaction in him.'

'It could have been someone infatuated with Alice,' I argued.

'Who?' He shrugged. 'Nathan, Ben, George? Even Percy's been questioned.'

'It wasn't George, Ben, or Percy.'

'And I don't think it was Nathan.' Elijah sighed. 'But I have to admit, I'm not as certain of that as I was.'

'We're going to the pub for a drink,' Elijah announced a few days later.

'What, now?' It was eleven o'clock. Too early, even by his standards. Did he think a trip to the Drunken Duck would cheer me up?

'Bring your notepad.' He plucked his jacket from the hatstand. 'We're meeting someone.'

'Who?'

'I don't know. Finlay will tell us when we get there.'

We arrived at the Duck to find Horace and Finlay sitting in the beer garden with a tray of glasses and a jug of ginger beer in front of them. The unsettled weather that had seen days of rain throughout the first weeks of September had given way to blue skies and the temperature was creeping upwards.

I was glad of the ginger beer although Elijah was unimpressed by the choice of beverage.

'Who are we meeting?' he asked.

'I can't tell you his name. I've promised him anonymity,' Finlay replied. 'He was based at Waldenmere Camp in November and December of 1918.'

A heavy-set man wearing workman's trousers, a white shirt and a red neckerchief appeared at the garden gate. Finlay gestured for him to join us. 'Thank you for coming. I appreciate you'd rather not be here.'

'I'll talk to you, but not the police.' The man had a gruff, low voice and smelt strongly of woodbine cigarettes.

'That's understood. I just want you to tell us what happened the night the tank went into the water.'

'We didn't know what was in it.' Sweat formed on his brow and he pulled his neckerchief loose.

'No one's suggesting you did,' Finlay said calmly. 'Just tell us what happened that night.'

'We was all getting a bit wound up. We wanted to get home for Christmas, but we was still stuck in that bloody camp. Pardon my language, miss.' He eyed me dubiously, his suspicion understandable. Horace, Finlay, Elijah and I made a strange-looking party.

'That's all right,' I replied. 'You must have been longing to go home.'

'We was. The food was diabolical and getting worse by the day. We couldn't understand why it was taking so long to get our papers. Then the colonel sends us all out on exercises.'

'The colonel?' Finlay queried.

'Colonel Thackeray.' He shifted nervously in his seat.

I felt a strange sensation creep over me. Elijah and Horace exchanged glances.

'Colonel Thackeray sent you on exercises?' Finlay prompted.

'The whole bloody camp on a route march to Aldershot, at night, in November. Stupid bastard. Didn't he know the war was over? We weren't having none of that.'

Finlay interrupted. 'We?'

'I ain't giving ya their names, if that's what you're asking.' The man folded his arms across his chest.

Finlay nodded. 'Understood. Carry on.'

'Three of us did about the first mile, then buggered off. It was too dark for the sarge to see us.'

'Where did you go?'

'Headed back to camp. But when we got close, we heard a noise coming from the lake. We couldn't figure out what it was at first. We got near to Mill Ponds and hid in the reedbeds.'

'You saw the tank?' Finlay asked.

'It had moved. Not by much, but enough to get it into the water.'

'Where had it been before?'

'On the banks near Mill Ponds. None of us knew how to drive the thing, so it was stuck there. It weren't of no use to anyone. It moved slower than a snail and never in the right direction.'

'Did you see who was driving it?'

'We saw the tank was beginning to go down in the mud. Then a man came out of the turret. We heard the hatch clang shut and he jumped into the water. He was holding a torch, but it died. I only caught a glimpse of his face, but it was Thackeray.'

Elijah inhaled and Horace made a tutting sound.

'Are you sure?' Finlay said.

'He was soaking wet and covered in mud, but it was him all right. You had to admire his guts. He was wobbling around all over the place. Never been the same since he got caught by that grenade, but he got the job done.'

'The job?'

'We assumed it was his orders. We'd been told to clear the camp out and we thought he'd been given the job of getting rid of the tank.'

'What happened then?'

The man shrugged. 'Nothing. We went back to camp. I don't

think I ever saw Thackeray again after that. I got my papers not long afterwards and was home in time for Christmas.'

Finlay let out a long sigh. He had my sympathy. Whichever way you looked at it, this would not go down well with his superiors.

'We had no idea someone was inside the bloody thing, I swear.' The man mopped his brow. Elijah offered him a cigarette and he took it gratefully.

'Is there anything else?' Finlay indicated to Elijah.

'When was this?' Elijah asked.

'To be honest, I'm not sure. Sometime in November, I think.' The man drew heavily on his cigarette. 'After Armistice.'

Elijah nodded. Horace passed an envelope to Finlay, who handed it to the man. He put it into his shirt pocket, nodded to us, then got up and scuttled out of the gate.

'Thackeray went to great lengths to dispose of Robert Elmes,' Finlay said. 'Sending the men out on exercises. And driving that tank can't have been easy.'

'What happens now?' I asked.

'I'll pass on what we know to Cobbe and continue working with him on this,' Finlay replied.

'That man could have been lying,' I suggested.

'Why would he?' Elijah said.

'For money. Mr Laffaye was paying him,' I replied.

'Paying him to tell us what he knows. Not to point the finger at anyone in particular,' Elijah countered. 'Why would he tell us it was Thackeray?'

'He may have had a grudge against him. It sounds like plenty of men had cause to dislike the colonel.' I was still battling with my emotions.

'I think he was telling the truth,' Elijah said gently.

'I do understand Miss Woodmore's doubts.' Horace looked

thoughtful. 'Colonel Thackeray would certainly kill for king and country, but shooting a man in the back in cold blood?'

'Shooting a possible deserter,' Finlay reminded him.

'Perhaps there was another reason?' Elijah suggested.

Before Finlay could reply, we were interrupted.

'Elijah. Thought that was you.' Nathan Cheverton was stumbling towards us.

Elijah sighed and motioned for him to sit down. 'Nathan, you remember Mr Laffaye and Captain Fortesque.'

'Of course.' It was clear from his bewildered expression Nathan hadn't a clue who they were. He sat down heavily next to me. 'And Thomas's girl. Interesting hair. Perhaps I can paint you? Dabbling in portraits, you know.'

I recoiled, remembering the sinister images of Alice in his paintings, but forced a smile. 'Portraits? How interesting.'

To my relief, he turned his attention to Elijah. 'I'm still not sure about the man in the tank.'

Elijah sipped his ginger beer and eyed him shrewdly. 'We think you may have known him. Do you remember Lieutenant Robert Elmes?'

'Rob? Yes, of course, lovely chap. Killed in action, wasn't he? Shame for poor...' He stopped and gave a guilty smile. He looked like a schoolboy caught in the act of pilfering from the tuck shop. It was the look I'd seen before at General Cheverton's funeral when he'd been about to say something indiscreet about Florence.

'Do you remember when you last saw Robert Elmes?' Finlay asked.

'If he says I was with him, I probably was.' Nathan gave a false, nasal laugh. 'Shocking memory.'

The three men looked at each other in bemusement.

'Oh.' I realised the reason for his strange answer. Fragments of conversation were starting to fit together.

'What is it, my dear?' Horace asked.

I leant towards Nathan and said in a conspiratorial whisper, 'Robert had a girlfriend, didn't he?'

The others stared at me in surprise.

'What? Oh, that. No.' Nathan shook his head vehemently. He moved closer to me, his head almost touching mine and put his finger to his lips.

'It was a secret, wasn't it?' I said quietly. 'You had to cover for him?'

He nodded. 'Never told a soul. Felt sorry for her, though.'

'Florence must have been heartbroken when he went missing.'

'Shhh.' He glanced over his shoulder in panic. 'Don't want the colonel finding out.'

38

'You look done in, love.' Lizzy stroked my hair.

'I didn't get much sleep last night.' I was sitting at the kitchen table in my dressing gown. I'd buttered a slice of toast but given up attempting to eat it. I stared into my empty cup, trying to summon up the energy to pour more tea.

'Why don't you go back to bed? I'll tell Elijah you're not up to working today.'

I shook my head. She was about to argue but was interrupted by a rap on the front door. To my surprise, she returned with Ben Gilbert.

'Do you mind if I have a private word with Iris?' he asked.

Lizzy nodded and left us.

'What's happened?' A knot was forming in my stomach. The last time Ben had sat at the kitchen table was after Alice's body had been found. Since then, his memories of that night had made him reluctant to come inside the house. I knew it must be serious for him to call.

He sat opposite me. 'Colonel Thackeray's gone missing.'

I stared at him. 'When was he last seen?'

'No one seems sure. The super hasn't been able to speak to Mrs Thackeray. The servants say she's unwell and none of them seems to know if the colonel was in his study yesterday or not.'

'Poor Florence. I don't think she'll be able to take much more.'

'The super is taking things slowly. He's made it clear at Sand Hills Hall that when the colonel reappears, they must contact him.' He paused. 'I wondered if you'd pay a call on Mrs Thackeray. Try to find out what's happening at the hall?'

I nodded. 'I should have gone before now.' I still felt raw from the interrogation I'd been subjected to at the funeral, but I owed it to Alice to offer what comfort I could to her mother.

'Thank you. I know it's hard for you. I'll stop by the office and let Elijah know where you are.'

I nodded. Elijah wouldn't be happy about my going to Sand Hills Hall, but if I went right away, it would be too late for him to stop me.

As it was, Lizzy insisted on walking with me. We made our way around the lake, pausing at the mudbank where the tank was found. I looked from the railway station to Mill Ponds and visualised the Waldenmere Hotel, with its promenade, fabricated bay and boathouse. I shuddered. Sir Henry had yet to resume work, but I wouldn't stay in Walden if the hotel went ahead. I'd talk to Father about moving back to London.

Lizzy walked with me as far as the old jetty. 'Such a dear, sweet girl.' She took a handkerchief from her pocket and dabbed her eyes. 'When your father said we'd be coming back to Walden, I was so happy. It felt good to be home. But now, everything's changed.'

I walked over to where Alice had lain. Part of me wanted to fall into the mud and weep. 'I'm sorry,' I whispered to the ground. The familiar feelings of guilt threatened to engulf me. Could I have done more to protect her? I'd seen those flashes of fear in her eyes more than once.

I climbed the slope to Sand Hills Hall, wondering what I was going to say to Florence. Nothing was likely to offer much comfort.

'Come straight home when you're finished,' Lizzy called.

The Thackerays' maid, Holly, welcomed me in. 'I'm glad you've come. None of us knows what's going on. Mrs Thackeray's in a fragile state and doesn't seem to understand that something could have happened to the colonel.' She showed me into the drawing room where Florence was in her usual place by the window, Bear curled on her lap.

Before she withdrew, Holly whispered, 'Could you try to explain to her that the colonel is missing?' She was clearly concerned that something had happened to him.

'Iris, how lovely to see you.' Florence placed the spaniel on the floor and held out her hands to me. 'Come and sit with me and tell me what's been going on. I've been shutting myself away because I can't bear people asking how I am. I don't go into town any more.'

Alice's paintings filled the drawing room, displayed on easels and propped up on the mantelpiece. I remembered how Alice had looked when she'd painted at Waldenmere, standing by the lake, engrossed in her work.

I swallowed my emotions and sat next to Florence. The cloying fragrance of her floral perfume had permeated the curtains and cushions of her favourite bay window seat. 'Do you know where Colonel Thackeray is?'

She shook her head. 'I've been taking my meals in my room for the last few days. I didn't feel well enough to come downstairs.' She whispered in my ear, 'We don't share a bedroom. Haven't for years.'

This didn't surprise me. 'Are you worried about him?'

'No. I don't care if I never see him again. Now Alice is gone, there's nothing left between us.' The desolation in her eyes was hard to witness, but there was also a glimmer of curiosity. 'Do you know why the police want to speak to Charles?'

I considered her for a moment, wondering how much to reveal. I decided there was nothing to lose. 'The man found in the tank has been identified.'

She looked puzzled. 'Who is it?'

'His name was Robert Elmes.'

Her body slumped. She seemed to fold in half as she sunk her head into her hands. A few minutes passed before she spoke again. 'How do they know it was Robbie?' she whispered.

'A compass was found in his pocket. It was engraved with the emblem of the Society for the Promotion of Nature Reserves.'

'An eagle with its wings outstretched,' she cried. 'I remember it.' Her distress was palpable.

'How did you know Robert?' I asked.

'He was posted to Mill Ponds in 1916. He never wanted to be an officer, although he felt it was his duty to do what was asked of him.' Her face was wet with tears, but she smiled at the memory. 'He stood out from the other men. It was his compassion. He was the kindest, gentlest man I'd ever met.'

'You became friends?'

She turned her watery eyes on me. 'You're a bright girl. I think you've guessed we were more than friends.'

I nodded.

'Such a sweet soul. And so handsome. He was twenty-four and I was thirty-eight, but our ages didn't matter. We knew instantly.'

'How long did your affair last?' Had Alice known what was going on, was what I wanted to ask.

'Nearly two years. Robbie became a second lieutenant and then a lieutenant. When he was posted to France, we wrote to each other. Occasionally, we managed to meet when he was on leave, but it was difficult.'

'Did your husband know about the relationship?'

'Not at first.'

'What happened?'

She shuddered. I guessed the truth was beginning to dawn on her. 'I planned to leave Charles. I'd written a letter to Alice, explaining everything, saying I would arrange to see her when we were settled. I couldn't take her with me and I'm not sure she'd have left her father anyway. Charles found the letter and threatened me. I think he already suspected and was looking for clues. He told me he'd make sure I never saw Alice again. I tried to get a message to Robbie to postpone things, but I'm not sure he received it.'

'You never suspected something might have happened to him?'

Florence shook her head. 'When I didn't meet him that night, I thought he'd realise I hadn't been able to get away and needed more time. I waited for a letter from him, but it never came. Then I heard he was missing in action.'

Her tears flowed, but my sympathy had withered. I was disappointed she'd been prepared to leave her lonely daughter here at Sand Hills Hall with no one but her tormented father to look after her.

'When the body in the tank was found, I asked Charles if he had any idea who it might be. He shouted at me. Told me not to ask such ridiculous questions.'

'You never thought it could be Robert?'

'It's silly, but I always hoped he was still alive.' Her hands trembled as she threaded a silk handkerchief between her fingers. 'He swore he'd never go back to France. He was so disillusioned. I wondered if he'd arranged to go missing. Somehow made it look like he'd been killed. I could understand why he would give up on me. I imagined him living in some quiet corner of France somewhere.'

'Juliet said something similar. She thought he was considering desertion when she spoke to him for the last time.'

She nodded. 'I knew she was Robbie's sister when I saw her at the garden party. He'd told me about her and how they'd founded the society. Fortunately, Charles had no idea who she was. He knew nothing about Robbie's background, least of all his interest in nature. I longed to talk to her about him, but I couldn't risk it.'

'Do you think Alice knew what was going on?'

'No,' Florence snapped. 'I kept it from her. I wanted to protect her.'

I didn't say anything. Alice was sharper than her parents had given her credit for. How much had she suspected? I would never know the answer to that. Was it possible she'd come to realise what her father had done when the tank was found and paid the price for that knowledge?

'I know what you're thinking.' Florence gripped my hand. 'But Charles would never hurt Alice. That's one thing I'm certain of. Sometimes he lashes out at me. But he loved her more than anything.' Her voice faltered. 'He once loved me, but I think those feelings have died.'

I felt another pendulum swing of emotions. I wanted to believe her. 'What about General Cheverton? Do you think he had any idea of what was going on?'

'No, I don't think so.' She sounded more doubtful about this.

'But Nathan knew?'

She nodded. 'He swore he wouldn't tell anyone.'

Nathan was hardly the most reliable person to trust, but I didn't comment. Instead, I asked, 'When did you last see your husband?'

'Yesterday, I think. It may have been the day before. He shuts himself away in his study most of the time. He's been drinking heavily.' Panic crept into her voice. 'The police want to speak to him about Robbie, don't they? Do they know about our affair? Is it all going to come out?' She sounded hysterical.

'It might be best if you told them about your relationship with

Robert Elmes. I'm sure Superintendent Cobbe will be sympathetic.' I needed to try to calm her down, or else the police wouldn't get anything coherent out of her.

Her shoulders suddenly drooped and she rested her head against the window. 'What does it matter? Alice is gone. They may as well know. In fact, I want them to know. My poor darling Robbie.'

I watched her face as she stared into the distance. The look in her eyes told me she was beginning to realise the consequences of the letter she'd written to tell Alice she was leaving and the dreadful truth of what had happened when she'd failed to meet her lover.

'Could you call Holly for me?' Her voice was a whisper. 'I'm not feeling well. I need to lie down in my room.'

I fetched Holly and watched from the hallway as she helped her mistress up the stairs. Florence's face appeared shockingly white against her red hair and she leant heavily on the maid for support. I doubted she had the strength to deal with what was to come. Because when he reappeared, the police were likely to charge Colonel Charles Thackeray with murder.

I walked across the hallway to the front door. As I was about to leave, I heard Florence call from the top of the staircase. 'Iris, how did Robbie die?'

I kept walking.

39

Had Alice known the truth about her mother's affair? It was possible. But what about her father's act of vengeance?

No. She hadn't shown any signs of distress that last morning. All she'd talked about was Ben. If Colonel Thackeray was behind the murder of his daughter, it wasn't because he suspected her of knowing what he'd done to Robert Elmes.

It was more likely Alice's relationship with Ben had been the trigger for any uncontrolled rage. When Florence tried to leave him, the colonel had committed murder to stop it from happening. If he thought Alice was about to run away to get married, would the thought of losing his precious daughter cause him to kill again?

What about General Cheverton? Had he known something? Elijah believed Mill Ponds held some of the answers. As I passed, I glanced over to the house. What would become of that beautiful red-brick building in Sir Henry's hands? I gazed sadly at the battered rose garden – then stopped walking. The doors to the general's study appeared to be open.

A thought occurred to me. Alice once told me that Mill Ponds had been a refuge for her father when he'd wanted to get away from the hall. Could this be where he was hiding out?

Or could Superintendent Cobbe or Finlay Fortesque be revisiting the crime scene? I needed to tell one of them Florence had admitted to her affair with Robert Elmes. I'd rather have left Florence to do the talking, but who knew how long she'd keep to her room? I hesitated, then decided to take a quick look. I'd stay in the garden and just peek into the study.

When I reached the open doors, I was struck by how quiet it was. I hovered outside, but no sound came from within.

After my nocturnal visit to Mill Ponds, I was reluctant to enter the house again and incur the wrath of Finlay Fortesque and I didn't want to risk coming face-to-face with Colonel Thackeray, either. In the end, curiosity got the better of me and I peered around the side of the curtain.

The room was in shadows and it took a moment to register what I was seeing. Blood was splattered over the ivory-framed photograph of General Cheverton's wife and a body was slumped over his desk.

I edged closer and saw the shattered skull. The ring and little fingers were missing from a hand that still clasped a revolver.

It was Colonel Thackeray.

40

'This isn't what I had in mind when I decided we should move back to Walden. I thought it would be safer here than in London.' Father was pacing up and down in front of the window.

The sweet tea Lizzy had insisted I drink made me feel sick. My head was pounding and I wanted to lie down but was afraid the image of Colonel Thackeray's shattered head would creep back into my mind if I closed my eyes.

I'd run from Mill Ponds to the railway station, where I'd found PC Sid King chatting with the station manager. After that, everything was a blur. Superintendent Cobbe had arrived and so had my father. I was back at home, being comforted and smothered in equal measures.

It was a relief when Elijah showed up. Lizzy went to the kitchen to make more tea while he headed to the drinks cabinet and poured me a large brandy.

'Thomas?' He gestured to the bottle.

Father shook his head. Elijah poured himself a glass and sat opposite me. 'What were you doing at Mill Ponds?'

'I was coming back from Sand Hills Hall. I looked up at the

house and saw the study doors were open and thought Superintendent Cobbe or Finlay might be inside.' I didn't mention I'd suspected the colonel might have been there.

Elijah leant forward. 'Are you sure Thackeray killed himself? That's what we first thought General Cheverton had done, but we were wrong that time.'

'The colonel put the gun to his head.' I took a sip of brandy. The burning sensation in my throat was infinitely preferable to the sickly taste of sweet tea.

'A pathologist will examine the body, but Superintendent Cobbe seems confident it was suicide.' My father stood by the mantelpiece, watching us.

'What did he use?' Elijah asked.

'His service revolver. A Webley Mark VI,' Father replied.

Elijah rubbed his chin. 'Another obituary to write. This one won't be easy. What was Thackeray doing at Mill Ponds?'

'According to Cobbe, the door had been forced. I assume Colonel Thackeray went there in order to spare his wife the distress of finding him,' Father replied. 'Poor Florence.'

I wasn't sure this was true. Since Alice's death, I believed Sand Hills Hall had become unbearable to her father. More likely, the colonel had chosen to end his life in a place that had once been a refuge for him.

I took another sip of brandy. 'Florence admitted she had an affair with Robert Elmes.'

Elijah lit a cigarette. 'What made you suspect?'

'George said there'd been a rumour during the war that Florence planned to run off with someone. It turned out that was true. She had. Then at General Cheverton's funeral, Nathan made some clumsy reference to a secret involving Florence. Juliet knew Robert had a girlfriend, although he never told her who she was. She thought it was because the woman was French, but it occurred to me that Robert might not have mentioned her name because she was married.'

'You've told Cobbe?'

I nodded. 'Do you think Colonel Thackeray knew he'd been found out? That's why he killed himself.'

'It looks that way,' Elijah replied.

'Perhaps he couldn't live with himself after what happened to Alice?' I posed this question apprehensively. 'Because of grief. Or guilt?'

Father shook his head. 'I didn't like the man, but I can't see him harming his own daughter.'

'Did you think he could shoot a man in the back and put his body in a tank?' Elijah retorted.

'Of course not,' Father replied irritably. 'I don't think this kind of speculation is helpful. It's a matter for the police, not something you or Iris should be involved in.'

'But we are involved.' I was frustrated by his lack of comprehension. 'And sometimes we hear things the police don't.'

'I understand that, but after what's happened, it's best you take a step back. The police will examine all the evidence and draw their own conclusions. We must resign ourselves to the fact that we may never know for certain what happened to Alice.'

I took a large gulp of brandy. Why didn't my father understand that not knowing was completely unacceptable to me?

'Thomas, we must do everything we can to find out the truth.' Elijah turned his glass around in his hand. 'Not knowing will make it much harder to recover from Alice's death.'

Father glared at him. 'I'm trying to protect Iris. And I'd like you to do the same.'

Elijah gave a slight nod but didn't reply.

I could feel the distance between Father and me growing wider.

* * *

Robert Elmes was publicly named as Tank Man and the story began to emerge. Soon, rumours were flying that Colonel Thackeray had been responsible for all the killings, including that of his own daughter. Some said Alice had witnessed Elmes' murder, while others claimed she'd rowed with her father over Ben Gilbert. After all, the gossips said, everyone had known they were sweet on one another.

When it was confirmed the bullet taken from Robert Elmes' body had come from Colonel Thackeray's revolver, Superintendent Cobbe began to wind down his investigation. Even Elijah no longer bothered to walk me home. There seemed to be a growing assumption that any threat had disappeared with Colonel Thackeray's suicide.

Leaving the office one evening, I was surprised to find George waiting for me in his old spot by the door of the printworks. He looked angry. I'd heard he'd lost his job with the council and thought he'd come to confront me.

'Is it true Thackeray killed Alice?'

'I don't know.' I kept walking.

'But he killed that bloke in the tank?' He kept in step with me.

'Yes.'

'Bloody hell.'

Out of habit, we took our old route down Queens Road to Waldenmere, walking side by side.

'I can't believe it. I'd never have thought that of him.'

'Neither would Alice,' I replied. 'I'm glad she never knew.'

'She was going to talk to her father about Ben, wasn't she? Did she do it that night?'

'How would I know?' Bitterness made my voice shrill.

When we reached Heron Bay, George put his arm in front of me, forcing me to stop.

'Do you think he did it?' he persisted. 'He was devastated when he found her. But maybe it was guilt?'

'I don't know,' I shouted. 'Why do you think I have all the answers?'

He hesitated, then put his arm around me. I rested on his shoulder and began to weep. 'It's the betrayal I can't bear.'

'I'm sorry. I never meant to hurt you.'

'No, Alice.' I stared into his confused eyes. 'She loved her father. She thought he was a good man. These accusations would have hurt her so much. I believe he killed Robert Elmes, but I find it hard to accept he would betray Alice by turning on her.'

George rubbed his face, hurriedly wiping away a tear. 'Come away with me. I don't want to leave you, but I can't stay here any more.'

'That night, when we were together in my bed, I thought I could live my life the way I want to, but I can't.'

'You can. Don't let what happened to Alice stop you from having the future you want.' He handed me a piece of paper. 'This is my mother's address. I won't be there for much longer. If you ever need to get hold of me, tell her and she'll get a message to me.' He touched my cheek. 'She knows about you. Knows how I feel about you.'

I slipped the paper into my pocket. 'I have to go.'

Summer was turning to autumn and it was beginning to get dark. We walked in silence to the end of Chestnut Avenue.

I wanted to say goodbye, but no words came. When I reached the front door, he was still standing on the footpath, watching me. I wondered if I'd ever see him again. The loneliness that had been present ever since Alice's death intensified.

41

Colonel Thackeray's funeral was a subdued affair, with no military honours. The army was noticeable by its absence. I stood next to Father, my heart grieving for Alice as her father's coffin was lowered into the plot next to hers. A short distance away was the still-unmarked grave of Robert Elmes.

The small huddle of mourners dispersed after the service. Florence politely thanked each one, her ghostly face devoid of emotion. This time, there was to be no reception back at Sand Hills Hall.

When I approached her, she grasped my hand. 'I'd like to speak with Mrs Rendall. Could you ask her to come to the hall?'

I nodded.

Juliet agreed to see Florence and I arranged to meet her outside Sand Hills Hall. It was a cold October afternoon and hurrying past Mill Ponds, I remembered the summer evenings I'd spent by the lake with Alice, George and Ben.

Alice had thought she'd been the unworldly one. But I'd come to realise how innocent we'd all been, oblivious to the danger that had been around us.

I reached the old jetty and was startled when a figure emerged from Willow Marsh. It was Percy. I guessed he'd been looking out for me. 'You know I'm on my way to meet Juliet at Sand Hills Hall?'

He nodded. 'I'm worried about how this will affect her.' He attempted to clean mud from his hands and, in the process, smeared it up his arms and even onto his forehead.

'Give me that.' I took the cloth from him and wiped the smudges from his face. 'Talking to someone who loved Robert might help her to come to terms with his death.'

'Maybe.' He pushed his hair over his forehead, spreading more mud. 'She doesn't know I'm here, but I wanted to be around in case she needs me afterwards.'

I smiled. 'She's lucky to have you.'

I left Percy in the marsh and climbed the slope to find Juliet waiting by the gates to the hall. She seemed nervous.

'How do you feel about seeing Mrs Thackeray?'

'I can't forgive him for what he did, though I don't blame her. I know she suffered at his hands.' She paused. 'It's going to be painful, but I want to understand Robert's last days. After all these years of uncertainty and self-doubt, I need to know the truth.'

I nodded. I felt the same way about Alice. Only when I knew what had happened to her could I start to accept it.

Juliet's face softened. 'And I'd like to talk to someone who knew Rob and cared for him.'

Holly showed us into the drawing room, where Florence rose to greet us. I noticed there was colour in her cheeks and she seemed to have gained some strength since the colonel's funeral.

'Mrs Thackeray. My condolences.' Juliet looked around at the paintings. 'Your daughter was an exceptional artist. I'm so sorry for your loss.'

I noticed she said loss rather than losses.

'I was sorry to hear of your parents' death. Your brother often spoke of them.' Florence paused. 'And you've lost Robbie all over again.'

Juliet nodded. 'Yes. That's what it feels like. I'm glad my parents never learned the truth of what happened to him.'

'I am so sorry. Please believe me when I say I had no idea what my husband did. I would never have believed him capable of such a thing.'

Juliet didn't reply, but at Florence's invitation took a seat next to her on the sofa. I watched them from an armchair by the fire.

'Robbie often spoke about you when we were together,' Florence said. 'Did he ever talk about me?'

'Not by name. He told me he'd fallen in love with a woman with glorious red hair, who he planned to be with after the war.'

Florence gave a faint smile. 'He didn't mention I was married?'

Juliet shook her head. 'I thought he'd met someone while he was in France and that's why I couldn't meet her.'

Florence gave Juliet an apologetic look. 'I knew you were his sister when we met at the garden party. I wanted to talk to you about him but I guessed Robbie hadn't told his family he was seeing a married woman and I didn't want to make things worse for you.'

'You were in love with him?' Juliet asked.

Florence nodded. 'We planned to run away. He couldn't bear the cruelty of war. Of being an officer and sending men to their deaths. He begged me to go abroad with him.'

'And you agreed?'

'Not at first. I was worried about Alice. But when she was nineteen, I knew it was time. I couldn't stay with Charles any longer. So, we began to make plans.'

Juliet's face was pinched, but she asked, 'What went wrong?'

Florence recounted the sequence of events that had led to the colonel's discovery of the affair. What happened after this was left to our imaginations.

Juliet remained impassive and it was difficult to judge her reaction. I didn't think Florence was going to receive the forgiveness I suspected she hoped for, but then Juliet reached out and took her hand. I stood up on the pretext of studying Alice's paintings while they cried together.

The light was fading when we finally emerged from Sand Hills Hall. Both women seemed to have taken some comfort from the meeting. While they'd shared their reminiscences of their beloved Robert, my thoughts had been with Alice.

Since Colonel Thackeray's suicide, I'd tried to figure out how Robert Elmes' death had led to the murders of General Cheverton and Alice. I'd come up with several different scenarios that might explain the sequence of events and I kept coming back to one particular theory. Listening to Florence and Juliet's conversation had convinced me it was the correct one. But it still didn't answer what I wanted to know more than anything else. Who murdered Alice? And why?

We descended the slope from Sand Hills Hall and I walked over to the old jetty where Alice had lain. Bedraggled flowers still floated on the water and the smell of rotting blooms hung in the damp air.

'Iris.' Juliet's voice was gentle. 'Come away. I'll walk you home.'

'I don't want to go home. I want to stay here and feel close to Alice.'

She came towards me. 'I know you're in pain. It's hard to lose those closest to you. But Alice is gone and you must try to accept it.'

'You've lost so many people in your life. I don't know how you cope.' Sweat was forming under my clothes, but I still shivered. 'Your parents died earlier this year, didn't they?'

She nodded.

'You told me you stopped trying to find Robert because you didn't want to cause them any more distress. After they'd gone, didn't you think of looking for him again?'

'I'd come to accept Rob's death by the time I left Wildmay Manor.' She gave that familiar stoical smile and I decided it was time to test if my theory was correct.

'I keep thinking of all those families that came to Walden when they read about the body in the tank. Some travelled for miles to see if he could be their son, or father, or brother.'

'It never occurred to me it could be Rob.'

'Even though he'd spent time in Walden?' I gave her a sceptical look. 'And you'd always had doubts about his death?'

She shook her head but began to look afraid.

I knew I had to carry on. 'You said you met with your brother at the Natural History Museum when he started his two weeks' leave in October 1918. You said that was the last time you heard from him.'

'That's right.' She looked curious.

'You knew that Robert had asked to resign his commission and was refused?'

'Yes,' she said, puzzled. 'He told me.'

'His records show that Robert spoke to his commanding officers about resigning on the last day of October. The day his unit disbanded. You could only have known he'd been refused if you'd read his records.'

'I can't remember how I found out,' she replied. 'You're reading too much into this, Iris.'

But I was certain I was on the right track. 'I think after your parents died, you started to look for Robert again. You knew he would never have gone back to France to fight. I think you went to Mill Ponds to look for his records.'

She was silent.

'I think you killed General Cheverton.'

42

'How did you know the records were at Mill Ponds?' I asked.

'You're tired and upset.' Juliet tried to take my hand, but I pulled it away.

'You didn't mean to kill him, did you?'

'You're being silly. It's getting dark. Let me walk you home.'

'I'm not leaving here until you tell me what happened.' I was prepared to stay there all night until she admitted it. 'You couldn't have known those things you told me about Robert trying to resign his commission unless you'd seen his records.'

'I didn't. I swear...' she spluttered. I could see conflict in her eyes.

'Did General Cheverton scare you? I know you didn't mean to kill him.' I tried to sound sympathetic.

'Please, Iris.' Her usually cool blue eyes had become overly bright and her pupils dilated. She had the appearance of a wounded animal.

'Tell me what happened. Why did you go to Mill Ponds?' The temperature was starting to drop and we were both shivering.

After a long silence, I heard her whisper. 'I never meant for it to happen. It was an accident.'

'I know.' I kept my voice soft and coaxing.

'I overheard General Cheverton's housekeeper chatting in Fellowes Emporium. She was complaining that the army hadn't taken the records away like they were supposed to. I called on the general to ask if he'd let me see Rob's papers. He wouldn't hear of it. He told me they were confidential. I asked what he knew about Rob, but he didn't even remember him.' She looked hurt and confused.

'So you decided to break in?'

'I didn't break in.' She regained some composure. 'I was bird-watching nearby when I saw the doors to the study were open. I'd thought about trying to talk to the general again, but when I heard him call out to say he was going upstairs for a nap and saw the housekeeper leave, I knew it was meant to be. I'd been given an opportunity and I took it.'

'You found the general's revolver?'

'It was on top of the filing cabinet keys in the desk drawer. I made a noise when I took them out. I'd unlocked the cabinet and found Rob's records, but then General Cheverton appeared. He pointed a shotgun at me and I panicked. All I wanted to do was get away. I must have fired the revolver, but I didn't mean to kill him.' She winced at the memory. 'The noise was deafening. I thought the whole town must have heard. Rob's papers were in my hand – I didn't even look at them till later – I ran and threw the revolver into the lake.'

'When you did read them, you saw it was Colonel Thackeray who'd issued the report saying Robert was missing in action?'

Her shoulders slumped and she gave a weak smile. 'I was stupid. I actually thought he'd helped Rob to run away. I didn't know anything about the man, but he seemed compassionate. He wanted to build a convalescent home.' Pain and despair ravaged her face. 'I thought Rob was still alive.'

'You wanted to find him?'

She nodded. 'I went to the garden party to try to speak to the colonel, but I couldn't get near him.'

'When the tank was found, you suspected it was Robert?'

'I told myself it couldn't be Rob. It just couldn't.' She shook her head slowly, as if she still didn't believe it.

'But you had to know for certain.' I could see the destructive sequence of events unfolding. 'You broke into the station house and saw the compass.'

Tears flowed. 'My beautiful little brother, trapped in that metal coffin all that time. Shut away from the sunlight. He would have hated it. He always wanted to be outdoors. Even as a child, he was never in the house.'

'You guessed Colonel Thackeray was responsible?'

She raised her head, her eyes heavy with tiredness. 'I'd found out more about him by then. His reputation for being a bully. His temper. I thought the colonel must have found out about...'

'About what? Robert's relationship with Florence? What was it you said earlier? Your brother had written to you, describing his lover as a woman with glorious red hair? You made the connection and realised your brother had never told you her name because she was married.'

'I wasn't sure. I decided to go to Sand Hills Hall to talk to Colonel Thackeray.' Her eyes were misty. 'But I was scared. I was in the garden, trying to calm my nerves, when I heard him arguing with Florence in the drawing room. She asked him if he knew who the man in the tank was. He told her not to be so ridiculous. He sounded so convincing that I left. But deep down, I knew he must be lying.'

'Did Alice hear them?' I was still desperate to know if she'd any inkling of what her father had done.

Juliet shook her head. 'No. She wasn't there at the time.'

'Why didn't you talk to Florence? When Colonel Thackeray wasn't around?'

'I wasn't sure if... I, I was confused,' she stammered, her eyes didn't meet mine. 'I didn't think Robert would have an affair with a married woman. It seemed so unlike him.'

'Then what did you think?' But as I said the words, the cruel truth dawned. 'Alice. With her beautiful red hair. You thought your brother had been seeing Alice?' The final piece fell sickeningly into place.

'I was confused,' she said again and I could see from her bewildered eyes that her mind was becoming clouded.

'You thought she knew what her father had done?'

'I couldn't understand why she hadn't said anything. Had she been involved? Had she known all this time?'

I gazed at the flowers rotting in the mud. 'Everyone believes Colonel Thackeray killed Alice.'

She nodded. 'I think he must have done, don't you?'

'No.' I shook my head emphatically. 'I was never convinced of that. The only person I really suspected was Nathan Cheverton.'

'I'm afraid it's more likely to have been her father.' She stared into the mud, her hair hanging limply in front of her face. 'That's why he killed himself.'

I took a step closer to her. 'When did you hear Florence and Colonel Thackeray arguing? How did you know Alice wasn't there?'

'Because I saw her. By the lake.'

'Here. You saw her here,' I hissed, gesturing to the mud around me. 'You heard that argument in the study on the evening Alice was murdered.'

She shook her head.

'Florence thought she'd seen someone in the garden – she was afraid Alice had overhead their row – but it was you.' I forced out the words. 'Did you kill Alice?' She shook her head. 'Of course, I didn't. I was with Percy. You can't think that.' Her eyes pleaded with me. 'What are you going to do? Will you tell the police?'

I didn't care about the police. All I wanted was the truth. 'I'm going to find Percy. He's in Willow Marsh.'

This startled her. I turned to walk away but she suddenly lurched forward. I gave a sharp intake of breath as she grabbed my arm. Then the last fragments of self-possession deserted her and she slumped down into the mud, taking me with her.

'Is this how you killed Alice?' I didn't attempt to stand. I needed to stay close to her, to force her to tell me everything.

'Don't,' she whimpered. 'Don't say it.'

'Did you do it for revenge?' My knees sank even further into the mud and the smell of wet earth filled my nostrils.

'Stop it.' She grabbed at me, her hands clawing up my body until they reached my throat.

I didn't care what she did to me. I had to know why Alice had died. 'Tell me the truth. Tell me what you did.'

Suddenly, she released her hold and stood up. 'I need to go.'

'No,' I screamed. 'You can't walk away.' I lunged forward and managed to grab her legs. I couldn't let her go until I'd heard everything.

Caught by surprise, she fell face down into the mud. Then I heard someone shouting my name.

'Iris. What are you doing?'

Percy ran towards us and tried to pull me off Juliet, but I wouldn't let go.

I screamed at him. 'She killed Alice. I know she did.'

He tugged at my arms. 'You're hysterical. You don't mean that.'

'Percy, tell the truth.' I gripped Juliet's legs even tighter. 'You weren't with her that night, were you? You didn't have supper at her cottage.'

He stopped pulling at me and managed to drag Juliet into a seated position. He sank down into the mud and cradled her in his arms. 'I'm here now, darling.'

'Percy, she was lying, wasn't she?' I spat the words. 'Tell me. Were you with her the night Alice was killed?'

He had one arm wrapped around Juliet, holding her against his chest. With the other hand, he tried to push me away. 'She said it to protect me.'

'No.' I gasped. 'She said it to give herself an alibi. Not to protect you.'

'Percy.' Juliet leant into him. 'I'm sorry.'

'Ssshh.' He stroked her hair. 'Why are you sorry?'

'I killed her.' It was a desperate wail. 'I killed Alice.'

43

Percy made a strange gasping noise but kept his arm wrapped around Juliet.

'Why? Why did you do it?' My hands still gripped her legs and I wasn't letting go.

'Leave her alone.' Percy tried to push me away again.

'I can't. I have to know what happened.' I scrabbled my way up Juliet's body until I had hold of her jacket. 'Tell me. Did you kill her for revenge?'

'No, no. I didn't. It wasn't like that.' Her eyes were full of pain. 'I was confused. I knew Thackeray had killed Rob and I wanted to go to the police, but I couldn't because of what I'd done to General Cheverton. I ran down the slope and she was there.'

'Alice?' My body swayed and I almost fell into Juliet's lap.

'With the policeman. They were kissing. I couldn't understand how she could betray Rob like that. I watched them together and when the policeman left, I confronted her.'

'What did you say?' I whispered. The scent of rotting flowers filled my nose and waves of nausea engulfed me.

'I told her what her father had done to Rob. She tried to walk away. She said she didn't understand what I was talking about.' Juliet stared at the mud on her hands. 'She kept saying she didn't know Rob. Then she started to scream. I'm not sure how she ended up in the water. She must have fallen. She tried to get up, but I pushed her down.'

Percy's mouth gaped and his hold on her loosened.

'I didn't mean for it to happen.' She sobbed into his chest. 'I didn't know what I was doing.'

My heart wept at the thought of Alice's fear and confusion. I tried to stand, but my left knee buckled.

Juliet continued in a whisper, 'Her father left my brother to rot in the water. That man destroyed my whole family. I was angry, but I didn't mean to hurt her. I knelt over her. I tried to wake her up, but she wouldn't move.'

A spasm shot through my body and I retched. I couldn't stand, so I fell forward, my hands sinking into the mud and withered flowers.

'Let her go, Percy.' The command from above took us all by surprise.

I looked up to find Ben standing over us. His face was contorted in fury.

Juliet made a whimpering sound.

'Ben, no.' I was afraid of what he would do. I didn't care what happened to Juliet, but I cared about Ben.

'Let go of Mrs Rendall, Percy,' Ben ordered, his voice low and hard.

'No.' Percy lifted Juliet to her feet, keeping his arms around her.

'Don't let them lock me up.' She gripped the front of Percy's shirt. 'You need to help me move Rob. He's been alone for too long. I'm going to take him to the woods. He loves it there. He doesn't like it in the churchyard.'

Percy closed his eyes for a moment. When he opened them, he said, 'I'll help you, darling.' I could see the anguish on his face. Juliet was clearly beyond rational thought.

'Please let go of Mrs Rendall.' Ben peeled Juliet's hands from Percy's shirt and snapped a pair of handcuffs on her wrists. 'Mrs Rendall, I'd like you to walk with me to the railway station. A car will be sent for and you'll be taken to Aldershot police station for questioning.'

'Can I stay with her?' Percy kept his eyes on Juliet's. His expression made me want to weep.

'For the time being.' Ben's voice was cold. 'Follow with Iris.'

I stood and groaned in pain. Percy took my arm and we trailed behind Ben as he led Juliet back to the footpath. Our progress was slow in the fading light. Juliet frequently stumbled and my left knee threatened to give way beneath me.

We eventually reached the ticket office and the station master stared at us in horror. He didn't move when Ben ordered him to phone Superintendent Cobbe. Juliet and I were caked in mud from head to foot. Percy was little better. Every time I blinked, I could feel more grit scratch my eyes.

When Ben barked the order again, the station master disappeared into his office to dial the operator. The four of us sat in a row on a bench. I shivered in my wet clothes but Juliet was as motionless as a statue. She seemed to have no feeling left. My eyes followed the trail of mud we'd deposited across the ticket office floor.

We sat in silence until two police cars arrived. Ben helped Juliet to her feet and led her outside. Percy and I followed to where Superintendent Cobbe was waiting. He told Ben to get into the first car with Juliet and pointed us towards the second.

Juliet turned to me. 'Keep trying to save Waldenmere, Iris. I'm sorry I won't be around to help you.' Her expression was calm, almost serene, like the Juliet I'd first come to know. She seemed to have given up on her life – a life she would lose if she were to be convicted of murder.

Ben gripped her arm. Before he could push her into the car, she reached out to touch Percy's face. 'I'm sorry, darling.'

44

'Juliet is likely to be sentenced to death.'

'I don't care.'

'I don't believe that.'

I shrugged. I gazed around Mrs Siddons' drawing room, remembering that first meeting with Juliet, when Percy had sunk comically low into the depths of the plush velvet sofa.

'If she does receive the death penalty, I'll help her appeal. I'll also continue to oppose capital punishment.' Mrs Siddons was calm but resolute. 'You used to agree with me on this issue.'

'I don't any more.'

'You think Juliet should hang?'

'She murdered Alice.' My voice was flat and emotionless.

'That's a tragedy that can't be undone. Juliet should be punished. She should also be helped.'

'I don't care what happens to her.' At that moment, it was true. I was yet to reach the point of acceptance. The pain of losing Alice was still too overwhelming for that.

'I liked Juliet very much,' Mrs Siddons continued. 'If circum- stances had been different, I believe she could have achieved great things, but the brutality of war took its toll. I don't think she ever intended to kill General Cheverton, but that act tipped an already fragile woman into a state of unbalance.'

I thought of the Matron at Wildmay Manor saying that women who'd served on the battlefields had been soldiers too. I could see how Juliet had become another casualty of war. Another lost soldier.

'I intend to continue the work I started with Juliet and Percy.' It was all I was prepared to concede at this time. 'I still support the aims of the Society for the Promotion of Nature Reserves.'

'Good. I agree. I still believe in the concept of nature reserves and I know many MPs share that view. There'll be more Sir Henrys in the future. We need to attain legal protection for places like Waldenmere.'

I stared frostily at my father over the breakfast table. He propped his newspaper against the coffee pot and began to read.

'According to *The Telegraph*, London and South Western Railway has agreed to sell Waldenmere to Walden Council. Sir Henry Ballard has made a statement saying he's sincerely sorry for the appalling sequence of events that followed the purchase of Waldenmere. He's quoted as saying that although the railway company can't be held accountable for the deaths that so tragically took place, they should have been more sensitive to the feelings of the local community when it came to their plans for the development of a lakeside hotel.' He took off his reading glasses and looked at me.

I knew Father had been using his contacts to instigate a campaign against LSWR. Journalists from different papers had taken the opportunity to lambast all of the large railway companies for putting profit above people.

LSWR and Sir Henry in particular, had been heavily criticised for their part in the 'Waldenmere Tragedy' as it had been dubbed. William Mansbridge and Aldershot Military Estates hadn't come out of it unscathed either. Following the article in *The Walden Herald*, several national newspapers had pointed the finger in their direction, suggesting money had exchanged hands to facilitate the deal.

'It's a shame you weren't here when Sir Henry first announced his plans to buy Waldenmere. Perhaps you could have stopped it from happening.'

Prevented Alice from being murdered was the unspoken sentence hanging in the air. I knew I was being unfair. Other things were going on in the world that made the problems of Walden seem insignificant. But I wasn't in the mood to be fair.

Never one to pick up on my mood, Father chose that moment to question me about George.

'Do you still see that chap who worked for the council?' He folded the newspaper in half and laid it by the side of his plate.

'He'll be leaving Walden soon.' The loneliness that was becoming a familiar companion crept over me.

He looked relieved. 'Do you plan to correspond with him?'

'No.'

'Good.'

'Maybe I'll go with him.'

'But...' he spluttered.

'I'm going for a walk.' I had to end the conversation before I made any more impulsive statements.

I put on my coat and went into the back garden to cut some late roses. I could see Father watching me from the kitchen window. I wrapped the flowers in old paper and headed to the lake.

Wind and rain had left the trees bare and the footpath was a haze of red, brown and yellow leaves. I walked past the railway station and on to Mill Ponds, wondering how Nathan Cheverton was coping with his debts. LSWR had not only shelved their plans to build a hotel, they'd also pulled out of the deal to buy Mill Ponds. The house was on the market, but with its tainted history, it didn't look like a buyer would be found any time soon.

To his credit, Sir Henry had put right the damage he'd done. Waldenmere was back to its normal level and the debris had been cleared from General Cheverton's garden. No trace of the activity that had taken place over the summer was left. The view of Waldenmere from Mill Ponds was as beautiful as ever, almost ethereal, with a low mist drifting over the lake. I remembered the comment George had once made about water hiding its secrets.

I forced myself to carry on towards the old jetty and knelt where Alice had lain. I breathed in the sweet scent of the roses before placing half of them on the ground. As I did, a gust of wind lifted fallen leaves and they swirled around my head. The motion made me feel that somehow Alice was close by.

I wondered if Mrs Siddons was right. Had the accidental murder of General Cheverton unbalanced Juliet? Or had it been the atrocities she'd seen on the front line, combined with the shock of losing her husband, brother and parents so close together? I remembered my last glimpse of her before she was led away. The look of weariness on her face suggested she was tired of the life she was shortly going to lose.

I walked to Heron Bay and then along Grebe Stream to the place I'd shared so many kisses with George. The surrounding oak trees had shed their leaves to expose our once private bench.

Taking the shortcut away from Waldenmere and through the woods into town, I headed to St Martha's Church. When I entered the churchyard, I saw a man kneeling to place flowers on Alice's grave. Swathes of tall Michaelmas daisies obscured my view and I thought it was Ben, but as I got closer, I realised it was George.

I walked towards him. 'What are you doing here?'

He looked up, startled, but his expression softened when he saw it was me. 'Paying my respects to Alice before I go.'

'You're leaving now?' Tears pricked my eyes.

'I don't have anything to stay for.' He leant forward to kiss my cheek. 'I care for you, more than you know, but you don't trust me and I don't blame you. Now your father's back, there's no future for us. I won't write, but if you ever need me, tell my mother and she'll get a message to me.' He turned and walked away.

I placed the remainder of the roses on Alice's grave and stared at the words on her headstone.

Alice Louise Thackeray
To live in our hearts is not to die

The town was returning to normal and the events of the summer would soon fade into memory, but Alice wouldn't be forgotten by anyone who'd known her. My dear, kind friend would be with me wherever I went. I didn't need to stay in Walden to remember her. Perhaps it was time for me to move on too.

'George,' I called.

ACKNOWLEDGMENTS

I'd like to thank the following people for their encouragement and support: my parents, Ken and Barbara Salter, for everything. Special thanks to Dad for his assistance with historical research. Thura Win for his advice and eye for detail as no. 1 beta reader. Jeanette Quay for acting as a sounding board during the years it took to develop this series. Barbara Daniel for her friendship, editorial guidance and advice.

Thanks to Emily Yau, my brilliant editor, for her advice and enthusiasm and to the whole Boldwood team for championing the Iris Woodmore Mysteries.

I enjoyed researching this book as much as I did writing it. I'm indebted to the numerous people, books, libraries and museums that contributed to my knowledge of this period.

I'd also like to thank past and present fellow trustees of the Fleet Pond Society, particularly Colin Gray, Jim Storey, Cathy Holden - and John Sutton for his advice on weirs, sluices and aquatic plants. And special thanks to all the volunteers who give their time to make Fleet Pond Nature Reserve such a special place.

MORE FROM MICHELLE SALTER

We hope you enjoyed reading *Murder at Waldenmere Lake*. If you did, please leave a review.

If you'd like to gift a copy, this book is also available as an ebook, hardback, large print, digital audio download and audiobook CD.

Sign up to Michelle Salter's mailing list for news, competitions and updates on future books.

https://bit.ly/MichelleSalterNews

Explore the rest of Michelle Salter's gripping Iris Woodmore series...

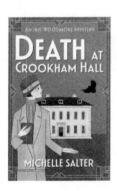  

ABOUT THE AUTHOR

Michelle Salter writes historical cosy crime set in Hampshire, where she lives, and inspired by real-life events in 1920s Britain. Her Iris Woodmore series draws on an interest in the aftermath of the Great War and the suffragette movement.

Visit Michelle's Website:

https://www.michellesalter.com

Follow Michelle on social media:

twitter.com/MichelleASalter
facebook.com/MichelleSalterWriter
instagram.com/michellesalter_writer
bookbub.com/authors/michelle-salter

Poison
& Pens

POISON & PENS IS THE HOME OF
COZY MYSTERIES SO POUR YOURSELF
A CUP OF TEA & GET SLEUTHING!

DISCOVER PAGE—TURNING NOVELS FROM
YOUR FAVOURITE AUTHORS &
MEET NEW FRIENDS

JOIN OUR
FACEBOOK GROUP

BIT.LYPOISONANDPENSFB

SIGN UP TO OUR
NEWSLETTER

BIT.LY/POISONANDPENSNEWS

Boldwood

Boldwood Books is an award-winning fiction publishing company seeking out the best stories from around the world.

Find out more at www.boldwoodbooks.com

Join our reader community for brilliant books, competitions and offers!

Follow us
@BoldwoodBooks
@BookandTonic

Sign up to our weekly deals newsletter

https://bit.ly/BoldwoodBNewsletter